i there,

At the age of seven, in the red plush seats of the Theatre Royal in Plymouth, halfway through a performance of *Oliver!*, I informed my father I had had an epiphany, and was going to dedicate my life to becoming an actress. But years of amateur operatics, school shows, and even a degree in drama failed to realise this dream. Instead, I ended up in swotty politics, as a special adviser to the Prime Minister and freelance speechwriter. I now live in Buttercup's home town Bath, with her my daughter Millie, where we spend much time re-enacting *The Sound of Music* and *Hairspray*, and singing rock ballads. I had so much fun writing **Buttercup Mash** and I hope you have lots of fun reading it.

Love

Jo x

Other books by Joanna Nadin

My So-Called Life
The Life of Riley
The Meaning of Life
My (Not So) Simple Life
Back to Life
The Facts of Life

My Double Life
Double Trouble
Double or Quits

Joanna Nadin

# Buttercup Mash

OXFORD
UNIVERSITY PRESS

OXFORD
UNIVERSITY PRESS

Great Clarendon Street, Oxford OX2 6DP
Oxford University Press is a department of the University of Oxford.
It furthers the University's objective of excellence in research, scholarship,
and education by publishing worldwide in

Oxford New York

Auckland Cape Town Dar es Salaam Hong Kong Karachi
Kuala Lumpur Madrid Melbourne Mexico City Nairobi
New Delhi Shanghai Taipei Toronto

With offices in

Argentina Austria Brazil Chile Czech Republic France Greece
Guatemala Hungary Italy Japan Poland Portugal Singapore
South Korea Switzerland Thailand Turkey Ukraine Vietnam

Oxford is a registered trade mark of Oxford University Press
in the UK and in certain other countries



First published 2011



British Library Cataloguing in Publication Data
Data available

ISBN: 978-0-19-275625-1
1 3 5 7 9 10 8 6 4 2

Printed in Great Britain

Paper used in the production of this book is a natural,
recyclable product made from wood grown in sustainable forests.
The manufacturing process conforms to the environmental
regulations of the country of origin.

*For Georgina and Nicola,*
*who are both full of glee*

# SEPTEMBER

**Friday 3 September**

11 p.m.
~~Dear Diary~~
Dear Dr Sven Magnusson

My name is Buttercup Jones. I am fourteen years old. *TODAY*. And I have *ISSUES*.

1. My mother is a 36-year-old failed conceptual artist called Lola who thinks it is *FUNNY* to gatecrash her daughter's party with a homeless man called Fergal O'Shaughnessy.
2. My best friend Imogen spent the whole evening refusing to speak to me because it is '*SO UNFAIR*' that I get a homeless man coming to my birthday party and all she got was Colin the Clown when she was seven, and he wasn't half as drunk.
3. My little brother Harry, who was dressed as the queen, and I am *NOT EVEN JOKING*, made everyone watch the video of his birth in *REVERSE* so we could see him going *BACK* into Lola and the sick going back into my mouth, which made Granny Jones disown us *YET AGAIN*.
4. My big sister Ruby didn't even *SHOW UP* because she 'like, forgot'.
5. Oh, and I would *TOTALLY* go and live with my dad,

only *I DON'T KNOW WHO HE IS*, and neither does Lola. But, given her track record, he is either *a*) broke, *b*) on prescription medication, or *c*) wanted by the police. Or, in the case of Fergal O'Shaughnessy, all three.

6. My home is not just metaphorically but *ACTUALLY* broken i.e: the fridge has alternative life forms growing in it, you cannot turn the kettle on at the same time as the microwave or the TV blows up, and there are chickens where chickens *SHOULDN'T BE*.
7. Oh, and I'm called *BUTTERCUP*. I mean, what kind of a name is that? You can't even shorten it. Try. See? At least Ruby and Harry are vaguely normal. Although to be fair Harry is short for Haroon and Ruby's middle name is Tuesday. But, the point is, Lola could have called us Tom and Kate and Rachel. But, *NO*, she is just determined to be *DIFFERENT*. Which pretty much sums up my life.

Seriously, it's my birthday. And I should be, you know, eating retro cupcakes in a vintage tea-dress. Or drinking Red Bull in a bus shelter, according to Imogen. But instead I am sitting in the dark with a chicken on my lap, writing a diary to an online shrink.

I mean, all I want is a *NORMAL* birthday. You know, with jelly and ice cream and candles.

I just want to be *NORMAL*, end of.

Lola says I don't know what normal is. And Ruby says normal is a media construct designed to sell washing powder. And Imogen says normal is for suburban-minded automatons like her mum and dad and I should think myself LUCKY.

But SERIOUSLY, Dr Sven, this is why I need you. Because I don't know how much more of this I can take.

Because, even if Lola is right, and I don't know what 'normal' is, I know that this SO isn't it.

**Saturday 4 September**

Dear Dr Sven,

OK. So I guess I've calmed down since last night. And maybe things aren't quite as bad as they seemed when Granny Jones was out cold on the floor with a chicken trying to peck a sapphire out of her cocktail ring and Harry in his wig trying to find her facelift scars. Because Stan came round and sang 'Build Me Up Buttercup' on his knees in a totally falsetto voice and comedy hat to cheer me up. Which kind of worked. And which also made me realize I had TOTALLY forgotten to tell you about Stan. I guess because he isn't an issue at all, he's my second best friend, (but only because Imogen made me sign a contract putting her first when we were in Year Six), and practically next-door neighbour (two doors up on opposite side of road, to be precise), and has known me for ever so is totally immune to Lola's mentalism (and my ISSUES).

So I admit, my life isn't a TOTAL car crash. But I do have issues. A LOT of them. Otherwise why would I be writing this

in the first place? Well, not writing a diary. I mean everyone has done that. Though possibly not on the scale of Imogen. Although she says it's not a diary it's a JOURNAL, and is COMPLETELY like the one Sylvia Plath wrote in when she was having suicidal *Bell Jar* thoughts (which Imo is not, at least not YET, because she does not want to die until she has done enough extraordinary things for someone to make a movie of her life). But usually it's some completely lame school assignment for a supply teacher, like Miss Harbutt-Reed, who we had for history last term when Mr Goldenblatt was off with a cold (not sleeping sickness, which is what Imogen claimed it was). Only Miss Harbutt-Reed accused me of *a*) harbouring an overactive imagination and *b*) missing the point, which was about historical record for future generations blah blah blah, and sent me to see Mr Kwame-Jones, who is our headmaster (and is no relation AT ALL). But, like I told him, it totally WAS a historical document because Lola really DID have to take Harry to a secret location for his custody visit, because Harry's dad, who I can't name for legal reasons, really is some kind of James Bond type spy at MI5, and it's really NOT my fault if Miss Harbutt-Reed is not familiar with my TRYING domestic circumstances. And Imogen was right: Mr Kwame-Jones totally IS progressive and cool, because he said it must be very difficult being from such an underprivileged background, battling against the day-to-day realities of the poverty line etc., etc., and changed the F to a B. I bet the Pennington governors are kicking themselves now, trying to be modern and attract overseas students by getting a multicultural head, even one who is an African prince and went to school at Eton, which makes Pennington look like Broadmead Comprehensive.

I've kind of gone off the point *AGAIN*. In fact I've forgotten what the point was. Oh, no, I've got it. That it is *WEIRD* to be writing to *YOU*. Because diaries are normally private and everything, so it's a bit freakish writing it for someone else to read, (especially a man who is at least 35, according to Imogen, who has Googled your picture seven times). But, according to your website, GoShrinkYourself.com (which is totally a great name by the way) the more I write down, the more I will be able to see for myself where my mental instability lies, and the more you will be able to help me when I send you the diary (together with my cheque for £500) for personal analysis and a free GoShrinkYourself pen. Though where I'm going to get £500 from is anyone's guess at this point. Because the reason I'm doing virtual therapy, rather than having normal lying-on-a-couch therapy, is that *a*) we have *NO MONEY* until Lola comes up with a new money-making scheme (and one that actually works, *NOT* like the time she tried to breed rare pigs, or become a Hedge Fund manager), and *b*) Lola says all therapists are either perverts or idiots and that your teenage years are supposed to be confusing and traumatic. But that's because she was expelled from Royal Girls for *a*) snogging her boyfriend Denzil on the lacrosse pitch, which indirectly led to her *b*) getting pregnant with Ruby at the age of seventeen. Imogen says she would cut off her right arm to get expelled from Pennington for doing anything on campus with a dreadlocked barge dweller. But that is because her parents are Welsh Methodists and also in the National Jigsaw Society and so she is totally repressed and covets anyone's home life where they don't spend the whole of Sunday either in church or searching for pieces of Van Gogh prints in the shagpile.

So, anyway, the point. Which is that Stan paid for a year's subscription to your website (£29.99 including VAT). He doesn't have money worries because even though his mum Celia is as flaky as Lola, she actually has a job, i.e. she paints nude pictures of celebrities, whereas Lola hasn't painted anything in years, let alone a B-lister's front bottom.

Stan also says there's no such thing as normal, but that if it makes me feel better, then he's totally behind it.

So I'm going to write it all down. All the WEIRD. And the CRAZY. Then it's up to you, Dr Sven. You have to make me NORMAL.

Or as normal as someone called Buttercup can be.

**Sunday 5 September**

Things That Are Compromising My Mental Stability Today

1. My height: i.e. I have grown ANOTHER three centimetres in the last two months, meaning I am now not just tall but FREAKISHLY tall (seriously, I can

actually see Mr Goldenblatt's bald spot and the fake hair-in-a-can he uses to fill it).

2. My stomach. Not in an 'Oh my God it sticks out' way. Because it totally doesn't. And anyway, I wouldn't care if it did. But in the way that butterflies seem to have taken up permanent residence in it. Seriously. I seem to feel SICK at the slightest issue. And, as I have explained, I have a LOT of issues. Hence a lot of butterflies. And vomit. Which I have already had to explain to Imogen is NOT bulimia.
3. School. Which starts tomorrow. And which is TOTALLY traumatic and butterfly-inducing. I mean, who doesn't get stressed by school? Well, maybe Sunday Henderson-Hicks, who is head of Year Ten, fashion editor of *Penny for Your Thoughts* (which is our PANTS school newspaper and is totally run by an evil clique of overprivileged clones and habitual joiners, according to Stan, who has made it his life's ambition to wrest control, change the totally LAME name to *Penny Dreadful* and turn it into a subversive webzine) and lead soprano of our Glee Club, i.e. Pennington Musical Society, i.e. PMS (now that Camilla St John Brice is back in the Manna From Heaven Christian Residential Unit for the Undernourished). PLUS she is going out with Blake Carrington who is the First XV rugby full back and OFFICIALLY the hottest boy in Year Eleven.

But the thing is I am so *NOT* Sunday Henderson-Hicks. *a*) I do not live in a four-storey Georgian townhouse in Lansdown, *b*) my father, whoever he is, is definitely *NOT* the owner of a chain of tooth-whitening salons aka Mr Britesmile, and *c*) I do not look like I walked straight out of a Gap advert. I mean, I am a giant, my hair is borderline ginger, and my lips are weirdly big (and not in a cool Angelina Jolie way), so that when I do wear make-up I end up looking kind of like a goldfish in drag. Which Sunday Henderson-Hicks and her sidekicks (or Sidehicks as Stan calls them, ha ha) never fail to point out. (By calling me Nemo. Again: ha ha.) At least they've stopped calling Imogen Puffer Fish, though, since she got breasts. I mean, it's not like she lost a bundle of weight, just that it moved upwards. They were like 34C the last time we measured them and I swear they grew again in the holidays. So Sunday and the Sidehicks are going to be totally spitting with jealousy because she will definitely make the upper boys' Top Totty list this year. And you think Imogen would be totally happy about it, but *NO*, she hates them. She says it is impossible to be an innocent ingénue type with large breasts. Stan said she could change her ambition to be more of a femme fatale type, but she says she is banking on Blake Lively playing her in her movie life story and that won't work.

Oh, sorry. How have I done this again? I started on school and I've totally ended up on Imogen's breasts. Note to self (which have also put on Post-it stuck to my computer screen, which is another of your excellent ideas): Concentrate on getting to point. Also, *CHANGE NAMES*, in case Imogen does not want you knowing breast size. Unless you know any screenwriters? Maybe you're like a therapist to the stars. Although I totally get that you can't disclose their names on your website. Oh, sorry, I've gone off the point again. Which is that school is hell.

*BUT* the alternative is worse, i.e. *HOME SCHOOLING*, which is what Harry is going to do, starting tomorrow. Though his father is in no way happy about this and I am kind of on his side. I mean, it's all very well home schooling if you are like some kind of total intellectual. But Lola didn't even show up for two of her GCSEs because she was in a yurt somewhere with Denzil.

Grandma Jones wants Harry to be put down for boarding school immediately where there will be less 'wayward' (i.e. Lola) influence. There is no chance of that. Lola says boarding schools hamper self-expression and creativity. I am lucky I am even at Pennington, which is private, but at least is mixed sex and has no scope for weird dormitory rules. Plus, according to Ruby, they will be totally non-private by the end of the year if her anti-private-school protest works. Although I do not rate her chances against the governors, because,

according to Ruby, they are all fascists anyway. Plus they have got Mr Kwame-Jones now. But Ruby says he is just a multicultural straw doll and it is the governors who are really in charge. Them and Miss Hutchinson, who is Mr Kwame-Jones's secretary, and is like the all-seeing eye, i.e. nothing gets past her (except when she is reading Mills and Boon, which she thinks no one knows about, because she keeps it inside a copy of *Caravanning Today*, only Imogen who *a*) has 20/20 vision and *b*) is always getting sent to see Mr Kwame-Jones, says there is no way *Caravanning Today* has ever contained the phrase 'Charles's breath was heavy in her delicate ear').

Anyway, my point, well one of them, was that I begged to go to school. Because there is only so much of Lola you can take. Even Ruby, who is like a mini version of Lola, only with blonde dreadlocks, went to school in the end. Although she got expelled from Pennington after three months and ended up at Broadmead, which is like this totally tough comp where they have to check you for weapons at the door. Plus she failed all her A levels and is at art college instead now, although mostly she is actually on her dad Denzil's barge, or at her boyfriend Spike's, which is where she lives, unless they have had a row. Which is quite often.

OMG. What is wrong with me? Seriously? So, the point, which is why Harry is being home schooled, which Lola told 007 (i.e. Harry's dad) is that *a*) there

is more to life than exam results, *b*) home schooling is less of a security risk, and *c*) he can hardly come round and do the school run given the whole 'being an undercover agent' thing, so it is tough luck basically.

4. Imogen's love life. This is like a subclause of number 2, because it's to do with school, but it's so big, and mental-instability-inducing, I've given it a number of its own. Because right now Imogen is totally in love with Milo Chirac who is Pennington's resident emo. She says he is definitely her ONE TRUE LOVE and she will not rest until they have signed their names in blood on each other's chests (she has been reading way too much vampire fiction again). But the thing is, three months ago she said the same about the boy who pushes trolleys around the car park at Sainsbury's, who she was convinced was actually the drummer in this band Talking Dolls. And before that it was Mr Rochester from *Jane Eyre* (though she couldn't lurk at his locker what with him NOT BEING REAL).
5. Lola i.e. my mother. Who warrants several subclauses of her own, for example (seriously, these are just the tip of the metaphorical iceberg. If I listed them all I'd be here until Christmas):
   i) Her total failure to set an example. I mean, I don't know anyone who is less like a role model

than Lola, except maybe Granny Jones, but only because she is *OBSESSED* with the seven signs of ageing (although not with eighth, i.e. owning a yappy dog called Geraldo, even though she knows I am totally allergic to dogs). And this is *NOT* because Lola is a single mother, which is completely normal now, whatever Granny Jones says, I mean even Princess Diana was a single mother, but the point is, I bet Princess Diana did not snog an international spy just because he had a mysterious beard, or eat a jar of maraschino cherries for breakfast, or let a man called Fish film her home birth with a camera he won in a bet over whether whales were extinct.

ii) The fact that I have to call her Lola, and that when I have tried to call her anything else, e.g. Mum, which you would think would not be so out there, she sticks her fingers in her ears and sings 'la la la I can't hear you' or screams and leaves the room. Plus Ruby is totally on her side because she says it is because Lola is a person in her own right and should not be identified purely by her relationship to us as her offspring. Which may be true but Lola isn't even her real name. It's Leona. And the thing is, if she hates the idea of being a 'Mum' so much, *WHY* did she have me?

iii) The Stuffed Mongoose. Which is like, a total symbol for *EVERYTHING* that is wrong with this relationship. I mean, normal mothers give their daughters book tokens for Christmas (Imo, although I am pretty sure she was *NOT* supposed to buy *Lady Chatterley's Lover*, although why I do not know because as far as I can tell it is mostly about gardening). Or ponies (Finty Goggins-Smith). Or memberships to Soho House (Sunday Henderson-Hicks). But no, last year I got a badly stuffed mongoose (i.e. it is not in a normal mongoose position, it has two legs stuck out like it's trying to do the splits or something, plus there is an inexplicable bulge in its forehead), which Lola said was to make up for not having a dog, but is frankly just creepy and now it is under my bed because every time I come in the room I can feel its beady glass mongoose eyes watching me. Which is why Stan calls it Hutch, as in Miss Hutchinson, the all-seeing eye. And this sums Lola up. She is just determined to *STAND OUT*.

And that's the point. I mean, what's so *GOOD* about standing out? Seriously, Dr Sven, *WHAT*? From now on, I don't care what Lola, or Imogen, say, I am totally going to concentrate on fitting in and being *NORMAL*. Starting tomorrow.

**Monday 6 September**

As predicted by *ME*, Buttercup Jones, Imogen has totally gone off Milo Chirac. She says this has nothing at all to do with the fact that he has developed a bad case of acne over the summer holidays, but that she is worried about their cultural differences, i.e. he is half French. This is rubbish, because normally Imogen is all for cultural differences in the hope that her mum and dad will ban her from seeing them and she will have to escape down her drainpipe to meet in secret. Anyway, I know what you're thinking, Dr Sven, which is that this should be a *GOOD THING*. But she has not sworn off men altogether, just Milo and his eruptions. And the problem is, *WHO* will she pick next? The prospects are not brilliant, given *a*) the gene pool at Pennington, and *b*) Imogen's liking for borderline psychos, fictional characters, and dead people.

<u>Imogen Pritchard's Top Five Ideal Men</u>

1. *HEATHCLIFF*, i.e. glowering antihero of *Wuthering Heights* fame. Which says it all. I mean, not only is he *MADE UP*, but he is a completely woman-hating self-pitying abuser (Ruby's phrase not mine). Although Imogen says he's just misunderstood and that it's all Cathy's fault for being an inbred prissy whinger.
2. *EDWARD CULLEN*. See above, i.e. *NOT REAL*, only with extra added threat to own life. And weird sparkly skin. Imogen practically *LIVES* in the paranormal romance

section in WH Smith. She was convinced that Freddy Fenton in 11C was really a werewolf, only it turned out he is just super hairy. Seriously, his chest is like an Alsatian. I mean is that normal at fifteen? Stan's is totally bare. He let me check and there is literally nothing. Imogen is hairier than he is.

3. JESUS. I have no idea. Really. I think this is some kind of genetic thing to do with her parents being Welsh Methodists.
4. BLAKE CARRINGTON who is *a*) going out with Sunday Henderson-Hicks, *b*) a total MUDHONEY, i.e. rugby-playing totty, i.e. not in ANY way edgy or paranormal, and *c*) wears deck shoes. Seriously. At least he's not fictional, I guess. Or the messiah. Although given his sport tendencies and limited IQ he might turn out to be a werewolf.
5. STEVE BUSCEMI, who is this weird-looking actor and WAY old for her. I mean, he's like forty-five or something. Which is TOTALLY GROSS. No offence. Because I guess you might be forty-ish (you really should have a better picture on GoShrinkYourself, it is totally blurry). But the point is you are probably married to someone who is also forty-ish. Or at least is not young enough to be your granddaughter. Or grandson. (I am totally pro gay marriage. Like Keith and Norm next door have been engaged for two years

but Keith wants to have the ceremony in the Jane Austen Museum and Norm wants a luau in Hawaii so they are locked in a no-win situation at the moment.)

Stan says Imogen is the one who needs therapy. And that, compared to her, I am totally *NORMAL*. And I guess it's true that I have never fancied a beardy prophet. But then again, I am fourteen, and apart from a crush on Tony Blair when I was eight, I have never fancied anyone. And is that normal? I mean, *IS IT*?

Oh, and on top of the Milo thing, Imogen is on a diet. *AGAIN*. This time it is Atkins Light, i.e. she is allowed some carbs but only brown ones, e.g. wholemeal bread and lentils, which she hates, so she is mostly just eating fat and protein, e.g. sausages with grated cheese, which doesn't sound that healthy to me. Imogen is always on diets. Last month it was Slimfast, which is *THE* diet of choice at Pennington, only she ended up having about eight milkshakes a day and actually put weight on. And the month before that it was food combining only that just ended in rows over whether or not Mars Bars counted as protein due to milk content. But the thing is, she's not even fat (unlike Patrick O'Hoolihan in 10D who is *TOTALLY* obese, only according to Lily Rubenstein, who is in ICT Society with him, and has seen the doctor's letter, it is his glands, not that that stops Scarlet Henderson-Hicks calling him Fatrick). Imogen is just curvy, which believe me, I would kill to be, only instead I got the stick insect gene, though where from is anyone's guess.

So all in all not a brilliant start with the normal.

Suddenly watching BBC Parliament with Harry in a bee outfit seems kind of attractive.

7 p.m.
Oh, I've just remembered something. We're getting a new head of drama. Which is totally a good thing because the old one, i.e. Ms Millington-Gypp, DID NOT LIKE me and Stan because she said we didn't take her, or the 'magic of theatre' seriously. Which is true, only how seriously can you take a woman who wore a unitard to work? Plus Stan has never forgiven her for making him be Jesus in the Year Seven nativity despite Stan claiming he was Muslim, which he isn't, but the point is, he could have been. Anyway Imogen says she's got the lead in a Royal Shakespeare Company production of *Othello*. Although according to Daisy Helmsley-Nougat, it is actually a bit part in *Casualty*, which seems more likely given that Ms Millington-Gypp was not in any way black or a man. Sunday Henderson-Hicks is totally NOT happy. I mean, it was guilt from eating Sunday's Krispy Kreme that pushed Camilla over the edge, but that's wasted if a new department head isn't wrapped around her Chanel-polished finger. Imogen says it is probably Anthony Head, who lives near here, and is in *Merlin*, and this old vampire show called *Buffy*, which Imogen is totally addicted to, because she thinks it is POSSIBLE that she actually IS Buffy. Imogen watches way too much TV. Which is a miracle given Mr and Mrs Pritchard's puritanical beliefs. Basically Imogen tells them she is watching Christian rock on the Bible Channel and they are too wrapped up in jigsaws to notice, so Imo says it

is their fault for letting her have a TV in her room and for being geeks. I mean, she could be self-harming with compasses for all they know. And I know for a fact she has thought about it.

But the point is (sorry, *I KNOW*) that school just got a tiny bit better.

**Tuesday 7 September**

Dear Dr Sven,

*UNSURPRISINGLY* our new Arts Head is *NOT* the man off *Buffy the Vampire Slayer*, it is not *EVEN* the woman in the Glade Plug-In advert, who was Imogen's second choice. It is someone called Mr Burton, who hasn't been in anything, except possibly a band called the Fruit Bats about fifteen years ago, according to Stan, who googled it in ICT. Stan is totally hoping it *IS* him, because Stan's second ambition (apart from wresting control of *Penny for Your Thoughts* etc.) is to be a session guitarist at Air Studios. Imogen pointed out that this wasn't properly ambitious and that he should want to be lead guitarist in a Grammy-award-winning band and then choke on his own vomit in the Chateau Marmont.

But Stan says this way he'll *a*) get to play with loads of different people, *b*) live, and *c*) avoid all the acrimonious falling out with the singer who wants to pursue a different sound or has snogged the bassist's girlfriend. This is because his old band The Free Radicals broke up after three weeks because Arthur Chen got off with Harriet Wicks who was supposed to be going out with Charley Grimshaw, who owned the drum kit, so no one could practise any more. So now me and Stan just mess around in the basement at Celia's. Not that I actually play anything. Unless you count 'Rehab' on the piano. Which seriously, if you heard me, you wouldn't. So I just sing. Which actually isn't TOTALLY bad. Stan says I sound like this Seventies singer Karen Carpenter. Which I thought was cool until it turned out she had killed herself. At which point IMOGEN thought it was cool.

Oh yeah. The new Head of Arts. So, Mr Kwame-Jones did the announcement in assembly this morning, and it turns out that Imogen and Norah Forbes, and most of the upper school (bar Lily Rubenstein, who makes Miss Hutchinson look visually impaired) were TOTALLY wrong and that Ms Millington-Gypp is not Othello, or getting mutilated in an improbable car accident on *Casualty*, she is taking over as Head of Drama at King James Boys. Which Imogen was totally cross about, but not as cross as Mr Kwame-Jones was with Imogen, who cried 'Oh, I am undone' just as he was about to reveal Mr Burton to the audience. Which is totally from Jane Austen, and which Imogen is always saying at totally inappropriate moments, although she claims it is just a manifestation of her need to invent drama in her otherwise mundane existence, which is what she told Mr Kwame-Jones when she got sent to his office after assembly. And Mr Kwame-Jones is obviously totally au fait with mundanity (is that even a word?) because he gave her a mint humbug and sent her back to class.

Anyway, I think my crazy rating is pretty good. Even though Imo stole my chocolate digestives at lunch. She says they are wholemeal so it is *TOTALLY* pro-Atkins (although she also got a Curly Wurly off Stan on the grounds that it is brown, which I am pretty sure is interpreting the rules a little *TOO* loosely). But she gave me her blueberries instead, which are a super food and totally good for your mental health, like oily fish, only edible. So apart from when Imogen spilt her hummus on Sunday Henderson-Hicks, who retaliated with a Strawberry Slimfast, which misfired and got stuck in my hair, nothing too mental happened today. Not compared to Harry. I asked him what he had done at 'school'. He said he got a raisin stuck in his ear and a chicken actually pecked it out.

See what I mean.

**Wednesday 8 September**

*OMG*, Dr Sven. It turns out that Mr Burton is taking over PMS. Imogen saw him putting up try-out posters outside the toilets and just asked him *STRAIGHT OUT* how come Mr Goldenblatt isn't in charge because he was deputy under Ms Millington-Gypp and is totally obsessed with musicals. But Mr Burton said according to Pennington rules PMS has to be run by the Arts department *NOT* the Humanities department, even if their head is totally gay (he did not say that bit, Imogen did). Only there is no way Mr Goldenblatt is going to take this lying down. When Michael Jackson died he wore a white glove for a week and tried to get a national holiday declared.

Oh, and Imogen is in a sulk because Stan gave me his doughnut at lunch instead of her. (It was America Day in the canteen, i.e. hamburgers, French fries—seriously—and grits, which I'm not even sure are food, which is another of the Pennington Board of Governors' concessions towards being more multicultural and inclusive.) Imogen got totally carb jealous, until I pointed out that she had two banana muffins. She says her mother is conspiring against her dream to be a skinny ingénue, and that Mrs Pritchard is possibly one of those 'feeders' who fattens people up in order to trap them and keep them under their power. She so isn't, she is just a NORMAL mum who knows how to operate an oven without it involving the fire brigade. Anyway in the end I gave Imogen half the doughnut, even though it is CLEAR that her diet is totally not working as one of the buttons on her regulation shirt pinged off during Religious Education. So it is either muffin-related or her breasts have grown AGAIN.

**Thursday 9 September**

Why can't I just be like Imogen and embrace weirdness, or even cultivate it? She is totally off the scale of happiness because today she got a STALKER. And I know this should be totally mentally compromising, but seriously she has been praying for this for a whole year, ever since Ruby got flashed

behind TopShop. She made me hang around the Southgate Centre every night after school for like two weeks after that happened, only someone saw us and reported us to Mrs Pritchard, who had thought we were at Junior Bible Study. Anyway, the point is that Imogen got this note stuck in her locker door, which she thought was a WeightWatchers leaflet from Sunday Henderson-Hicks, because she has totally done that before, but it turned out to be this anonymous poem (typed, not cut out of newspaper letters, but still, untraceable and menacing, i.e. GOOD in Imogen's eyes) all about how beautiful Imogen is and how she is Rubenesque, i.e. has big breasts. She is convinced it is from Blake Carrington. Although *a*) I don't think he has even heard of Rubens, and *b*) I totally saw him outside the chem. labs with Sunday's tongue inside his mouth. (Which, if you're wondering, which you're probably not, but, anyway, was pretty gross.)

Also, it is way more likely to be Titus Pelling, who eats bees (I am NOT EVEN JOKING), and who has had a crush on Imogen since Year Eight. But Imogen says he's not edgy enough and that stalkers have to be totally older and sinister, i.e. a potential murderer. Which I pointed out Blake totally wasn't, but she said he is in Year Eleven, which is good enough for now. She is totally hoping he starts lurking outside her house or sends her a chopped-off finger in the mail. Which I pointed out she might be confusing with kidnappers, but she says I am just trying to 'rain on her parade'. Anyway, my point is I haven't seen her this happy since she thought she had scarlet fever (it was an allergic reaction to

Marks and Spencer knickers). So why aren't I like that? *WHY, I ASK YOU, WHY???*

Although I note that Mr Burton is not so gleetastic either. This is because so far, only Sunday Henderson-Hicks, the Sidehicks, and the Asian entrepreneurs (membership two) have signed up for PMS. Stan says this it is the fault of reality TV giving the masses false hope that they can bypass the hard work route and rely on Simon Cowell and *Heat* magazine instead. But I think it's probably that they value their reputations, and possibly lives, too much.

**Friday 10 September**

2 p.m. (Geography)
Dear Dr Sven, I am in Geog, which is why my handwriting is totally *NOT* looking that of a sane person, because I am actually supposed to be learning about Belgium so I am smiling and looking definitely interested in chocolate exports, but am actually writing like mad under the desk. Anyway, the thing is, Imogen had the idea to carry the journal around in case I felt like having a breakdown and needed to 'unburden' myself, and for once she is totally right, because there is definitely a whole lot of unburdening to do. And most of it is down to Imogen, i.e. she has decided that we *HAVE* to join PMS in order to fulfil her fantasy love life. I am *NOT EVEN JOKING*.

This is because, for some inexplicable reason, Blake

Carrington has signed up. Imogen saw him writing his name under Sunday Henderson-Hicks's when she was stalking him in first break, and she thinks he was doing it 'as a sign to her' because he could totally see her behind the Rugby Club trophy cabinet (contents negligible) so she wants to sign up too only she says she can't do it unless I do because there is only so much weight-related abuse she can take from the Sidehicks without me as back-up. And it is only going to get worse, because she is NOT great on stage. Seriously, Dr Sven. She does this thing where she frowns, and makes her lip wobble, and looks like she is receiving catastrophic news, e.g. that a close relative has died, or been maimed in an accident, even when she is only supposed to be being a tree or something.

This is SO not good. She is totally going to make a fool of herself, and me, and possibly end up doing a Camilla St John Brice (although she has tried anorexia before and she only lasted three hours, thirty-seven minutes, and then she ate an entire packet of Jaffa Cakes, but that's not the point). Please, Dr Sven, let her catch laryngitis and totally lose her voice on a permanent basis. Or start fancying Titus Pelling. I mean, I know he eats insects, but at least he's SINGLE.

**Saturday 11 September**

Weird stuff I have found in the fridge today

1. A jelly in the shape of a headless monkey.
2. A new life form, growing on top of what I

think might once have been a half eaten yoghurt.

3. A hammer.
4. A urine sample belonging to 'Mr L Osgood'. WHO is he? And why is he leaving his urine in our fridge? WHY WHY WHY? When I asked Lola she said it might have been from when she read that drinking urine was good for your immune system. At that point I resolved never to ask her stuff like that again because the answer is always worse than you think it can possibly be.

On the plus side, Harry has gone on a custody visit with 007. He got picked up in blacked-out BMW half an hour ago, which personally I feel was an ill-advised choice of car as NO ONE has tinted windows round here so it totally drew attention, especially from Carl and Denny Potts who live in the flats, and who spent several minutes leaning on it pretending they were in *The Wire*. Anyway, the point is, Lola has gone round to Celia's to sulk. (Did I mention they were best friends? They were at art college together and have been pretty much inseparable ever since. Which is nice only Celia is totally an ENABLER, i.e. she just encourages Lola's unmother-like behaviour plus she is equally messed up. I mean, she is married to a gay American art dealer called Troy, who lives in LA, only he's not Stan's dad, that's Govindas, who works in a vegetarian Hare Krishna restaurant, only he used to be called Che and lived in an anti-capitalism squat in London, and is actually called Rupert. I know. Confusing, right?) Anyway, the

point is Stan and Imogen are coming over to watch DVDs. Which is most definitely a GOOD THING.

11 p.m.

Except that I forgot to factor in the now traditional Imogen versus Stan 'There is no way I am watching that film' fight; sample dialogue:

Stan: WHY would I want to damage my eyes with the sight of Hugh Grant flopping his fat lips and absurd hairdo all over Julia Roberts? Seriously, Imo, you are the one who needs medical help, not Buttercup.

Im: Oh right. So let's just BORE OURSELVES TO DEATH with some totally OBSCURE Japanese anime.

Etc.

Because Imogen ONLY likes films that involve *a*) paranormal romance, *b*) close-harmony song and dance numbers, *c*) makeovers, or *d*) Steve Buscemi.

<u>Imogen Pritchard's Top Ten Films</u>

1. *Twilight*. Because she thinks she is Bella. Which she SO IS NOT.
2. *New Moon*. As above. Plus Taylor Lautner gets his chest out in almost every scene. Which, personally, made me do a bit of sick in my mouth, but then I'm clearly a FREAK.
3. *Ghost World*. Which is also on Stan's top ten list because he says it is the closest adaptation of a comic

book ever, bar *Scott Pilgrim*. Whereas Imogen likes it because *a*) it involves Steve Buscemi and *b*) I once told her she looked like Scarlett Johannson, i.e. she has breasts and blonde hair.

4. *Brief Encounter*. Which does not involve any of the above but is a black and white film about a doomed affair, both of which are high on Imogen's favourite ever items. I mean, she actually wishes the world was in black and white because she says it is totally more dramatic and moody. Which is weird but not as weird as the phase where she wanted a permanent voiceover for her life and started referring to herself in the third person, e.g. '"Oh, where are my black pants," said Imogen as she fell back on her black satin sheets and pouted mysteriously.' She does not have black satin sheets. They are yellow cotton. But this kind of detail has never bothered her.
5. *Notting Hill*. Imogen thinks London is ACTUALLY like this. She is deluded. The last time I went to London, which was to see Stan's dad Govindas at the vegetarian restaurant, a dead pigeon fell on my head. And I am NOT EVEN JOKING.
6. *ET*. Which even I like. Although I'm not totally sure as to why Imogen does. I mean, there's no makeover. Or singing. So unless she also fancies wide-headed aliens with glow-in-the-dark fingers, which I guess is entirely

possible given her track record on vampires etc., it is a total mystery.

7. *Hairspray*. John Travolta in a fat suit. What's not to like? Actually, maybe Zac Efron. EEEW. I actually did a shudder then.
8. *The Princess Diaries*. Because she is ACTUALLY convinced that this will happen to her. That, any day now, Mrs Pritchard will admit that she is heir to the throne of some made-up European principality and that Julie Andrews is in fact her grandmother.
9. *Camp Rock*. She will not watch horror, because she says it is too UNREALISTIC. Yet she has seen this twenty-seven times. TWENTY-SEVEN! Despite Stan pointing out that there is no way that an internationally famous guitarist would have to teach street dance.
10. *Barbie Fairytopia: Magic of the Rainbow*. Which I cannot even bring myself to comment on.

Seriously. This CANNOT be healthy. How is reality ever going to live up to the dialogue that I know for a fact Imogen rehearses in her head at every available opportunity? Especially if reality is Blake Carrington. I mean, have you HEARD him speak? Well, obviously not. But let me tell you, it is usually stuff like 'AWESOME' or 'MAAAAATE' or 'LATERS'. Which you have to admit, is kind of a let down.

11.30 p.m.
Oh, in the end we watched *The Wizard of Oz*. Not because Imogen won. But because it was the only DVD that didn't have Harry's (or Lola's) sticky fingermarks on it, or chicken-related damage. It was actually OK. Even Stan got into the flying monkeys. He said it had a graphic novel feel about it.

1 a.m.
Lola hasn't come back from Celia's. Which means I am TOTALLY home alone. Or I would be if Stan hadn't offered to stay over. Is this even legal? The home alone bit, I mean. Not Stan staying. Because nothing funny is going on there. He's like asleep on the floor, in Ruby's protest sleeping bag. NOTE TO SELF: Check legal age of being left unsupervised in house.

1.10 a.m.
Actually he's not asleep. He says the sound of my pen is keeping him awake. So I'm stopping now.

**Sunday 12 September**

I KNEW it was a mistake watching *The Wizard of Oz*. All that 'Over the Rainbow'ing has TOTALLY fuelled Imogen's determination to join PMS and win Blake over with her Dorothy-like charms.

This is SO NOT good. I mean, all I want to do is kind of fade

into background somewhere. But if I join PMS I might as well walk around with a sign on my back saying '*FREAK*' (which Titus Pelling actually did one year, only Blake Carrington stuck it on him, he didn't actually do it himself. But that's not the point). And anyway, why is Blake even in PMS? I mean, he plays *RUGBY*. Stan said it's because he's actually gay. But Imogen said *a*) Stan is just trying to be anti-competitive sports (which he is, but mainly because rugby could compromise his guitar fingers) and also that it is totally clichéd to assume all men involved in musical theatre are homosexual, except Mr Goldenblatt, who is *TOTALLY* gay, but is a history teacher so he is actually breaking the mould, and *b*) Stan has *NO* gaydar, which he has totally inherited from Celia, whereas she has totally clear reception when it comes to gayness. (Which is so not true because for a bit she thought Ruby was a lesbian but it turned out that the person with long hair who she had been snogging outside the Mung Bean vegan café was Spike. And Celia totally knew that Troy was gay when she married him. It was a visa thing.) Stan said, 'Whatever, but I'm telling you, he's gay.'

But even I think Stan's wrong on this one. I mean, Blake shops in Jack Wills for crying out loud.

**Monday 13 September**

It turns out that no one sent Imogen a chopped finger in the post over the weekend or lurked outside her bedroom window (she double checked with the Post Office and Mrs Larkin next door) so now she is totally convinced that Blake is her stalker, on the grounds that he has all his fingers intact. Which I pointed out was insane, because so does everyone at Pennington (except for Juno Platt who lost one in a freak accident with a Hoover) plus the fact that he hadn't sent anything, or done any stalking, means he is not in fact a stalker at all. But then she accused me of peeing on her bonfire, which reminded me of the whole urine in the fridge thing again, which then Imogen got TOTALLY jealous about, and so I ended up standing outside the boys' changing rooms for two hours after school to make up for it. Which it turns out was a total waste of time because rugby practice was called off on account of the pitch being waterlogged, and, according to Lily Rubenstein, Blake had gone to TopShop with Sunday to look at strapless prom dresses. Which Imogen said was a sign because she has wanted a strapless prom dress for ages, only Fashion Stylist Guru person Gok Wan says she can't have one. I agreed it was definitely a sign, i.e. give up on Blake, he is TAKEN, and possibly a cross-dresser. But Imogen got even more excited about that possibility because that would make him TOTALLY deviant in Mrs Pritchard's eyes, as if stalking didn't already tick that box.

Anyway, the result is, Imogen is even more determined that PMS is the answer to pretty much everything:

*a*) her love life,

*b*) her insane desire to have a movie made about her,

c) her belief that she is, actually, a reincarnation of Marilyn Monroe.

And I have tried to point out that it is the unanswer (is that even a word?) to all of my issues, i.e.:

a) I am too tall,
b) I am too nervous,
c) I am too crazy.

But she says if I loved her even a little bit then I would do this one simple thing for her. Which may not be fingers in the post but is TOTALLY blackmail. So what do I do, Dr Sven? WHAT?

**Tuesday 14 September**

OH. MY. GOD. I have done it. I have just signed over my soul to the devil, i.e. Pennington Musical Society. I am NOT EVEN JOKING. The only plus side is that, if I go down, Stan goes down with me. I said I thought he was totally opposed to it on account of habitual joiners and jazz hands. But he said he's going to take them down from the inside, Ruby-style. Plus he reckons Mr Burton might actually turn out to be pretty cool, because he has a shaved head and a Ramones T-shirt. But how cool can a man who runs a glee club be? I ask you.

Seriously, Dr Sven, I think life, as I know it, just got a whole bunch worse.

**Wednesday 15 September**

The war has begun. So far today Sunday Henderson-Hicks has tripped me up, spilt Slimfast Chocolate on Imogen's maths homework, and left a box of goldfish food in my locker. Imogen says it is just further proof why Sunday is so wrong for Blake and she is so right. Stan said if anyone is right for Blake *HE* is, but Imogen threatened to stick chocolate-flavoured quadratic equations in his amp socket so he shut up after that.

This is so *NOT* good. And I feel sorry for Mr Burton. Seriously, Dr Sven, I really don't think he's cut out to deal with the horror that is PMS. I mean, I saw him go into Miss Hutchinson's office earlier and I could totally hear her giving him a five-point list on why his Ramones T-shirt (actual vintage, not mass produced for Urban Outfitters) is totally inappropriate for Pennington. And he didn't even *TRY* to argue back, despite having height advantage because he is totally over six foot, and Miss Hutchinson is four foot eleven. (Not that he would have won because she is totally immovable when it comes to uniform. She once sent Imogen home for her skirt being too tight, even though it wasn't Imogen's fault, it was having macaroni cheese for lunch.)

He is *SO* going to get crucified.

As am I.

**Thursday 16 September**

As predicted by me, Mr Goldenblatt is *NOT* taking the PMS thing lying down. He is totally forming his own all-male show choir, which will exclusively perform Michael Jackson hits, and a Mariah Carey ballad. According to Lily Rubenstein, Mr Burton has gone to Mr Kwame- Jones to complain that it is petty, and sexist. But this is a school that *STILL* refuses to let girls join the football team on the grounds that our breasts will be distracting.

Oh, and to make matters worse, Imogen got another secret admirer note. (Have stopped referring to him as a stalker as I think that just encouraged her.) I'm beginning to think it might be Blake, because anyone with an ounce of intelligence would know this is *NOT* helping. I mean, Imogen already lives in fantasy land, and this is just pushing her over the edge of some fictional/reality quantum leap thingy. Although given the fact that Lily Rubenstein says Blake and Sunday were snogging in her mum's hot tub at the weekend, maybe it actually *IS* Edward Cullen, after all.

**Friday 17 September**

Mr Kwame-Jones says there is no way he can endorse the Jackson Twenty, i.e. Mr Goldenblatt's all-male all-Michael Jackson show choir. According to Lily Rubenstein, it is not the sexism, it is the demands for exclusive use of the piano, a make-up artist, and a redesign of the school theatre to allow them to emerge on a giant white-gloved hand from beneath the seats.

So Mr Goldenblatt's dream is over already. Though he should be kind of used to it. I mean, it is totally not his first:

<u>Mr Goldenblatt's Broken Dreams</u>

1. The time his boyband You've Got Male got booed off stage at the Battle of the Bands.
2. The time he tried to demonstrate box splits to the Year Sevens and ended up in the emergency room with groin strain, and on YouTube with his trousers ripped. (*WHY* would you wear thong to school, Dr Sven? *WHY*?)
3. The time he thought he had been talent spotted by Sharon Osbourne in last year's pantomime, only it turned out to be that red-headed emo from the bookshop.

**Saturday 18 September**

Ugh. Bad start to Saturday. I have just rediscovered the note I found in my locker yesterday and then immediately tried to block from my memory. I guess at least this one was not from a secret admirer/stalker, but was still pretty mentally compromising, i.e. it was from Mr Burton reminding me that the first PMS meeting is on Monday after school and that he

is looking forward to meeting me and all the other LOSERS who have signed their lives away.

OK, so he didn't say that last bit, but he might as well have. I mean, it's not that I don't love to sing. I do. In the shower. Or at Stan's. But in front of actual people? Not so much. And in front of Sunday Henderson-Hicks? Seriously, I'd rather chew tinfoil. I mean, her entire EXISTENCE is devoted to musicals. According to Lily Rubenstein she has a signed photo of John Barrowman next to her bed and does dancercise to the *Les Miserables* soundtrack every morning before school.

Imogen says she will just have to make way for fresh new talent, like Madonna, who is totally stepping aside gracefully for Lady Gaga. Only I am pretty sure that *a*) Sunday Henderson-Hicks would not step aside gracefully for Lady Gaga let alone me, I mean, she is the one who started the rumour this morning that I am actually a hermaphrodite, i.e. half female half male, and *b*) we are not, by any description, talent.

Ruby says I have got my priorities totally wrong and in fact I should be devoting my extra-curricular time to her and Spike's anti-private school protest, i.e. to stop Pennington only admitting students who are either loaded and/or Gifted and Talented, and let everyone walk the hallowed halls and play lacrosse, even if they wear jeggings and eat Monster Munch.

I should clarify at this point that Lola is not loaded and neither am I amazingly gifted or talented. It's just that the entrance paper had loads of stuff about co-ordinates on it and me and Stan had been playing Battleships obsessively since we were eight. Anyway, Ruby says it is class war and I have to sign up to it. I said I'd think about it. I mean, I am totally against not letting people in just because their dads don't play golf with Mr Ledbetter-Morpeth or any of the other governors. It's just that the last protest I went on with Ruby was outside Mr Shamsie's Food Emporium (it is not an emporium, it is a corner shop with own brand baked beans and five kinds of Pot Noodle; he has ideas way above reality, although Imogen says it is good that he is dreaming big) and was against him selling misogynistic, i.e. woman-hating, magazines, only it turned out it was *Nuts*, which is just rubbish rather than completely women-hating, and he banned me from shopping there ever again which means now I have to walk all the way to the giant supermarket to get Sour Skittles (which are totally my favourite sweet and I once ate eleven packets in one day, only I got a bit sugar high and sang 'Pokerface' to Miss Hutchinson when I was waiting to see Mr Kwame-Jones for eating sweets in Citizenship, so I am limited to one packet now for mental health reasons).

At least I am not the only one with troubles though. Granny Jones rang (who has clearly forgotten she has disowned us, in less than two weeks, which is a new record) and is in a bad mood because Mr Cement (I am NOT EVEN JOKING), who lives downstairs (and who is actually this totally nice man who used to run an art gallery, but who Granny does not like because he votes Lib Dem and wears yellow trousers) has complained about Geraldo (who is not a gay hairdresser, he is a whippet, and who she has *EVEN THOUGH* she totally knows I am allergic to him, because she says no one was allergic to dogs when she was my age and I just need to buck up). Mr Cement says he can hear Geraldo barking through the ceiling, but Granny says Mr Cement is lying because *a*) she has the expensive kind of underlay and *b*) Geraldo does not bark. But the thing is Geraldo totally does bark. Because Granny leaves the telly on for him when she goes to Dr Jolly's Eternal Youth clinic for tri-annual botox injections (because Dr Jolly does not allow dogs, which Granny says is contravening her human rights, but it turns out she would rather be wrinkle-free than just plain free), but she always puts it on the Shopping Channel, because there is non-stop talking, only he has this weird hatred of the Diamonique slot, and barks like crazy, which I know for a fact because once I was walking past on my way to stalk the shopping trolley boy with Imogen, and we could hear the yapping all the way from Sainsbury's.

**Sunday 19 September**

5 p.m.

*OMG*. Have just remembered *PMS* starts tomorrow. And I swear I feel like I swallowed the urine sample right now. And the thing is, if I feel this bad now, what is it going to be like when I'm doing high kicks to something out of *Chorus Line*?

Stan says I need to be more positive and think of it as an opportunity to subvert PMS. This is because he lives to subvert things. Like, even when we were seven he was trying to get a T-Rex song into assembly. But I am pretty sure there is no way he is going to get Mr Burton to agree to put on *Marc Bolan, The Musical*. Which I totally told him. But he just said 'Oh, come on, Buttercup, do it for me.' Which is unfair. Because he knows I completely will.

10 p.m.
OK. So I have done some positive thinking, i.e.:

1. Maybe I can just do it for one week.
2. Maybe even Imogen will be put off by the level of freakness that pervades all school societies.
3. Maybe there won't even be a show this term.
4. Maybe we'll just sing scales and do those trust games where you fall backwards and hope someone catches you. I mean, even a fractured coccyx is probably preferable to a full-on *Mamma Mia* fest.

Stan says this is *NOT* what he meant by positive. But I said it was all he was going to get until I am sure no one is going to make me harmonize 'There's No Business Like Showbusiness' in a catsuit.

**Monday 20 September**

This is when I wonder whether positive thinking is really all it's cracked up to be, Dr Sven. Because, seriously, spinal injury might be preferable to the *HELL* I have somehow got myself involved in. I so should have double-checked that sign-up sheet, i.e.:

<u>PMS Membership List</u>

- Sunday Henderson-Hicks (needs no explanation)
- Poppy Pringle, Alicia Beaufort, Finty Goggins-Smith (aka the Sidehicks)
- Lucinda Ledbetter-Morpeth (father is head of board of governors)
- Titus Pelling (who, it turns out, can totally act, although Imogen says it does not make up for the fact that he eats bees)
- Fintan Riley (has enormous head. Not hair, head. Seriously, it is alarmingly big.)
- Blake Carrington (apparently not gay as definitely saw him stare at Imogen's breasts during the warm-up jumping, although she was springing so vigorously right in his face I thought he might sustain breast-related injury at one point).
- Norah Forbes (partially sighted).
- Daisy Helmsley-Nougat (junior gymkhana champion of the south-west)

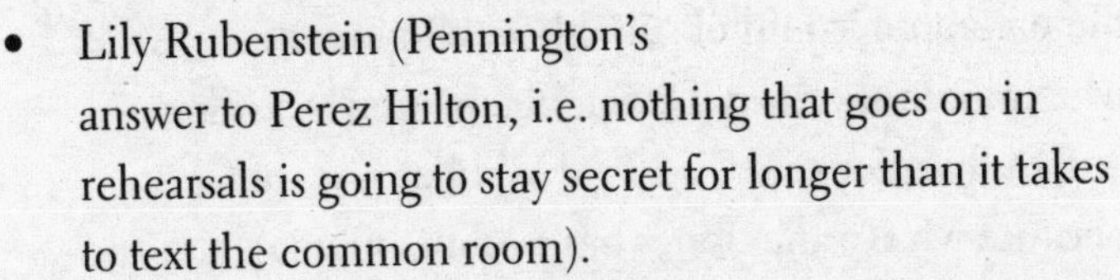

- Len Cho (president of Asian Entrepreneurs, Maths Club, Chess Club, and others too numerous and pants to mention)
- Lily Rubenstein (Pennington's answer to Perez Hilton, i.e. nothing that goes on in rehearsals is going to stay secret for longer than it takes to text the common room).

And that's just the ones I can remember. I swear I have blanked half of them out to avoid further trauma.

Oh. And it TOTALLY gets worse. Because we are not just doing singalongs and trust games for the rest of term, because they've already been BANNED after one of the Sidehicks refused to catch Len Cho on the grounds that he 'like, smells' (which he kind of does, because he has this addiction to cheese and onion crisps but that is not the point). No, Dr Sven, we are doing a full-scale, open to the public, ROCK MUSICAL, as written by Mr Burton. Seriously. The only good thing is that there is a whole list of other people who are so not happy with this, e.g:

1. Sunday Henderson-Hicks, who says that she cannot perform substandard work because it might damage her vocal cords and CV.
2. Alicia Beaufort who says she was totally told by Mr Goldenblatt that they were doing *Sound of Music* and she has been rehearsing Maria for the whole summer including pretending she is a nun (which, frankly,

I can't see, given what she does with Clint Cooper-Willis behind the cricket pavilion).

3. Lucinda Ledbetter-Morpeth who says that her father says PMS is supposed to perform something from the pre-approved list of suitable entertainment, which includes *Salad Days* and anything by Gilbert and Sullivan or Andrew Lloyd Webber (except *Cats* because Mr Kwame-Jones has a feline phobia).
4. Mr Goldenblatt, who is off with swine flu/disappointment at the premature end of the Jackson Twenty dream, only Poppy Pringle texted him with an emergency alert and he issued a warning from his sick bed that he will fight this to the high court if he has to, once he is out of quarantine.

Mr Burton told us that the songs will be totally written by professionals because they will all be Top 40 hits from the last three decades (which Stan is totally gloating about, although I have told him that this means they are going to be CHART PANTS not Indie kid shoegazing or prog rock), that he totally understood that change is always tough, but that it was time to bring Pennington into the twenty-first century (which I swear is NEVER going to happen, I mean we play lacrosse, for God's sake, LACROSSE!). But Sunday and the Sidehicks, and Blake by default, are threatening to boycott PMS until there is regime change. Which I pointed out to Imogen was a good reason to leave, i.e. what is the point of being members if Blake isn't even in it. But she said, *a*) There is no way Sunday will not do PMS, because the only other society she can join, that she hasn't already, is Asian Entrepreneurs and they won't have her on the grounds that she thinks Taiwan is in China, and *b*) that Imo wants more than Blake, she wants stardom as well, and as her best friend I should be totally supportive of her dreams instead of trying to undermine them with my self-obsession.

Which is pretty impossible because her dreams change on a regular basis. Like last term she wanted to be the first ever woman President of the United States. And in Year Seven she wanted to be Mary Magdalene. Seriously, the only person who has more diverse ambitions is Harry, who has so far wanted to be a doctor, an orang-utan, and the first boy on the moon. And anyway the point is I'm NOT self-obsessed, or trying to undermine her. I'm just trying to save myself. And her. Because, apart from Sunday Henderson-Hicks, she is TOTALLY her own worst enemy and this is only going to end in tears. Which is something I possibly should not have told Imogen, because now she is not speaking to me. I have tried to phone but Mrs Pritchard says she is busy memorizing Psalms. Which I know is a total lie. She is watching *Hollyoaks* and sulking.

9 p.m.
Maybe I am self-obsessed. I mean, not wanting to do PMS is mostly about me. And I hardly ever give money to the homeless guy selling the *Big Issue* outside Tesco (although

that is because I usually don't have any plus his dog weed on Imogen's Ugg boots once). Plus, I'm writing this diary. Which is *COMPLETELY* about me.

9.10 p.m.
Except the bits that are about Imogen and Stan and Lola etc. And which I will definitely edit. Or get permission for or something.

10 p.m.
I think Imogen is right. I am too self-obsessed. So I am going to be more supportive of her dream. Because she IS my best friend. And because she will probably change her mind in a week anyway.

10.10 p.m.
Oh, and I will definitely buy a *Big Issue* next time I am in town.

10.15 p.m.
And happen to be wearing wellies.

**Tuesday 21 September**

Except that Imogen totally does not make it easy for me to be supportive, i.e. this morning she said the Atkins Light thing is totally failing, for some inexplicable reason (only it is totally explicable when you take into account that she has been averaging two bags of chocolate raisins a day on the grounds that they were once fruit) so she is now on the Lemon Detox, which involves only consuming large quantities of water mixed with lemon juice, maple syrup, and chilli powder. She said Beyoncé lost a stone and a half in a week on it and she is aiming for at least that by the auditions on Monday, so under no circumstances was I allowed to feed her carbohydrates, not even if she begged and threatened to kill herself, or me.

Except that at first break she told me if I didn't give her a Nutella sandwich she would tell Sunday Henderson-Hicks that the rumour she made up about me being a hermaphrodite is actually true so OBVIOUSLY I gave in only now she says I am ruining her chances of leading ladydom by feeding her junk food. I told her that Mr Burton totally does not look like the kind of man who has an issue with REAL women, but she said she doesn't want to be real she just wants to be Edith Piaf. You see, Dr Sven? There is no winning with her. This is what I have to put up with.

**Wednesday 22 September**

10 a.m. (Citizenship)
OK, so honestly, Dr Sven, I really wanted to support Imogen's Blake/*High School Musical* dream thing today (i.e. let her come to mine after school to rehearse, because she can't do

it at her house due to Mr and Mrs Pritchard's silent scripture contemplation thing) only it turns out I have to go to Granny Jones's after school to pick up Harry because he is having lessons there for the day. (Lola says it is really important for him to learn skills and wisdom from the older generations. This is a TOTAL lie. She is going round Celia's.) So Imogen is STILL refusing to speak to me, which is totally annoying, especially as she is sitting next to me. In fact I am writing this in huge writing in the hope she will read it and see that I am BEING VERY SUPPORTIVE AND NOT AT ALL HUNG-UP OR SELF-OBSESSED ABOUT MY OWN MENTAL HEALTH. EVEN THOUGH IT IS TOTALLY BEING PUT AT RISK.

*Oh my God. I can't believe you wrote that. You so ARE NOT being supportive. What about my own mental health? I am totally at risk of perishing with love for Blake. I can barely eat. I might even WASTE AWAY by Monday and it will ALL be YOUR FAULT. And you had better cry at the funeral. And make sure they play 'She's the One'.*

Sorry. Imogen wrote that bit. I am writing really small now, so she cannot read me pointing out that she is NOT going to waste away because she had a Snickers at first break (for the peanut protein, i.e. she is back on Atkins Light because the chilli did bad things to her wee) and right now she is sucking a fruit Polo that she found in her coat pocket. And more importantly, I am trying to be supportive, but my completely hopeless family is ONCE AGAIN ruining my life plans.

**Thursday 23 September**

Imogen is still sulking. I know this because there was another note in our lockers this morning telling us to come to an 'Impromptu PMS Singalong' at lunchtime to 'get our heads in the game' for the auditions on Monday, which, like *EWWW*. Anyway, I *TOTALLY* went, and so did Stan, even though he would rather have been in the ICT room trying to hack into the Pentagon, and I would rather have been anywhere in the world, even a rat-infested Mumbai slum (which Imogen would always rather be in), only Imogen absolutely refused to stand next to me and actually opted to 'buddy up' (again, *EWWWW*) with Len Cho for the duets, despite the fact that he is now on two packets of cheese and onion a day. Which meant I got Stan, which is actually kind of cool, because we did 'Ice, Ice Baby'. Which was meant to be ironic. Only Titus Pelling actually started breakdancing. He has no shame.

Nor, it turns out, does Mr Goldenblatt. According to Lily Rubenstein he has submitted his own musical to Mr Kwame-Jones, which he has written on his swine flu sick bed. It is called *Off The Wall* and is the life story of a troubled Jewish pop star called 'Michael Jacksonberg', with himself playing the lead role and Sunday Henderson-Hicks as his sister Janice. I am *NOT EVEN JOKING*.

**Friday 24 September**

<u>Things I learned at school today</u>

1. That Belgium's biggest export to America is diamonds.
2. That Imogen is still sulking. Which is, like, a *TOTAL* record. Normally she only manages three hours before she has to tell me something earth-shatteringly important.
3. Mr Burton totally knows who I am, and weirder, thinks I am, in some way, good at something. I am *NOT EVEN JOKING*.

So I was at the water fountain, minding my own business, and trying *TOTALLY* to ignore the fact that Sunday Henderson-Hicks was singing 'Ebony and Ivory' with Poppy Pringle, neither of whom are darker than St Tropez medium, when he came right over and said, 'Hi, Buttercup. So, I . . . er . . . hope you're, like, auditioning. You've got a totally strong . . . er . . . alto,' which is a kind of voice (though I guess you knew that, although I didn't—I totally had to Google it). And which is weird, because *a*) I really didn't think he knew my name because I totally, like, mumbled my way through the cheesetastic 'hi my name is' introduction thing, plus *b*) how can he tell I've got a really strong anything from me rapping 'I rock a mic like a vandal'. Seriously, *HOW*?

Only now of course I feel like I totally *HAVE* to audition because otherwise I am letting him down. Which maybe is what he wants me to think. Maybe it is all Jedi mind tricks to force me

into humiliation.

Or maybe he's just a nice guy.

Oh God. Now I'm even more mixed up than before.

10 p.m.

PS I may have been totally wrong about the home schooling thing. I mean, when am I going to need to know about Belgium's trade deficit in the real world, *WHEN*?

**Saturday 25 September**

Hi, Dr Sven. I can't write much as a Good Thing has happened. Or at least mostly good, because *IMOGEN IS HERE*, i.e. she is totally talking to me again. This is because I texted her and told her she could come over for the whole day and that Harry's dad might show up and she totally cannot resist a chance to risk getting herself blown up by fundamentalists. The Bad Thing is that now I have to *REHEARSE*. Imogen has decided that she cannot suffer Len Cho's crisp breath, because it is 'torturously reminding her that she can never eat macaroni cheese again', and wants me to duet with her on 'Islands in the Stream'. Only she gets to be full-breasted blonde Country and Western legend Dolly Parton, and I have to be beardy old man Kenny Rogers. Which I have agreed to *ONLY* because I am being supportive, otherwise, Kenny Rogers? Seriously?

Stan is here too. Him and Harry are going to be the judges. Lola wanted to know what we were doing so I told her, including the Blake bit, in the hope that she might actually exert some parental influence and ban it. But she is *ALL* in favour. She said she once joined the Conservative Party purely because she fancied someone called Gideon. She has *NO SHAME*.

5 p.m.
The judges have spoken: Stan says we will win on originality, only I should wear a fake beard to look more convincing and Harry asked to marry Imogen (I think even he is mesmerized by her breasts). Anyway, it totally pleased Imogen, thank God, because she asked Harry when his dad was coming and he said he wasn't as he was in a safe house in Kuala Lumpur until next Tuesday. And then I could totally tell Imogen was about to accuse me of *LYING*, but I quickly said, 'That's what he *WANTS* you to think, Harry. It's to throw any potential kidnappers off the trail.' Which was clever, no? Anyway. I am totally being more positive, which should please you and Stan. Because, like he says, by this time on Monday it will all be over.

**Sunday 26 September**

10 a.m.

Oh. My. God. The auditions are only, like, *HOURS AWAY*. Hours before I lose any shred of dignity I had left by pretending to be an old man with a beard called Kenny. Hours before Mr Burton wonders what *PLANET* he was on when he begged me to audition. Hours before Sunday Henderson-Hicks actually laughs so hard at my *PANTSNESS* a bit of pee comes out (this happened to me once, and I am *NOT EVEN JOKING*, only it wasn't at Sunday, because I am so not that mean, it was at Stan doing his impersonation of Prince in a launderette, which, like, you would totally get if you saw it, but it kind of doesn't work on paper, so I'm not even going to try).

And after that, then there's the show.

This isn't the end. This is just the beginning.

Damn. I knew this positive thing couldn't last.

2 p.m.
Now they are less than hours away. Actually that's not true. They are still hours away, just fewer than before. I must stop exaggerating, I'm starting to sound like Imogen. I'll be claiming I'm undone next.

Stan says I'll be fine, and anyway, I'm not really auditioning, I'm just backing Imogen up. Which is totally true in theory. Only why doesn't it feel like it in practice. Plus I'm not at all sure Imogen is going to thank me for my performance if part of it involves barfing.

**Monday 27 September**

8 a.m.
OK. On the scale of craziness thing, I am at, like 8. Which is

so *NOT* good. I keep replaying Stan in my head telling me I am only doing it for Imogen. Which is totally true. But I still want to hurl. The only positive I can find in this situation is that in a few hours it, and possibly my existence at Pennington, will be over.

5 p.m.
OK. So that didn't totally go according to plan.

1. I mean, I *TOTALLY* told Mr Burton that I was only there to back up Imogen and that I wasn't really singing at all so not to really look at me, or listen or anything. But I totally caught him looking. And not just idly glancing, but totally *STARING*. And *THEN* he made me sing *AGAIN*. Only this time with Stan, even though Stan was only supposed to be there for moral support, (and to remind me which way I was supposed to be facing), because he said the song didn't 'show my voice off' and he needed to hear me with a male. So I said we couldn't because we hadn't rehearsed anything except 'Ice, Ice Baby'. But then *STAN*, of *ALL* people, says 'We can do "Fairytale of New York"' which is true, because we are always singing it at Christmas because it totally makes Celia cry, and so we end up doing it in front of everybody, including Sunday Henderson-Hicks who is looking at me like I have just spat Hubba Bubba on her Manolos, and Imogen who is looking like she wants to spit something worse

on my Converse. So then I had to spend twenty minutes afterwards sucking up to her and pointing out that *a*) as I didn't even want to be in PMS, Mr Burton was hardly going to give me a role, *b*) Stan is really the one at fault because he offered to sing with me, for some INEXPLICABLE reason, and *c*) realistically neither of us is going to get a lead because Sunday Henderson-Hicks did 'I Am Beautiful' and Poppy Pringle actually passed out. Only no one will know anything until Friday when the casting is done, so now I have four days of Imogen sulking purgatory to get through.

2. It turns out Blake Carrington can actually sing. I mean, he looks like a meat-head rugby bore, but he kind of sounds like a very young Frank Sinatra. Weird, huh?

**Tuesday 28 September**

Sometimes, Dr Sven, I am totally grateful for Imogen's wish to live inside a soap opera script, because she got another letter in her locker today and now she is WAY too consumed with secret admirer love to worry about me overshadowing her performance. If it wasn't for the fact that it was four pages long, in Times New Roman 10 point, I would write the whole thing out for you here, because you would TOTALLY have a field day analysing it. I mean, whoever wrote it has ACTUALLY

compared Imogen to Gabriella Montez and himself to Troy Bolton (i.e. from *High School Musical*, which, according to Ruby is Disney's MOST evil, world-dominating output EVER, even beating *Hannah Montana*, and according to Stan is just pants). Imogen says it is definite evidence that Blake is her secret admirer because according to Lily Rubenstein he went to the Odeon seven times in two days when *High School Musical* 3 came out and has a poster of Zac Efron above his bed. And I totally would argue against this, only we saw him in the canteen and his gaze was definitely pointed in the general direction of Imogen's breasts (although they are quite hard to avoid. I have seen Miss Hutchinson make eye contact and she walked into a door she was so COMPLETELY transfixed), which meant he totally DID NOT see Imogen wink at him, but Sunday Henderson-Hicks, who was in the salad queue, DID and asked her if she had something in her eye, and Imogen, who spends, like, entire days thinking up lines like this to throw into conversation, said 'Just Blake' and then flipped her hair in what I think was supposed to be some kind of seductive manner, but it ended up hitting Arthur Chen in the eye and then he had to go to see Miss Hutchinson for Optrex and Imogen had to see Mr Kwame-Jones about her aggression. She totally didn't care though because *a*) she has been waiting two years to use the line about the eye, and *b*) Blake (allegedly) thinks she is Gabriella, i.e. lead girl material, and *c*) Mr Kwame-Jones said it is unsurprising that she is aggressive coming from such a violent poverty-stricken background (he has never met

Mr and Mrs Pritchard), and that it is society to blame, not her.

Anyway, that wasn't the bad bit of today. That happened right after, when me and Stan were deconstructing the incident in ICT (this wasn't the lesson, we were supposed to be differentiating between ROM and RAM, but seriously, what is *THAT* about?) and Stan said at least it meant Imogen will still be talking to me on Saturday. So I said, 'Why, what's happening on Saturday?' And then *STAN* totally stopped speaking to me. And now I have checked on the Chickens of the World calendar in the kitchen and it turns out that Saturday is *STAN'S BIRTHDAY*! Seriously. I cannot *BELIEVE* I forgot it. This is *ALL* because of PMS distracting me and compromising my mental health more than it is already compromised by Lola and her genetic mess. So now I only have four days to redeem myself because *a*) even if he is, according to the contract, my second best friend, that is just a piece of paper, which I was forced under Guantanamo conditions to sign, and in *REAL LIFE* Stan is *TOTALLY THE MOST IMPORTANT PERSON IN MY LIFE EVER*. I mean, he's like my brother, or something. Plus *b*) his parties are totally cool, i.e. they do not involve homeless men, or birth videos.

*BUT* the thing is I have no money to buy him a present. And as Lola still hasn't come up with a new genius money-making scheme, I don't know when I'll be getting any. Which totally kind of sucks, Dr Sven.

**Wednesday 29 September**

OK, so I may be being paranoid, but *I SWEAR* Mr Burton just winked at me outside the chem. lab. And, like, what does this *MEAN*? I am totally not asking Imo because she will totally tell me it is because he is a pervert, or stalker, i.e. a good thing. But I think, unless he has some sort of nervous twitch, like Hatty Perrin in Year Thirteen, who touches her right ear every thirty seconds, it is definitely audition-related. So either it could be that I have his sympathies because I was so appalling that he regrets ever asking me to sing in the first place. Or that he actually liked it. Which, frankly, is *WORSE*.

Oh. But on the good side, I've totally solved the Stan birthday present thing. I'm going to make him a mix CD. Which is totally unoriginal, because it's what I do every year, but in the current economic climate, i.e. total recession, I *REALLY* don't have a choice. But because I do it every year, I figured it's kind of upholding a tradition, which would emphasize how important Stan and all our stuff together is, don't you think? And I know he totally loves mix CDs, especially theme ones, which are kind of like my speciality. Like one year the theme was animals, so there was The Doves, and Gorillaz, and also the Beatles 'Blackbird' (which was double points for band and song). And last year the theme was 'Stan', so I had 'Stan' by Eminem, and Paul Weller's 'Stanley Road', and loads of stuff by Stan Getz, who is this lounge artist guy. Oh, and also 'I'm Still Standing' by Elton John, which is a total cheat, but Stan thought was genius. And I have thought really hard (well at least for the whole of *Homes Under the Hammer*, which is what Harry is currently watching, and which Lola claims is teaching him financial and construction skills) and this year's theme is going to be 'love'. Which I know sounds lame, and I did want to do 'Mongoose', but that would mean buying obscure hardcore house off iTunes, which I can't afford, and is also illegal because we are banned from anything to do with Apple after Ruby and Spike sent ninety-two threatening letters to Steve Jobs in some anti-capitalism protest, so I needed something totally generic, but totally meaningful, and which can be found easily in Lola's extensive, if oddball, CD collection. So far I have got nine out of ten tracks:

1. 'I Love Rock 'n' Roll' (Joan Jett original version NOT Britney Spears cover)
2. 'Hello, I Love You' (The Doors, who are like Stan's second favourite dead band, after T-Rex)
3. 'Ten Storey Love Song' (Stone Roses—total Nineties classic, according to Lola)
4. 'How Deep Is Your Love' (Bee Gees—total Eighties cheese according to me)
5. 'Last Night I Dreamt that Somebody Loved Me' (The Smiths, who are this depressing Eighties band from Manchester, but Stan says their guitarist Johnny Marr is a living GOD)
6. 'Whole Lotta Love' (Led Zeppelin—no explanation

needed. Even I think this rocks.)

7. 'To Love Somebody' (Nina Simone—this song makes me cry, and I have *NO* idea why. Although I cried at a Coca-Cola advert last week. But I think it might just have been because I was due on.)

   *OH MY GOD. TMI.* Will never mention periods again.

8. 'You Don't Know What Love Is' (White Stripes—that whole thing was weird, huh? When everyone thought they were brother and sister and it turned out they were married. But they *TOTALLY* looked the same. I mean, what is *THAT* about? Whereas most people don't think Harry and me are related at all. Although this can be a good thing. Especially when he has decided to go shopping naked but for a policeman's helmet.)

9. 'Love is Like a Cigarette' (Duke Ellington—which he totally won't have heard of, which always makes him happy. Though how exactly is love like a cigarette? Unless it is life-destroying and vile. Which, on reflection, is possibly true.)

And I did want to use 'Slave to Love' but the Roxy Music box has got a Captain Beefheart CD in it, which is *NOT* unusual for Lola. I mean, I tried to alphabetize them once, because, you know, then we'd be able to actually *FIND* what we wanted to listen to, but it was impossible because only about ten CDs were in the right box, plus Lola had a total flipout and mixed them all up again because she said she couldn't handle that level of order and control in her life any more (this is something to do with Granny Jones and socks, only I can't get out of her exactly what because every time I ask she does the fingers in the ears lalala thing).

And I know it's one track short, but I'm hoping Ruby will have something, only all her music is at Spike's, so I have to wait until she comes round tomorrow. But I've texted her with strict instructions that it cannot involve folk rock and this is a long shot, believe me.

But, anyway, cool mix CD? Although, actually, come to think of it, I don't know why I'm asking you because for all I know you could be this total classical geek. Plus, it's not like you can answer me yet, is it. Not until I have £500. And if I had that sort of money I'd be able to buy Stan a present, wouldn't I.

**Thursday 30 September**

The whole PMS casting thing is totally MESSING WITH MY MIND. Actually mostly it's Imogen messing with my mind, but you get the picture. Seriously, she is off the scale with her West End/Blake ambition thing and says if she doesn't get a lead role opposite him she is going to throw herself off Pulteney Bridge. I told her she was being overdramatic but she said duh, that is the point of PMS.

Thank God all this will be over tomorrow, and normal (i.e. completely ABNORMAL but at least without show tunes) service can resume.

9 p.m.

Oh, I forgot. I got my last song. For Stan, I mean. For once Ruby totally came up with the goods without me having to traipse to the canal at midnight thus risking murder/rape/ Weil's Disease (which is this gross thing you get from rat wee, according to Imogen, which is why swimming in the river is *NOT* a good idea. Only when it's hot, it is *TOTALLY* easy to forget about the wee). It's 'You Got the Love' (Florence and the Machine version). How great is that? It is because Florence is currently on Ruby's positive female role models list:

Ruby Tuesday Jones's Top Five Women to Emulate

1. Emily Davison (suffragette who threw herself under the king's horse to win women's right to vote, but who could have saved herself a lot of bother if you took Lola as your barometer of participation, i.e. she can't vote because she isn't on the electoral register because she says it is Big Brotheresque and they will use it to trace all her unpaid bills etc. (of which there are many)).
2. Former tennis legend and lesbian Martina Navratilova (not that Ruby wants to play tennis, or be a lesbian, just that she says she admires Martina for doing both and 'railing against the homophobic and sexist world of professional sport' by being gay and unglamorous).
3. Florence Machine (although I don't think that is her surname), and this is kind of

a 'music' subset also featuring Kate Nash and Marina and the Diamonds, but no longer including Amy Winehouse due to *a*) her 'willingness to subordinate herself to patriarchal concepts of marriage, i.e. begging Blake to take her back and *b*) wearing ballet flats (which is a shame CD-wise because I totally heart 'Back to Black').

4. American Secretary of State (and wife of former President Bill) Hillary Clinton (although she is apparently treading a fine line due to her trouser suits and helmet hairdo). Personally I am surprised she ever made it this far, given her 'willingness to subordinate herself to patriarchal concepts of marriage', i.e. going back to Bill after he cheated on her with the one who looks like Kirstie Allsop, but Ruby says sticking with Bill meant she was nearly the first ever being a woman President so she totally used the scandal to her own advantage which is, apparently, GENIUS and cancels the other stuff out.
5. Lola. I am NOT EVEN JOKING. Sometimes I wonder if Ruby and I are related at all. I mean, this is a woman who considers drinking other people's urine. How can anyone want to emulate that, Dr Sven, HOW?

## OCTOBER

**Friday 1 October**

*NOOOOOOOOOOOOOOOOOOOOOO.*

Seriously, Dr Sven, this cannot be happening. In fact, maybe it isn't happening. Maybe I really have lost it this time and I am now living in a catastrophic projection of my own imagining. I will pinch myself to check.

No. That hurt, and now I have a bruise on my arm to add to the horror, which no doubt Imogen will assume is some kind of self-harming and get all over-excited about.

The thing is, Dr Sven, *I GOT THE LEAD ROLE*!

Oh God. I actually felt sick coming up when I wrote that. I mean, seriously, Dr Sven. *WHY IS THIS HAPPENING TO ME*? *WHY WHY WHY WHY WHY*? I wasn't even auditioning. I was only doing it for Imogen. But she's not even the second lead. Look:

<u>'The Boy Next Door' Cast List</u>

| | |
|---|---|
| Buttercup Jones: | 'Girl Next Door' (*UGH*. I just did that sick thing again.) |
| Stan Romer: | 'Boy Next Door' (*I KNOW*! *HOW* is this possible? Not that he's not good. I mean, he is totally *AMAZING* at music. But he *HATES* musicals. He says they are crimes against music, if not humanity.) |

| | |
|---|---|
| Sunday Henderson-Hicks: | 'Bad Best Friend' (which at least makes sense, although she totally doesn't think so and is demanding a recasting once Mr Goldenblatt is back). |
| Blake Carrington: | 'Too Cool Boy' (again, total sense. Because from what I can make out, he has to spend most of the time leaning on stuff looking aloof, and 'vacant' isn't that far a stretch to aloof when you think about it, is it?) |
| Imogen Pritchard: | 'Mother of Girl Next Door' and Main Understudy (i.e. she is *MY MOTHER*. Which she says wouldn't be so bad if the role actually was like Lola, but *NO*, my mother (fictional version) is like Mrs Pritchard, or Granny Jones, i.e. totally repressive and prone to wearing cardigans. And to make matters worse, she is married to . . . ) |
| Titus Pelling: | 'Father of Girl Next Door' and Main Understudy. (Titus is totally happy with this arrangement, even though Sunday pointed out that the only reason he got it is because his head is normal-sized.) |
| Lucinda Ledbetter-Morpeth: | 'Headmistress' (which she is also happy about, and is already lobbying Mr Kwame-Jones to be allowed to shadow him so she can do |

method acting and immerse herself in the role, though frankly, if I were Mr Kwame-Jones I would totally say no. For so many reasons.

Poppy Pringle: 'Pipette 1'(which is not some kind of science thing. The Pipettes are like Gladys Knight's Pips, or Diana Ross's Supremes or something. Which you would think would make the Sidehicks totally happy but Alicia said she doesn't see why she has to be Pipette 2 when she has longer hair and a 32B bust and Poppy's is 36A. So Poppy said at least she doesn't have split ends and a sticky-out belly button. And then Finty offered to show everyone her belly button, which she claims is psychic, and they all got sent to Mr Kwame-Jones.

Alicia Beaufort: 'Pipette 2'

Finty Goggins-Smith: 'Pipette 3'

Fintan Riley: Caretaker

Lily Rubenstein: Admirer of Boy Next Door and set designer

Len Cho: Owner of soup kitchen (which, like, *WHAT*?)

| | |
|---|---|
| Norah Forbes: | Chorus |
| Daisy Helmsley-Nougat: | Chorus |
| Etc. | |

Not that I actually know what 'Girl Next Door' does. Or her mother for that matter. Because Mr Burton said he will save the details for the read-through on Monday. But it is clear that Imogen is totally less significant.

Oh my God, Dr Sven, it was awful. And it *TOTALLY* didn't help that Imogen did her 'I am undone' thing just as Mr Burton was about to read out the roles. Because it turns out she totally was. And seriously, I am trying to find the positive but maybe, *JUST* maybe, there are times when *THERE IS NO POSITIVE AND LIFE JUST SUCKS*.

9 p.m.
OK. I take that back. And I totally apologize for *EVER* questioning your therapeutic techniques, because I've just realized that, because Imogen hasn't been cast anywhere near Blake, then she is *NEVER* going to get to kiss him, stage or otherwise (unless he miraculously *a*) turns out to be her secret admirer and *b*) dumps Sunday Henderson-Hicks), then it is *TOTALLY* a waste of time being in PMS at all so *WE CAN LEAVE*! So overall my crazy rating is definitely back down to manageable levels. It would be better, but a chicken just did something vile on my duvet.

**Saturday 2 October**

*Stan's birthday*

Crazy rating: DO NOT EVEN ASK.

I KNOW! How did this happen? Well, let me explain:

It all started out totally well. Stan got a tonne of good stuff:

1. New amp (Celia)
2. Jimi Hendrix's ACTUAL plectrum (gay stepdad)
3. A mantra T-shirt and 'I heart Hare' beads (Govindas, aka Che, aka Rupert)
4. Totally excellent 'Love'-themed mix CD (me, and I know he liked it because he put it on immediately and played it five times throughout the night to the point at which Celia said if she heard the Bee Gees again she was going to have a panic attack).
5. £500 (Grandma Romer, who arrived three hours late because she got lost on the M4 and had to be police escorted for thirty-five miles. HOW she is allowed to have a licence is questionable. I mean, she can barely see over the steering wheel. Plus she is totally losing more marbles than me. For an hour she thought she was in 1975.)
6. DVD of *Charlotte's Web* (Imogen, on the grounds that it is a cartoon, and Stan loves cartoons. This is NOT why she got it. She got it because the rat is played by STEVE BUSCEMI.)

But that is when it all started to go wrong. Because when Imogen showed up (which, even given her monumental sulking was always going to happen in the remote chance that either one of Stan's dads showed up. I mean, when he first told her about Troy, I swear she had a minor heart attack) it turned out she was totally *NOT* speaking to me. So our entire conversation had to be relayed via Stan, i.e:

| | |
|---|---|
| Imogen: | Tell Buttercup that I cannot forgive her for stealing my limelight so cruelly. |
| Stan: | Buttercup, she is hacked off with you. Even though it is *NOT* your fault. |
| Imogen: | Oh my God. I might have known you'd take her side. And, like, shut up. It so *IS* her fault. |
| Stan: | You shut up. |
| Imogen: | No *YOU* shut up. |
| Buttercup: | Oh God, both of you shut up. And tell Imogen that I will be handing in my PMS resignation on Monday now that the whole Blake thing is *OBVIOUSLY* off. And then none of this will matter and we can all go back to being normal misfits, as opposed to ones with jazz hands and spirit fingers. |
| Stan: | Seriously? I mean, I know it's not our thing, but you're good. |
| Imogen: | No she's not. It's just Mr Burton trying |

to prove a point and give the underdogs a chance. It's like when Ms Nugent picks Norah Forbes for netball captain even though she is totally partially sighted. But anyway I am *NOT* leaving PMS. Because *a*) I am volunteering to do Front of House and then if anyone gets a heart attack or dies then I get to go up on stage and do a heartbreaking but reassuring announcement. Plus *b*) if you have a heart attack then I can take over your role. Plus *c*) it is a Saturday, at a party, yet we are playing Who'd You Rather [which was totally true, and is this game where you have the options of snogging two people and you *HAVE* to pick one on pain of death, which I guess sounds kind of lame, except that we always play it. It's like one of our traditions. Only when we were little it was 'Who Would Win', i.e. who would win in a fight between Mickey Mouse and Daffy Duck. Which, in case you're wondering is Daffy, because of flight advantage.] instead of actually being

| | |
|---|---|
| | engaged in romantic trysts [she actually said this]. At least I have my sights set on a prize; you two only ever hang with each other. It's NOT NORMAL. |
| Stan: | Oh, I am undone. |
| Imogen: | I am being SERIOUS. This is my courtroom argument thingy as to why we CANNOT leave PMS. Because at least we might get to snog someone REAL [which is rich, coming from someone whose ideal man is Heathcliff]. And that is totally inappropriate use of 'I am undone' by the way. |
| Buttercup: | But I don't WANT to snog anyone REAL. At least not anyone at Pennington. And anyway men TOTALLY MESS WITH YOUR MIND. I mean, if Lola had stayed away from men she would never be half as messed up as she is. |
| Stan: | But then you wouldn't be here. |
| Buttercup: | Maybe that would be a good thing. |
| Stan: | No it really wouldn't. Imo . . . ? |
| Imogen: | Then I'd get to be Girl Next Door. |
| Stan: | Imo? |
| Imogen: | Oh all right. No. But you're wrong about Lola. She isn't messed up because of men. She just makes bad choices. I read about it in *Cosmo*. She is totally |

| | |
|---|---|
| | drawn to brooding rogues. [Again, rich, coming from someone who fancies Heathcliff and a vampire.] |
| Stan: | Where is Lola anyway? |
| Buttercup: | She's at a yogathon [which is totally true. Only not because she is trying to get in touch with her body, rather she is trying to get in touch with Jake, the man who teaches downward-facing dog]. |
| Stan: | So who's babysitting? |
| Buttercup: | Ruby and Spike |
| Stan: | Is that even legal? |

At which point I decided it was probably time I went home. And Imogen had to go as well because she has a 10 p.m. curfew unless she is at Covenanters (which is a church youth group and makes PMS look cutting edge), which she never is, because she says she is allergic to that much gingham. Anyway I TOTALLY should have stayed at Stan's because when I got back it turns out that Spike has eaten meat and Ruby has dumped him because she says he has violated his body, and her rights as a vegetarian woman, only Spike says it was organic so it doesn't count and he ate it by mistake because he thought it was a Linda McCartney sausage. But Ruby says he didn't spit it out he swallowed which meant that he liked it which means he is a BETRAYER.

So she has moved back in *TO MY BEDROOM*, because she cannot bear to be alone, and also because her old room is full of hamster cages from one of Lola's money-making ventures. So now I am lying awake, with the sound of snivelling in one ear and the smell of patchouli up my nose and the overriding fear in my brain that Imogen is going to try to poison me.

And I am *NOT* being overdramatic, because believe me, she will totally think about it. I mean, she has seen *Heathers* fourteen times. Plus she is always googling hemlock and stuff. Admittedly it's to fake an internet history of suicide in case the police ever seize her computer. But even so, she could totally turn her knowledge to other uses.

**Sunday 3 October**

Ruby is in total agreement about the men thing. She says they are the root of all *EVIL*, e.g. George Bush and Walt Disney, and she is *NEVER* getting back with Spike. Not even if he turns vegan and has a sex change. Now she is watching *Supernanny* with Harry and eating cereal out of the box. In the interests of self-preservation, I am going round to Imogen's. Hopefully she will have calmed down since last night. Plus they have nice normal Sundays. With Radio 4 and roast beef and discussions on ornithology. As opposed to naughty steps, Coco Pops, and sex changes.

5 p.m.

OK, so Imogen's house wasn't quite the haven of peace and reflection I had imagined:

1. Because a piece of Mr and Mrs Pritchard's jigsaw of Henry VIII had mysteriously gone missing so that there was a hole where his codpiece should have been. If it had been in our house, I would have blamed the chickens, whose eating habits are totally getting worse. Seriously, yesterday one of them ate a Lego helmet and a false nail (presumably Granny Jones's). I think they have pica—you know, where you have the urge to eat weird stuff (Lulu Hoffman in 8C had it and had to go to A&E after eating four scratch and sniff erasers) but as they barely leave the vicinity of the TV, let alone walk the half a mile to Imogen's, I can only assume that the missing piece is one of her attempts to create drama. Which totally succeeded because there was a moratorium on entering the dining room while a search was carried out, which meant that Sunday lunch was an hour late, plus all sorts of claiming it was evidence of devilment. Which it wasn't.
2. Because Imogen has a *NEW PLAN* to wrest Blake out of the clutches of Sunday Henderson-Hicks and into her own. It is that, as lead girl, I will infiltrate the Sidehicks, win the trust of Sunday, then evilly sabotage her and Blake, who will be compelled to turn

to Imogen as a shoulder to cry on. Seriously. She has been watching *WAY* too much *Mean Girls*, because there is *NO WAY* this will work. I mean, sabotage *HOW*? Which I totally said. But it turned out she has thought of this, i.e. I can big up Imogen to Blake, while Stan can flirt outrageously with Sunday and lure her away. So I said this was even more far-fetched because *WHAT* would Sunday see in Stan. So she gave me a list:

Reasons why Stan Romer is Totally Hot (objectively, I don't fancy him), by Imogen Pritchard

1. His hair is long enough to be breaking school rules, and his head is normal-sized.
2. He does not eat bees, unlike some people I could mention.
3. He can play the guitar, like *ACTUAL* guitar, and not just mime to 'Guitar Hero'.
4. He has muscle definition, without doing the Vince Vaughn neck-too-wide-for-head look.
5. He has that weird Steve Buscemi geek charm thing going, I mean have you *NOT SEEN Ghost World*?

Which is all kind of true. Except for claiming he is like Steve Buscemi, which he is *SO* not, because, as I keep pointing out, Steve Buscemi is, like, *ANCIENT*. And his eyes are all buggy, like frogs, or someone being strangled or something (not that I have seen this happen except on ER once) and Stan's are more cow-like, you know. Except not in a bad way. That sounds bad. They are just kind of big and brown. I am so not selling them, am I? OK. So how about Stan also knows every single chord change Jimmy Page ever wrote, and can play them too, which is pretty cool when you think about it. And also I really like the way he always sings the Buttercup song when I am feeling *REALLY* subnormal. I mean, he totally rocks, I guess, if you like that sort of thing.

But that's *NOT THE POINT*. Because I really don't think Sunday is going to fall for weird geek charm. She is more of a 'total obvious preppy hottie' kind of girl. But I didn't tell Imogen that because I so could not deal right then with the whole 'not supporting my dream' thing. And also, because then she gave me another list. And this one was way worse:

<u>Prospective boyfriends for Buttercup Jones by Imogen Pritchard</u>

1. Daniel Radcliffe aka Harry Potter. Unless he is being a wizard, which you should totally avoid because I think the death eaters could send you over the edge.
2. Mr Sylvester, who teaches Biology and totally looks like an old Corey Monteith. Only just try and blank out the *CRIMINAL* button-down shirt.
3. Edgar Linton, i.e. the *BORING* one that Cathy marries instead of Heathcliff.
4. Hugh Cooper-Willis, i.e. the one with the mole on his

left cheek, not Clint Cooper-Willis, who is, like, gross.

5. Len Cho. Unless he has been eating cheese and onion crisps again.
6. Thomas the Fisherman (the one out of the Bible, not that friend of Denzil's with the eels).
7. Titus Pelling. Because you are always telling me that he is not that bad so *YOU* go out with him.

Which, after you have crossed off the *TEACHERS* and *FICTIONAL* characters and *CELEBRITIES* and *DEAD PEOPLE*, basically leaves Titus Pelling, Hugh Cooper-Willis, who totally does have the whole Vince Vaughn fat neck thing going on (plus I am pretty sure it is Clint with the mole not Hugh, though why this makes him *NOT* gross I have no idea) and Len Cho, i.e. captain of the Mathletes, co-founder of the Asian Entrepreneurs Society, and possessor of cheese and onion breath. Which, like, *NO*! So I said that Imogen had obviously been so preoccupied with the mini sausage rolls last night she had not heard me point out that I was avoiding men at all costs henceforth on mental health grounds. But she said duh, she totally thought of that and these are all *NON-MENTALISM-INDUCING* boyfriends, i.e. *DULL* and *BORING*, plus relationships with the opposite sex are a normal healthy part of adult life, like a musical mash-up, i.e. bringing together two individuals and creating something better and more interesting at parties. And that shutting myself off from them can only send me further into the dark pit of my own psyche. Which is *a*) straight off BBC3, and *b*) *RICH* because she is not at all interested in *HEALTHY* relationships, but only in ones that involve stalkers, messiahs, or vampires.

Plus I am pretty sure that me in combination with anyone else would *NOT* be a mash-up. Just a big fat Buttercup Mash.

**Monday 4 October**

1 p.m. (Latin)
Mr Kwame-Jones has vetoed Mr Goldenblatt's Michael Jacksonberg extravaganza. According to Lily Rubenstein it is because it contravenes copyright, libel, and pyrotechnic laws. And according to Stan, it is because it is pants. But whatever, it means we are definitely doing Mr Burton's original *Boy Next Door* thing. Which means I am definitely Girl Next Door, i.e. the lead. Which, like, *NOOOOOO*. Even Mr Goldenblatt agrees. According to Lily he emailed Mr Burton to tell him that I am an unproved quantity, with a poor genetic background (this is because Ruby once chained herself to him in a bid to free some dolphins, or save them, or get them new swimming pools or something) and freakishly long legs. Only, still according to Lily, Mr Burton emailed back to say there was something about me, and that Mr Goldenblatt needed to trust him. Which is kind of nice, only I'm pretty sure Mr Goldenblatt is right.

Oh, and I told Stan about the plan. You know, about him seducing Sunday, not me going out with Len Cho or Hugh

Cooper-Willis or anything. Because *a*) I know for a fact Stan thinks Hugh is a moronic Mudhoney with a superiority complex and bad taste in v-neck jumpers plus *b*) that is NEVER going to happen. Which is pretty much what Stan said to the Sunday thing.

Only then he made the 'and what would she see in me anyway' point. So I told him about the list, you know, the guitar and the hair and the geek charm thing. And he went a bit quiet and then said, 'Do you really think that?' And I said, 'Duh, no, Imogen wrote it. Well, most of it anyway. I mean, I think you'd probably need to start working out or something.' And then he said, 'I'm not changing myself for Sunday Henderson-Hicks.' So I said, 'Do it for me, then. Because otherwise Imogen is never going to shut up about this thing and it's totally doing my head in.' And then he got really weird and said, 'Whatever, I'm not changing for anyone. You either get me as I am or you don't get me at all.' Which is totally the kind of thing Ruby would say, not Stan. I mean it's way out of character. What is WITH him? So now he is sulking, and I'm going to have to do serious sucking up after Latin to make up for it. I would do sucking up IN Latin only *a*) it is Latin and I can barely recite the alphabet, *b*) it is Mr Ough and he has weirdly good hearing. Seriously, he once heard Finty Goggins-Smith tell Alicia Beaufort that Lily Rubenstein said that Clint Cooper-Willis had impetigo (although Finty thought it was a character in *The Tempest* and was something to do with English Lit homework) and *c*) I have to sit behind Fintan

Riley and it is impossible to see past his head. Seriously. It's like a spacehopper or something.

5 p.m.
OK, so Stan has forgiven me. Just about. But only because Imogen admitted it was all her idea. He is still not at all keen on the plan, but I begged and begged and in the end he caved. Which is totally nice of him really. Plus there is still an outside chance that Imogen will go off Blake once rehearsals start and she sees that he *DOES NOT* have hidden depths but is, in fact, the *NEANDERTHAL MORON* he so brilliantly pretends to be.

**Tuesday 5 October**

2 p.m. (Geography)
Why, why, *WHY* did I not stand up to Imogen on the PMS dream thing? Seriously, Dr Sven, my mind is supposed to be consumed with Belgium's tractor imports but all I can think about is just how bad I am going to look in sequins and a top hat. Please God, don't let there be top hats. I will actually hit my head on the lighting bars.

*PLUS* I have just seen one of the Cooper-Willis twins (to be fair I am not sure which one as I was not in mole-spotting distance) actually head butt a wall four times to prove his superior strength. Does this sound like the kind of boyfriend who would be good for my mental health. *DOES IT*?

5 p.m.
Ruby is still here. Which means she and Spike have now officially split up for three days, which is a *RECORD*. I mean, normally he totally caves after one day and comes round promising to be a better man and respect her womanhood and right to reject all forms of animal cruelty etc. but this time he has *NOT EVEN TEXTED*. I said maybe his phone has run out of credit, as he is an impoverished art student, but Ruby says his mum put £80 on there last month in case of emergencies and apart from the time they got arrested for spray painting a sobbing Chinese factory worker on the window at Gap there haven't been any, so that is *NOT* an excuse and that this just proves he is unworthy of her affections.

Lola for one is happy though. She says it is wonderful to have all her offspring under one roof again, and it is especially excellent for Harry as there is a lot he can learn from his eldest sister. This is so not true. Ruby has done nothing but watch television since she came home. Although Stan says actually he's learned loads of things from TV that he would *NEVER* have learned at Pennington, e.g:

Things Stan Romer has Learned from TV

1. That the earthquake in Chile shortened the length of a day by 1.26 microseconds (*Newsnight*).
2. That communism is doomed to failure by its own goal, because if all income is equal then no one will bother working (Open University).

3. That police-sanctioned drug use areas are an effective way to control dealing (*The Wire*).
4. That Chris Moyles has weirdly small hands for a fat man (MTV video awards).

Imogen has a list as well. But I'm not sure it proves the argument:

Things Imogen Pritchard has Learned from TV

1. That it is NOT illegal to marry your cousin (*EastEnders*). (Which she was totally happy about because she has a crush on her cousin Dafydd who is eighteen and is thinking of becoming a priest. Which in my opinion does not make him in any way a good prospect, but Imogen says it is just a challenge.)
2. People with busts larger than a B cup should NEVER wear ruffles (*How to Look Good Naked*).
3. Peach stones contain arsenic (*Murder She Wrote*).

In fact, apart from reigniting my 'Imogen is going to do murder' fear, I'm pretty sure this just confirms that Harry's education is totally in JEOPARDY. Seriously, I'm thinking of calling 007. Or Granny Jones. One of them needs to stage an intervention or something. Or does that only happen on TV? Oh God. I think I may be as bad as Imogen. Even I am confusing soap operas and real life now. Seriously, TV is bad for your health. You should add that to your list of things to avoid. Though, seriously, Dr Sven, that list is debatable. Like, number one is 'People who raise anxiety levels', which

I can see makes sense, most of the time. Only what are you supposed to do when that person is your own mother, and you are condemned by regressive custody laws to live with her for at least the next two years? I bet you didn't think of that, huh?

**Wednesday 6 October**

8 a.m.

Oh, I am doing that sick thing again, Dr Sven. Seriously, any minute I am going to bring up a whole bowlful of Chocolate Stars, which is going to be so much worse coming out than it was going in.

And I can't even make use of the fact that Lola is totally happy to fake sick notes because Imogen is on her way over to escort me to school to make sure I don't bunk and miss the first *Boy Next Door* read-through and thus doom her to a Blake-free existence for the rest of her life. I warned her if I did chocolate vom all over Sunday Henderson-Hicks then that would pretty much doom us all but she says I just need to hold my breath because you can't be sick with air in your lungs. She learned it on *Casualty*, and she is adding it to her 'Things I have Learnt From TV' list.

OMG. This is so NOT good. And don't tell me to do positive thinking, because I swear the only way from here is down.

5 p.m.

OK. So, from what I can remember, because believe me, I

am totally doing my best to blank a lot of this out in case it traumatizes me for the rest of my adult life, the gist of the musical is that Boy Next Door, i.e. Stan, is totally hung up on Girl Next Door, i.e. me, only she, I mean me, doesn't think of him that way because I am going out with Too Cool Boy (Blake). Only it is *TOTALLY* obvious that he is not the one for me as I am kooky and different (yawn) and he is a total boy slut (double yawn). Only then Bad Best Friend decides she wants Too Cool Boy and seduces him, just as I find out I am pregnant. At which point I row with my repressive parents, i.e. Imogen and Titus, and decide to run away. Only Stan saves the day by pledging eternal love (gak) and offering to raise the baby as his own.

All of which *a*) is *TOTALLY* dodgy storyline-wise, which Lucinda Ledbetter-Morpeth is already hyper about and issuing governor warnings left, right, and centre, only Mr Burton said it is not dodgy, it is realistic teen drama. Which it is *NOT*. It is straight out of *90210*. I mean when does this happen in real life? *WHEN*? And *b*) means I have to kiss *i*) Blake and *ii*) *STAN*. *I KNOW*! I mean, it's not even hygienic. Which I totally told Mr Burton, but he said we can deal with that at a later date, which is not *EVEN* an answer, it is just passing the buck.

Oh, and it gets worse. I have to sing. And not just one song. A *LOT*! Like, this is just some of the playlist:

1. 'Endless Love' (Lionel Richie)—a duet with Blake (gak gak gak);

2. 'Jolene' (Dolly Parton) which I sing about evil Sunday Henderson-Hicks when she tries to steal Blake;
3. 'Papa Don't Preach' (Madonna) when I find out I'm pregnant;
4. 'Total Eclipse of The Heart' (Bonnie Tyler)—when I find out Blake has cheated on me;
5. 'You're My Best Friend' (Queen)—a duet with Stan;
6. 'It Must Be Love' (Madness)—full company including harmonies and rounds. Which, like, NOOOOOO.

Sunday Henderson-Hicks is totally OVER threatening to leave because she gets to sing 'The Tide is High' by Blondie and 'You Know I'm No Good' by Amy Winehouse which she says are WAY more testing vocally than any of my 'amateur' numbers. And Stan is happy because he gets 'I'll Stand By You' by the Pretenders, and Chrissie Hynde is his favourite female rock vocalist of all time.

Even Imogen is totally cheered up because now she gets to do a dirgey Beatles solo which she says is TOTALLY Sylvia Plath and she is brilliant at looking bereft and borderline suicidal.

The only person who is as not happy with this as me is Mr Goldenblatt, who stormed in in this totally dramatic entrance thing (he swung the double doors too hard and one of them hit Fintan Riley in the face (which is not that difficult) and blood gushed everywhere; seriously, it was like a scene from *House*, and he had to go to Miss Hutchinson for first aid) and told Mr Burton to STOP RIGHT THERE because he was suspending all rehearsals until he had approved

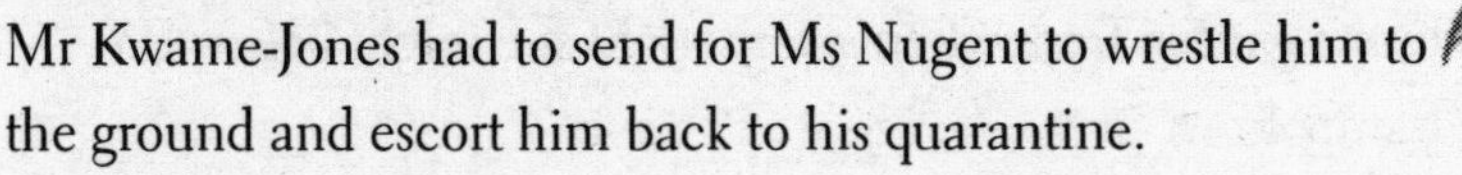

song choices (which there is no way he will do because he only likes Michael Jackson). Only it turns out he is still totally contagious and Mr Kwame-Jones had to send for Ms Nugent to wrestle him to the ground and escort him back to his quarantine.

On the plus side, I didn't throw up. But that doesn't make up for the hell my life has become. Not by a long chalk, Dr Sven.

1 a.m.
And to add insult to my misery (which I know is not actually a saying, but when I elaborate you'll understand why I am **TOO TIRED** to even care), I have just been woken up by Spike banging on the bedroom window, in a desperate bid to win back Ruby. Which was *a*) utterly pointless because Ruby is on the top bunk in Harry's room because he is more tolerant of patchouli and snoring than I am, and *b*) terrifying. **SERIOUSLY**, I could have had a heart attack. I mean, what is wrong with texting, surely that is the point of living in the twenty-first century not in the middle of a Shakespeare tragedy, which I totally told Spike (once I realized it was him and not a murderer, or Fergal O'Shaughnessy) only he said he had ceremoniously melted his mobile to symbolize the potency of his and Ruby's love for each other, and his mum won't buy him a new one until he has mown the paddocks for four months. Then I asked him how he was managing to be suspended several metres above the ground anyway, given that my bedroom is on the third floor, and he said he had used

the ladder. Only then I reminded him that it is out of bounds for health and safety reasons, i.e. several rungs are wobbly, and then, as if to prove this, he fell off.

It is totally lucky that Lola's old mattress is still festering in the garden from when she thought she might become a trampolinist.

See how dangerous love is, Dr Sven?

**Thursday 7 October**

Imogen says it is not dangerous it is utterly romantic and the only thing that could have improved on the gesture would be if he had actually been hovering at the window instead of on the ladder. She is lucky that I am too tired to even TRY to explain to her, YET AGAIN, that vampires are NOT REAL.

And DEFINITELY too tired to try to infiltrate the Sidehicks. She will have to *a*) wait until next week, when I do not look like I have been up all night arguing with a lovesick nineteen year old with a symbolically melted mobile and *b*) I have the strength to tell her that her plan is NEVER GOING TO WORK. I mean, seriously, we are talking about people who have been au fait with leg wax and lip primer since the age of ten, whereas the first time I shaved my legs was two years ago when I realized I was making Stan jealous. I am not even joking, Dr Sven. He has almost NO body hair. Which I told him he could totally make use of by becoming an Olympic cyclist or some kind of manfish person. Which I'm not sure exists, but if it doesn't then it should. Only Stan just shrugged and said he'd stick to wearing jeans, thanks.

**Friday 8 October**

Mr Goldenblatt is not taking the whole PMS takeover thing lying down. According to Lily Rubenstein he has sent a list of demands to Mr Burton and Mr Kwame-Jones including that they employ J-Lo's choreographer for the group numbers, and that the entire cast is given lycra catsuits for rehearsal purposes. Which is so *NOT* going to happen. I mean, for a start there is no way Fintan will get one over his head. Or Imogen over her thighs. Which I did not say. But Sunday Henderson-Hicks totally did. Which you would *THINK* she would be upset about but, *NO*, because Blake actually told Sunday to take a chill pill. So now Imogen is taking this as yet another *SIGN* that he is not so secretly admiring her. The only positive is that I was left out of it, because I am in no way allowed to disagree with Sunday because of the infiltration thing. Which, so far, is just about do-able by pretending I am deaf, or interested in something on the floor. But what do I do when she tells people I have man chromosomes again. Seriously. *WHAT*?

**Saturday 9 October**

Spike is in the building (via the normal route this time, i.e. the back door, which is always unlocked, if not actually wide open, to allow chicken access). He and Ruby are in Harry's bedroom having coalition talks, i.e. complex negotiations over some sort of power-sharing relationship. Harry is also in the bedroom to act as a witness and troubleshooter in case of actual physical threat. He is very good at this kind of thing. Like, once, when the chickens were having a fight over a Cheesy Wotsit he totally solved it by opening a packet of Twiglets, which they all hate, so they ran and hid in the washing machine. He is *SO* going to be a UN diplomat when he grows up. Or a head at an inner-city comp.

God knows what I am going to be, though, Dr Sven, other than *MESSED UP*.

I mean, when I was little I wanted to be God (totally ambitious, I know, I have reined it in since then).
And then I wanted to be a wizard, because of the whole Harry Potter thing. Which I *KNOW* sounds like Imogen, but I was seven, and she is fourteen and still has 'princess' on her top job list.

<u>Imogen Pritchard's Top Three Career Choices</u>

1. Princess (only *NOT* by marrying royalty, but because it turns out she is secretly in line for the throne of some tiny but totally rich principality, and will get a huge makeover and Sunday Henderson-Hicks will be spitting mad with jealousy).
2. Forensic criminologist (not the *REAL* kind, but the kind who are impossibly glamorous, and in love with their co-workers,

with whom they solve uncrackable murders on a weekly prime-time basis).
3. Member of Girls Aloud (this is dependent on all sorts of factors including Cheryl Cole having a freak accident that facially disfigures her for life, and Simon Cowell spotting her talent while she is humming to herself on the packing line of a biscuit factory).

I have pointed out she should add 'Writer of Top Soap Opera', because seriously, Dr Sven, *NO ONE* could imagine more absurd cliffhangers or random long-lost relatives than Imogen. But she says she does not want to write about other people, she wants to be written *ABOUT*, e.g. be the star of her own eponymously titled hit comedy series 'Imogen', about a kooky but beautiful girl and her slightly less gorgeous friends in their Notting Hill flatshare.

At least I'm realistic. I mean, for a bit I did think I could maybe be a doctor. Because I am very sympathetic to illness of all kinds. Except that I got sent to Mr Kwame-Jones for not concentrating in Science *FIVE TIMES* last term. Although, like I told Mr Kwame-Jones, *YOU* try concentrating when there is a nit scare and Fintan Riley is your lab partner. Only then we did genetics, and it turns out I may have inherited certain cognitive skills and behaviour from my parents. Only, as far as I can see, the only thing I have inherited is a tendency to *BRING THE CRAZY*.

**Sunday 10 October**

Although I guess there's an outside chance my dad can actually sing. Not that I am giving it the Big I Am or anything, which, as you kind of know by now, is *SO* not me. But the thing is, I'm really not totally hideous. Which is kind of a shock. I mean, I was singing 'Papa Don't Preach' in the shower, where admittedly the acoustics are kind of favourable, and there was a lot of running water in the background, and the sound of a chicken who for some reason has taken to nesting in the bath, but it was actually OK. Not X *Factor* stuff, but, you know, I wouldn't throw me off the karaoke stage. Not that I'd go on one in the first place. I mean what is *THAT* about? Not that it makes me feel any better about tomorrow though. I mean Camilla St John Brice could sing but Sunday still gave her an eating disorder. Plus singing in the shower is one thing. Singing in front of Mr Burton screaming at me through a megaphone about my lazy arms and left feet in the workshop tomorrow is another.

5 p.m.

Oh, and Spike and Ruby have reached an accord, and are back together on a trial basis, with the following rules:

1. No eating meat, *NOT EVEN* organic.
2. Snails count as meat.
3. So do eels.
4. No eating of any products made by Nestlé, Kraft or other evil conglomerates.

5. No Disney.
6. Pixar counts as Disney.
7. No ogling the girl on the printer ink counter at Office World and claiming you are planning a boycott of Canon.

Lola says the house is a hollow shell without Ruby but, personally, I can live without the snoring and the constant banning of stuff.

She'll be back anyway. I give them a week. There is no way Spike can survive without *Toy Story* 2.

**Monday 11 October**

OK. So I take it back about Mr Burton. He is totally *NOT* the shouting through a megaphone kind of director. In fact, he is not a shouting at all kind of director. Seriously, he ums and ers more than I do. I am *NOT EVEN JOKING*. Although I do not think this is grounds for dismissal, which Sunday claimed because she says no one with that level of self-doubt should be anywhere near a professional stage and the sooner Mr Goldenblatt is back the better. Which according to Lily Rubenstein is Wednesday.

Only now everyone is fully expecting some kind of insane sing-off between him and Mr Burton and is taking sides and Len Cho is getting the Asian Entrepreneurs to make Team Goldenblatt and Team Burton badges and sell them for £1 in the senior toilets.

Oh, and I asked Lily how she knows all this stuff, because seriously, Dr Sven, she makes *Gossip Girl* look clueless, and it turns out she has *HACKED* into Mr Kwame-Jones's email account.

<u>Interesting things Lily Rubenstein has found out from Mr Kwame-Jones's email</u>

1. Miss Hutchinson wants to introduce psychometric testing for the new intake to weed out dodgy applicants. (This is very worrying, because, seriously, Dr Sven, I would never pass. I mean, I have done one of those ink blot things at Imogen's in her Freud phase, and I *ALWAYS* see dead animals.)
2. Mr Kwame-Jones is internet dating and has been out with Maureen (42, GSOH, looking for fun and frolics) and Brenda (47, likes line dancing, looking to mend her achy-breaky heart). Neither emailed again. (Which is kind of sad, because Mr Kwame-Jones may not be Denzel Washington, but he is totally cool for a headmaster.)
3. Miles Pitt-Dullforce has a recurrent urinary tract infection (which totally explains a lot of things).
4. Ruby has emailed forty-seven times in the last two weeks alone, demanding the school is handed over to the 'people' and that the governors turn themselves over to the police for crimes against the proletariat.

5. Mr Burton's MSN name is 'axeman'. (Though I am pretty sure this is to do with guitars, not murdering, which is what Imo thought.)

Imogen said Lola should join the dating site then she could go out with Mr Kwame-Jones and he could be my new dad, which would mean I would RULE SCHOOL, and I could get him to expel Sunday leaving Blake at her mercy. I said I would not put Mr Kwame-Jones at Lola's mercy, plus he is totally not her type, i.e. he has a job, and neat hair.

So we are back to Plan B, i.e. infiltrating the Sidehicks. Which is pants. But is better than Mr Kwame-Jones experiencing the full horror of my mother.

**Tuesday 12 October**

Reasons why Imogen's plan to infiltrate the Sidehicks is NOT going to work

1. I do not LOOK like a Sidehick, i.e. I do not possess a single Alice band, pair of over-the-knee socks, or anything from Abercrombie and Fitch, as Sunday Henderson-Hicks reminded me when she pointed out that I dress like a blind transvestite. Plus I am ginger and a borderline giant. (She didn't say this bit. It's an objective observation.)
2. I do not THINK like a Sidehick. I mean, I know I'm

*NOT* on a genius par with Harry, due to my defective inheritance, but I actually heard Finty Goggins-Smith ask Mr Sylvester if cows were 'like, horses crossed with pigs'. I am *NOT EVEN JOKING*.

Imogen says that clearly writing to you is not helping me at all because I am still being completely *NEGATIVE*. But it's not that, I'm just being *REALISTIC*. I mean, seriously, Dr Sven, she is totally expecting that by the end of rehearsal tomorrow, I will have usurped Poppy Pringle as top Sidehick, convinced Blake that Imogen is his *ONE*, while Stan and Sunday will be exchanging saliva behind the props cupboard. Plus I'm not even sure there *WILL* be rehearsal because Len Cho is taking bets on the sing-off with Mr Goldenblatt beating Mr Burton eleven votes to ten due to Mr Goldenblatt's infamous Shirley Bassey impression, and the fact that I am being forced by Imogen to vote *WITH* Sunday Henderson-Hicks, i.e. Team Goldenblatt, even though I am definitely a Team Burton kind of girl. I mean, he may live for the music and all, but at least it's better music than 'Goldfinger' sung vibrato.

9 p.m.

Oh, and writing to you is helping. At least I think it is. Either that or I am becoming co-dependent in a virtual relationship with a man who may or may not be medically qualified. Which I guess doesn't sound so good when you think about it, does it.

**Wednesday 13 October**

Things I learned at school today

1. Mr Goldenblatt can be bought for the price of two Michael Jackson numbers and a choreography credit. He has dropped all other demands after Mr Burton offered to write 'ABC' (chorus number, combining the themes of love and education) and 'Man in the Mirror' (Blake solo, when he has revelation that vanity isn't everything and decides to volunteer at a soup kitchen) into the show. Thank God Mr Burton refused 'We Are the World'. Seriously, Dr Sven, that song makes me feel like I'm going to hurl. The total downside is that Mr Goldenblatt is now in charge of all the dance routines, and there is no *WAY* I can do Fosse fingers or any of the other weird contortions he has already mentioned. I mean, when I dance, I totally look like a giraffe having a seizure. And that's not even me saying that, that's Stan.
2. It is going to take longer than two hours to fulfil Imogen's Blake Carrington fantasy. I mean, most of rehearsal was spent trying to learn the harmonies for 'It Must Be Love' so I didn't get a chance to talk to Blake on his own, and when I tried to stand near the Sidehicks Alicia Beaufort sprayed me with foot deodorant (she has overactive sweat glands according

to Lily Rubenstein, and has had Botox in her armpits four times and even *THAT* didn't stop it). Imogen says I am just going to have to try harder come Monday when I have a duet rehearsal with Blake. She has offered to come as my personal assistant but I pointed out that would make her seem kind of *FREAKISH*, which is so *NOT* a look she wants to channel in front of Blake.

3. Mr Burton has decided to throw a PMS disco next Friday so we can bond in the wake of the whole Team Burton/Goldenblatt hoo-ha. I know. *A DISCO*. Thank God I signed Imogen's boycott when she decided that school discos/dances/proms of any variety were totally *LAST YEAR*.
4. Steel is an alloy of iron and carbon. Seriously, *WHEN*?

**Thursday 14 October**

Stan is right, Imogen *SO* needs mental help. I mean, if you therapized (is that even a word?) her obsession with creating drama, then I totally wouldn't be in such a *MESS*. *SERIOUSLY*, Dr Sven, she is in plan *OVERDRIVE*.

This time it is her 'Get Buttercup a Boyfriend' scheme. She has revised her list, and we are starting tomorrow with Hugh Cooper-Willis. She has not made it completely clear what, exactly, we are starting, but as I have just seen Len Cho sing the periodic table off by heart in

Combined Science, I am being grateful for the small mercy that he is at number three. Seriously, it was like one of those bad acts on *Britain's Got Talent* that they let through just so Simon Cowell can humiliate them. Do you watch this? Although, I'm guessing with a name like Sven maybe you get *Sweden's Got Talent* or something. I mean WHAT was Mr Sylvester thinking? Alicia Beaufort laughed so hard she coughed a piece of Special K bar into Poppy Pringle's hair. Finty Goggins-Smith didn't laugh. She thought it was the Japanese National Anthem. Even though it is *a*) Chemistry, not music and *b*) he is half CHINESE.

I am blaming PMS. There is no way he would have done that if Mr Burton hadn't compared him to Elvis. And NOT the one who sings in Gracelands Palace Chinese Takeaway on the London Road and who is actually called Alan.

**Friday 15 October**

10 a.m. (Latin)
Am in Latin so am writing this QUIETLY. Although Mr Ough is busy arguing with Miles Pitt-Dullforce about getting a toilet pass out for the seventh time in forty minutes. Seriously. Anyway, the point is, Imogen said IT has started. I said WHAT has started? And she said OPERATION HUGH COOPER-WILLIS. She has just told Norah Forbes, who sits next to Carey Cardew in second period French, who is goal attack

to Lily Rubenstein's goal shooter in third period netball, that I fancy him. So it will be all over Penn by lunch, as long as Ms Nugent doesn't swap netball for lacrosse given that it is unseasonally sunny, because Carey Cardew has a note to excuse her from lacrosse on account of a phobia of small balls.

1 p.m. (canteen)
OPERATION HUGH COOPER-WILLIS did NOT go according to plan. Stan has just asked me if it's true that I fancy Clint Cooper-Willis. I said duh, no, it is Hugh Cooper-Willis, although I think Imogen has got it wrong and it is Clint who has the mole. Stan just gave me a weird look and went to get a focaccia sandwich. (He has no battle with carbs. Seriously. He is totally skinny. Not in an emaciated way. Just in a kind of Stan way.)

2 p.m. (French)
I have found out what went wrong. It turns out that Carey Cardew was off games today because she has strep throat, so Norah Forbes just told Ava Parker instead who was standing in on the netball squad, only Ava is deaf, so Norah had to sign, only she only knows the words 'hello' and 'milk' and the letters a, j, and m, so she just made stuff up. And ANYWAY both Cooper-Willises are off school with strep throat too. So it was *complètement* pointless. *Alors*.

Imogen is undeterred. She says it gives us time to improve our plan. I pointed out it wasn't my plan but she did the scary 'not supporting me' sad eye thing, so I ended up agreeing, mainly because I have two hours of PMS to get through after school and it's bad enough with Sunday and the Sidehicks trying to trip me up without Imogen doing it as well. I mean, her legs are twice the width, there is no way she can miss.

5 p.m.
I think I might have broken something. I am NOT EVEN JOKING. Literally every time I moved, which believe me, is quite a lot in 'ABC', due to some seriously overambitious box steps, I SOMEHOW impaled myself on the waxed and tanned limb of a Sidehick. It is lucky we are boycotting the disco next week or I swear I would be in a total body cast.

**Saturday 16 October**

2 p.m.
Imogen has been forced to go to some giant jigsaw shop in Cardiff for the day, which means absolutely NO Cooper-Willis/Sidehick infiltration/world domination via the power of musicals talk WHATSOEVER. She is totally not happy but says she has stocked up on *Harpers*, *Vogue*, and *Elle* to try to detract from the fact she is in WALES looking at TOYS.

Stan says in fact Wales is musically rich and she should go and check out the place on the Severn Bridge where Richey

Edwards from the Manics killed himself (*ALLEGEDLY*). Only Imogen says she thought of that, *OBVIOUSLY*, but her dad is refusing to stop and they have childlocks on the door.

Oh yeah, I'm at Stan's. I think we're actually going to rehearse. Which, like *I KNOW*. But Stan says if we're going to do this thing, we might as well not make *COMPLETE* fools of ourselves.

Which is totally true. Though not as inspiring as it could be.

11 p.m.
I'm still at Stan's. In fact, I think I'm going to stay the night. Because *a*) he has a toaster that works and *b*) we are about to watch *Summer Stock*, which is this musical with Judy Garland in. I know, right? Because Stan *HATES* musicals. Which I told him. Only he said 'Yeah, but you don't.' Plus he says I remind him of her. I mean, Judy. Which I said did not sound in any way like a compliment, given that she committed suicide. But he said not the craziness. Just the way I sing. Like, when we were rehearsing earlier, he said I looked like I was lost in the music. Like totally at home. Which I guess I was. But that's because it's easy with him, here, in the basement. Because it almost is home. And because then I'm OK being me so I forget to worry about the tallness, and the weirdness and everything.

He says I just have to keep thinking like Judy and I'll be fine on stage.

It would be nice to think he's right. But I think it's going to take more than believing in Judy to save me.

**Sunday 17 October**

10 a.m.
Imogen is coming over. She has just texted to say she has '*HAD AN EPIPHANY*!!!!!!!!!' This does not bode well. The last time I had a text with that many exclamation marks it was when she decided we should become nuns.

Stan says she's probably just realized she fancies Dracula.

I hope he's right. I still haven't told him everything about *OPERATION HUGH COOPER-WILLIS*. Or the rest of the list. Even though we were up till about four talking. I mean, it's bad enough me thinking it's totally crazy without him confirming it.

Luckily he's not coming back with me. He says he doesn't think he's had enough sleep to cope with Imo in epiphany mode. Plus they're showing all the Spiderman films back to back on SKY.

11 a.m.
*OH. MY. GOD*, Dr Sven. Imogen is here and her epiphany is totally *NOT* anything to do with vampires, it is to do with her second favourite thing after Steve Buscemi, i.e. *MAKEOVERS*.

*SERIOUSLY*, Imogen says the only way that *a*) I can infiltrate the Sidehicks and *b*) get a boyfriend who does not have some ginger giant fetish, is to totally submit myself to a packet of L'Oreal, some hair straighteners and a wardrobe revamp. I said I have completely *NO* money for any Gok-style spending

sprees but she says I am lucky because vintage is no longer the province of the mental or poor, even Cheryl Cole wears it, it is just a question of weeding out the wheat (Celia's Chanel cast-offs) from the chaff (Lola's hemp-woven and fancy dress cast-offs). Plus she has brought me a pair of over-the-knee socks that she got in her Lindsay Lohan phase (only they gave her total thigh muffin tops, and Sunday Henderson-Hicks started singing the muffin song out of *Shrek* every time she walked past so she has been back in control tights ever since).

This is *SO NOT GOOD*, Dr Sven. I am having to hide in the bathroom while she gives Harry false eyelashes and some breast-enhancing highlighter, but I am running out of time to think up an escape plan because *a*) he has a playdate with someone called Tigger at half ten and *b*) there is no lock on the door and I am pretty sure Imogen will remember this from the time Denzil walked in on her on the toilet.

Oh, I can hear the stairs creaking, and it is definitely *NOT* chicken-related as they do not carry that much weight despite the weird eating habits.

6 p.m.

OK. Something *VERY WEIRD* has happened (and I don't mean Imogen doing a fanfare when she swung the mirror round, because believe me, I have heard that about a million times). And I am not sure if it is weird in a *BAD* way, or just weird in a *DIFFERENT* way. The thing is, I look kind of *NORMAL*. Or, at least, normal by Sidehick standards. I mean, my lips are still huge, and I am still five foot nine and a quarter, i.e. freakishly tall for a fourteen year old. But my hair isn't ginger any more, it's this kind of caramelly colour. I mean, it's almost Pantene advert hair (or at least it would be if Imogen hadn't tried to tong it into 'tumbling waves' because the result is sort of more sproinging at angles than tumbling, but she says it will have definitely flattened down by tomorrow). And I'm not entirely sure about the outfit, i.e. I am wearing a Westwood bustier and skinny jeans (more of Celia's hand-me-downs, which I got because *a*) Stan does NOT look good in a bustier, and believe me, we tried once, and *b*) Ruby is too short, plus she will only wear military surplus and recycled organic cotton and says that flaunting labels is blatant support for capitalist fascist governments everywhere and I am condemning millions to death with a pair of Calvin Klein knickers) which Imogen says is totally retro vamp, although I am wondering if it is not more contemporary hooker. But I'll be back in uniform tomorrow, only with the over-the-knee socks (barely on the knee on my legs, although Imogen says this is very Japanese and ironic).

Lola is totally NOT impressed. She says I am breaking the Jones family tradition of standing up against conformity and that I look like someone else, i.e. not Buttercup Jones. But *a*) it is not a total tradition because Granny Jones HEARTS conformity and *b*) maybe it's a good thing that I look like someone else. Like someone who doesn't live in a house where chickens spend more time in the beds than humans. Or whose little brother is trying to cross-breed ants and worms to create a new world dominating super-species. Or whose mother actually knows what that role involves.

And maybe if I look like someone else, I will be someone else. Someone *NORMAL*. Maybe Gok is totally right, and happiness is as simple as better hair and a pair of jeans that fit.

**Monday 18 October**

11 a.m. (French)
Stan is completely *NOT* in agreement with Gok. He says he preferred the way I looked before. Or at least he did once he had managed to stop choking on the piece of toast he was eating when I walked into his kitchen this morning. He said he can barely stand to walk to school with a Sidehick clone, that I am in danger of tarnishing his reputation as an edgy loner, and that I am totally prostituting myself and Imo is my *PIMP*.

I said surely me being a ginger giant was more damaging to his reputation but he said actually that was pretty much integral to the whole thing.

He is wrong though. It is a definite improvement. I mean Sunday Henderson-Hicks actually did *NOT* try to trip me up and then shout 'timber' when I walked past her at the lockers. And Finty Goggins-Smith thought I was her twin (although not sure this is a reflection of my look, or her lack of brain cells, as she totally does *NOT* have a twin).

Also, Imo says she is not a pimp, she is a Makeover Artiste and is thinking of pitching her own show to Channel 5 called *Ten Years Older*.

And I am definitely *NOT* a prostitute. Although Mrs Hockerill (maths) did send me to Mr Kwame-Jones for excessive thigh exposure. But, like I said to Mr Kwame-Jones, it is *NOT* my fault if my legs are freakishly long and in fact I am thinking of suing the sock manufacturers under the Trades Descriptions Act, which Mr Kwame-Jones said showed excellent initiative and confidence for someone from the working classes.

And also I have to go now because Monsieur Leclerc is about to *frapper mon oreilles* or something, but I will totally report back after my rehearsal with Blake after school.

5 p.m.

Gok is *TOTALLY* right, Dr Sven. I mean since changing my look, the following brilliant things have happened:

1. Blake said my hair looked 'like, really, like, shiny, or something', which meant I could say, 'Yeah, Imogen did it, she's totally amazing at that stuff, and loads of stuff in fact.' Which means Imogen is now *TOTALLY PLEASED*.
2. Mr Burton is totally *NOT* pleased. He says I will have to either dye my hair back or wear a wig for the show as the whole *POINT* of my character is that she is *NOT* 'your average run of the mill private school clone', which if you think about it, is a *COMPLETE*

*COMPLIMENT* because he is actually saying I look *NORMAL*!

3. Mr Goldenblatt is also *NOT* pleased. Only this is nothing to do with my hair or clothing but because the Sidehicks got tangled up in 'The Tide is High' because Finty does not know which way is left, which meant we didn't have any time to do 'ABC' and for me to get more injuries because Mr Goldenblatt was trying to unsnag Finty's Rolex from Poppy's Tiffany necklace.
4. Hugh Cooper-Willis (who *IS* the one with the mole after all) is going out with Poppy Pringle. According to Lily Rubenstein, she went to see him on his sick bed and gave him more than just a bunch of grapes. Although now she is off school with strep throat and three hickeys. Which is *BRILLIANT*!

**Tuesday 19 October**

Day two of my new look has not been *QUITE* so fabulous:

1. Imogen called an emergency strategy meeting at lunch and has decided that I need to refocus my *NORMALIZING BOYFRIEND* efforts on Titus Pelling (now that Hugh Cooper-Willis is out of the running for at least three weeks until he realizes that Poppy Pringle has man hands) and that I need to flirt with him in rehearsal tomorrow and then, once he

is completely sucked in by my feminine powers, ask him to the PMS disco on Friday. I said *a*) I am not at all sure I have feminine powers and *b*) he will be going anyway so why do I need to ask him and *c*) I thought we were boycotting the disco on the grounds that *i*) they are so last year and *ii*) we will get Slimfasted. But Imogen said *a*) everyone has feminine powers, even Ruby, it is utterly instinctive, it just needs a new hairdo to bring them out, *b*) that is SO not the point, and *c*) she has made a major reassessment of the boycott and, statistically, more teen movie heroines whose plotlines involve meeting their ONE TRUE LOVE attend their school proms than don't, so, unless we are telekinetic or possessed by the devil (i.e. like Carrie, and, believe me, Imogen has tried this one) we should start going.

2. Mr Goldenblatt has got permission from Mr Kwame-Jones to DJ the disco (MC Goldenboy, and I am NOT EVEN JOKING), which means it will be 'Thriller' on repeat and some insane Liza Minnelli number, at which point the decks will 'accidentally break down' forcing Mr Goldenblatt to sing a cappella.
3. Ruby came over (to *a*) tell me that the date is set for their anti-private school protest in December and that I am duty bound as a Jones to attend, and *b*) borrow a saucepan because Spike has been using Denzil's in

some kind of art project and it is stuck on his friend Ludo's head) and she is completely *OUTRAGED* at my new look. She says I am not just letting Ruby down, I am letting myself down, and the whole of the female sex, and that women did not chain themselves to the railings at Greenham Common so I could have the right to look like a rah. I said I didn't think women tied themselves to anything over hair dye, I thought it was nuclear weapons, but Ruby said *WHATEVER* and stormed back to Spike's (without the saucepan, because ours are either broken or dirty or being used as chicken baths).

But I am thinking *POSITIVE*, Dr Sven. Because Alicia Beaufort let me hand her an eye mask in Chemistry today. I mean, she hasn't done that without using gloves and complaining to Mr Sylvester that she might catch fleas since Year Seven (when to be fair, a flea actually did jump off me on to her but it totally *WASN'T* my fault, it was because a chicken had been sleeping in my bed again).

**Wednesday 20 October**

Oh my God, Dr Sven. *ANOTHER* good thing has happened.

It turns out that Titus Pelling is *GAY*!

I am *NOT EVEN JOKING*. I found out in rehearsal, when Sunday Henderson-Hicks and Blake

were practising their snogging scene (like they need any rehearsals) and all the other girls bar me were learning the steps to 'ABC' (I will explain this in a minute).

So, what happened was that Titus and Miles Pitt-Dullforce were playing magnetic travel chess (they have to use the magnetic kind because all the missiles from the Sidehicks cause chaos with the chessmen) and Miles had to go to the bathroom for like the fifth time so I sat down and said I would take over for a bit (only Titus got annoyed because I made an illegal move with a horse, which is completely *NOT* my fault because at home we don't have actual chessmen we have Sylvanian families and Lego people, and the ponies are totally allowed to fly wherever they want to), and *THAT*'s when I asked him to the disco on Friday. Only instead of looking all smitten and flirted with, he went pale and said, 'I . . . er . . . you're not my type.' i.e. because he is *GAY*.

Which is what I told Stan when he demanded to know exactly what I was doing twiddling my hair manically, so I said, 'Flirting, duh.' And Stan said, 'Is that what it was?' And I said, 'Yes, only it didn't work because I am not boy.' And Stan said, 'Oh for God's sake, Buttercup, did you bleach your brain as well as your hair, Titus is *NOT* gay.' And then he stalked off because he had to sing Lionel Richie stuff to Mr Burton.

Imogen says Stan is just jealous because he secretly wishes he was gay because it is so much more edgy than just having a gay dad. I am not sure this is true but I did not argue because

I don't want to spoil her happiness about the Titus thing, because she has wanted a Gay Best Friend ever since she saw *Will and Grace* and she is going to recruit him starting tomorrow. And I think she kind of deserves to be happy, especially after *a*) she had to watch Blake and Sunday swap saliva for seven minutes thirty-two seconds (this was not actual, it was rehearsal, but even so, it is a total Pennington record) and *b*) Mr Goldenblatt banned her from dancing during 'ABC' as well. He says it is down to costume changes and she won't be able to put on her downtrodden housewife outfit if she is in an ironic Britney, but Lily Rubenstein says he emailed Mr Kwame-Jones demanding the right to enforce a strict dietary regime for 'certain cast members' in order to maximize fitness and minimize unsightly bouncing in lycra.

Mr Goldenblatt is a total body fascist. He is making me do the boys' part (see above) because he says my height is too distracting and that I ruin his sightline. Although at least I am not Fintan Riley. He has to wear a supersized collar and have his hair shaved to disguise his enormous head. Personally, I think shaving it is a huge mistake. It will just draw attention. He would be better off in a hat. Or off stage.

10 p.m.

I have just had a panic, Dr Sven. Maybe yesterday wasn't such a GOOD thing after all. Maybe Stan was right. Maybe I CANNOT flirt. I mean, even given that Titus is gay, his level of shock was totally HIGH, I mean he had NO IDEA that I had been trying to lure him with my feminine wiles. Maybe I don't even have feminine wiles!

Oh God. I need lessons. I will text Imogen. I know for fact she has studied the entire *Gossip Girl* box set and probably laminated a list of techniques.

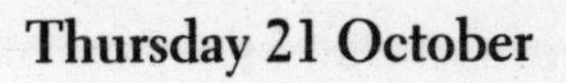

**Thursday 21 October**

I have just seen Mr Burton wheeling a crate of Coke along the corridor for what I can only assume is some kind of refreshment stand for tomorrow's disco. He is crazier than I am if he thinks anyone but Fintan Riley is going to stick to that. And Fintan is not supposed to go near artificial colours anyway after the time he went a bit ADHD and stuck his head in the school gate and Miss Hutchinson had to grease him out with some Nivea.

Oh, and I was totally right. Imogen had already done a list (*NOT* laminated, but when she was in Year Five, which I am not *EVEN* going to say anything about because I am just grateful right now).

The rules of flirting, according to Imogen Pritchard

1. Lick lips so they look wet and kissable.
2. Touch the flirtee on the arm frequently.
3. Constantly laugh.
4. Have a copy of a book with 'kiss' in the title in your hand at all times.

She says I can totally use them on Len Cho at the school disco. Although I am *REALLY* not sure that this is a good idea, Dr Sven, because in maths, he actually nearly cried when he worked out that x was the square root of pie or something. I mean, is *THIS* the kind of boy I want to touch on the arm? Let alone near my kissable lips? *SERIOUSLY*, Dr Sven, *IS IT*?

**Friday 22 October**

*I DO NOT* feel well, Dr Sven. The thing is, I have practised everything Imogen said, i.e., the touching and the laughing etc., only I just look completely *CRAZY*. And, anyway, even if I could flirt, I'm pretty sure *I DO NOT* want Len Cho as a boyfriend. I mean in rehearsal today he spent the entire time trying to contact aliens by beaming the sound of Blake singing 'Man in the Mirror' into space using his iPhone. I mean, even if it were possible, which it is *NOT*, *WHY* would aliens want to hear that? Is that a sign of intelligent life on Earth? I so think not.

Imogen says I am just getting first night nerves and that once I am there I will realize that Len is my ticket to mental calm and stability, plus I *HAVE* to go because *a*) I am wearing vintage Lacroix and it is *CRIMINAL* not to show it off in front of Sunday Henderson-Hicks and *b*) as well as snogging Len, I have Blake duties to attend to (i.e. engineer it so that he and Imogen somehow find themselves alone in a dimly-lit corridor, with the sound of Stevie Wonder filtering through the jasmine-scented night air), because Stan isn't going (he is sticking to the boycott on the grounds that *a*) the likelihood of them playing any Doors is about 100–1 against and *b*) there is an anime marathon on the Cartoon channel) so he can't get off with Sunday (like *THAT* would ever happen). I did point out that, given that all is quiet on the stalking front, maybe Blake has changed his mind about his secret love for Imogen, but Imogen said, duh, he is just playing it cool because probably Sunday has threatened to kill herself if he does not stay with her.

She has been watching soaps again. Seriously, I am thinking of grassing her to Mrs Pritchard, because I think it may be worse for her health than the four Curly Wurlys she ate at last break.

OK. Here goes nothing. Wish me luck, Dr Sven.

11.45 p.m.

<u>Things that DID NOT happen at the PMS disco</u>

1. I did not snog Len Cho;
2 Imogen did not snog Blake;
3. Mr Burton did not turn out to be a good dancer. (Seriously, it is like watching myself on the dance floor, only with less hair. He is like totally unco-ordinated. Which you think would stop him but *NO* he totally got down to 'Dirty Diana'. Which, like, *EWWWWW*.)

Things that DID happen at the PMS disco

1. Len Cho called an ambulance because he thought I was having some sort of nervous breakdown (symptoms excessive drooling, jittery hands, hysterical laughter) and I only managed to convince the paramedic I was fine when he called Lola, realized that he knew her from a party at Denzil's, and said, 'Oh, it runs in the family then.'
2. Me and Imogen got sent home early for *a*) locking Sunday Henderson-Hicks in the girls' toilets (Imo) and *b*) removing the lightbulbs in the backstage area thus causing a health and safety hazard (me—due to height advantage).
3. Finty Goggins-Smith snogged Miles Pitt-Dullforce but she said it was only because of the blackout, and thought it was actually Mr Burton.

Imogen said in fact it was a complete triumph because now Blake will realize that Sunday is the kind of B-lister who gets locked in a toilet, while she is the misunderstood heroine who gets expelled and then reinstated in a blaze of authority-trumping glory. Plus it is *NOT* my fault that Len Cho is breakdown-sensitive ever since his uncle was adversely affected by his hayfever medication and thought he was Napoleon (according to Lily Rubenstein).

I said *WHATEVER*, it is totally a sign that the boyfriend thing is a *HUGE* mistake. Because *I DO NOT WANT A BOYFRIEND*. I mean, the only boy I want to hang out with, who doesn't make me stutter, flap my hair idiotically, or want to hurl, is **STAN**. Which is what I told Imogen. Only **THEN** she went so red in the face I thought **SHE** was having a breakdown, only it turned out it was another **EPIPHANY** because she said:

IMOGEN: Oh my God. I am such a fool. It has been staring me in the face for years, but I have only just seen it.

BUTTERCUP: Seen what? Are you quoting from *Jane Eyre* again?

IMOGEN: No, duh. Seen that Stan is your **ONE TRUE LOVE**! It's like in *Pretty in Pink*. Only if she actually went out with Duckie, instead of Blane, which, when I direct a remake, will totally happen.

BUTTERCUP: But you **LIKE** Blane because then it is a wrong side of the tracks love story. And **NO HE ISN'T**.

IMOGEN: Whatever. And **YES HE IS**. He is totally your **BOY NEXT DOOR**!

BUTTERCUP: He doesn't even live next door. He lives two doors up, on the other side of the road. But that **ISN'T THE POINT**. He is like family, or something. Like a cousin. And **DON'T** start on the 'you can marry your cousin' thing because this is **SO NOT** like you and Dafydd.

IMOGEN: *OH MY GOD*. You are right. It is even *MORE* complicated and *BRILLIANT* because now it is totally clear that he is like your replacement father figure. You have unresolved man issues. *WHY* did I not see this? We *HAVE* to find your real father or you will never be able to have a healthy relationship with yourself, with Lola, or with a man. Oh, I am undone . . .

And then I would have argued back, only at that point Imogen had to hide behind a topiary whale while she changed, because she had told her mum she was going to a Covenanters prayer meeting, and I am pretty sure not even Mrs Pritchard believes you wear hot pants to praise the lord in.

Anyway, the point is, on the good side, the whole boyfriend thing is *OFF*. But on the bad side, the *HUNT DOWN MY FATHER* thing is *ON*.

Not that we have any chance of actually finding him. I mean, I have asked Lola, several times, usually when she has done something so colossally Lola-like that I have to contemplate leaving home, but she *TOTALLY* does not know.

So the whole thing is *CRAZY*, right? Like thinking Stan is my *ONE TRUE LOVE*. I mean that's just off the scale, isn't it?

11.55 p.m.

Isn't it?

**Saturday 23 October**

8 p.m.

It so is.

<u>Reasons why Stan Romer is NOT my ONE TRUE LOVE</u>

1. He is Stan.
2. He is my second best friend (on paper) and my real best friend (do *NOT* tell Imogen!).
3. When I first got a bra, he did not start pinging it, or offering me 50p to see it, like the Cooper-Willises, he just tried it on to see what it felt like.
4. He is Stan.
5. He has seen me wee into a paddling pool naked.
6. He has *NEVER* tried to kiss me, not once, in the entire fourteen years I have known him.
7. The last girl he fancied was Princess Amidala, which despite the height thing, I am totally *NOT*. I mean, have you seen her hair?
8. When I told him that no I did *NOT* get off with anyone last night because, like, why would I want to, I am *NEVER* getting off with boys, they are all vile etc., plus apparently my flirting looks like I am having a mental breakdown so I am completely ungettoffable with anyway, he did not say 'Oh, but yes you are gettoffable with', he just said 'oh'.
9. He is *STAN*!

And right now, he is asleep, in my bed, recovering from the

anime marathon, and I am not in any way feeling *ODD* about this.

Actually that's not true. I am feeling odd. But only because I am thinking about thinking about it being odd. Which doesn't make it odd. Does it? Oh God. Now I'm just totally confused. So I will move on to the next list, which is the one that Imogen brought round about five minutes after Stan arrived.

Buttercup Jones's suspected fathers by Imogen Pritchard

1. *SULTAN KOSEN* (the world's tallest man);
2. *DENZIL* (because he is Ruby's dad, and Lola is always 'accidentally' ending up on the barge, even though he has a girlfriend called Fiona Moon Twitchett);
3. *STEVE TYLER* from this ancient band Aerosmith (huge lips, and groupie habit);
4. *RONALD WEASLEY* (ginger);
5. *STRINGER BELL* (from *The Wire*, who is Lola's number one fantasy TV crime overlord).

Reasons why Imogen Pritchard's list SUCKS big time

1. Lola has never been to Turkey.
2. Denzil is five foot four, plus there is no way Ruby and I share all the same genes, I mean she is not allergic to dogs, she is not ginger, and she actually *LIKES* pickled eggs.
3. Ronald Weasley is *NOT REAL* and if she means Rupert Grint, then he is, like, nineteen or something, which

would mean he would have been five when
I was born, which, like, *NOOOO*.

4. Stringer Bell is *BLACK*.
5. Although I admit Steve Tyler is
   a possibility.

Imogen got totally cross about this and said if I didn't want her support she will go and help someone who does appreciate her many talents, e.g. Ms Nugent, who is totally crying out for a makeover. But, like I said, Ms Nugent's tracksuits are just sensible and the Joan of Arc haircut is probably totally hot in the lesbian PE teacher community. And anyway I *DID* want her support, but maybe we should take a more practical approach, which doesn't involve giant Turks or boy wizards.

At which point she totally cheered up and said, 'Oooh. Maybe we could find her diary. It will totally be like in *Mamma Mia*, only obviously you look nothing like Amanda Seyfried, you are more the slutty older friend of Meryl Streep, but that's not the point. Oooh, maybe your dad is Pierce Brosnan! *WHY* didn't I think about that?'

But before I could point out that Lola does the fingers in the ears lalala thing whenever Pierce Brosnan comes on the TV, Imo had gone off on one again, i.e. '*OR* how about regression therapy, I have seen it on *The Mentalist* and Lola will be able to reveal all her deepest buried secrets and possibly even turn out to have been Queen Victoria in a past life.' At which point she stopped to swallow the four M&Ms that had been in her mouth the whole time, so I seized the opportunity and said if

Lola was anything in a past life it was *NOT* Queen Victoria, it was more likely to be Marie Antoinette. *BUT* why didn't we:

1. Interview Lola,
2. Interview Lola's known associates.

Which Imogen got totally excited about because she is convinced she is Oprah and can get anyone to confess to anything, and said we should start tomorrow on Lola.

You know, I totally think this might be *GOOD* after all, Dr Sven. Because maybe my dad will turn out to be a total positive influence type person. Maybe he will be able to fix stuff around the house, and persuade Lola to be normal. Maybe he *WILL* be like Pierce Brosnan. Or George Clooney. Or even Steve Tyler, now that he has given up the groupies, and bad videos.

10 p.m.

But then again, knowing my luck, it will turn out to be Sultan Kosen or Ron Weasley.

**Sunday 24 October**

Transcript of interview with Lola Jones, as recorded on Harry Jones's Fisher Price tape recorder

IMO: Testing, testing. Does this thing actually work?

LOLA: Is this homework? Because they should have given you a recorder or something, shouldn't they? God, I

| | |
|---|---|
| | mean, I pay them enough. |
| BUTTERCUP: | You don't pay them anything. |
| LOLA: | Riiiight. Sorry. What is this again? |
| IMO: | We are going to find Buttercup's dad so she can forge meaningful relationships with the opposite sex. Or the same sex. Because I am totally pro-lesbianism. Once I thought I was one. But it turned out— |
| BUTTERCUP: | God, Imo. *STOP*. |
| IMO: | OK. Question 1. |
| BUTTERCUP: | No hang on a minute, Imo. Lola, don't you even mind if we find my dad? I mean, aren't you going to lecture me on how I don't need anyone else but you etc., etc. |
| LOLA: | Oh, yeah. That, all of it. Only I could really use the child maintenance right now. Because, like, Harry's dad— |
| BUTTERCUP: | *DON'T SAY IT THIS IS BEING RECORDED*. |
| LOLA: | Riiight. Sorry. Carry on. |
| IMO: | OK. Fabbity fab. |
| BUTTERCUP: | *DON'T* say that. It makes you sound about five. |

IMO: *GOD*. OK. So, Lola: first question.

LOLA: What were we talking about again?

BUTTERCUP: Give me strength.

IMO: Shut *UP*, Buttercup. Lola: look into my eyes. Who is Buttercup's father?

LOLA: Wow. Your eyes are, like, amazingly blue.

IMO: Answer the question, come on, Lola. Just answer it. *ANSWER THE QUESTION, LOLA*.

LOLA: What was it again?

BUTTERCUP: Oh, for crying out loud.

(Sound of tape recorder being wrested from Imogen's control. Interview ends.)

I am going to try Granny Jones tomorrow. She is like an elephant, i.e. she remembers *EVERYTHING*.

Although if elephants remembered *EVERYTHING*, you'd think they'd have sussed a way out of the zoos by now, wouldn't you, Dr Sven.

## Monday 25 October

10 a.m.

Imogen is *NOT* coming to see Granny Jones. She had to go to a jigsaw convention in Yeovil, which she totally got out of by claiming she had a viral infection, only then Mrs Pritchard said she had better go to bed with plenty of fluids and York

notes. Imo says she is going to downgrade it to a mild cold by teatime tomorrow and will be back on Oprah form by Wednesday latest. Anyway, it is actually a *GOOD* thing because Granny Jones does *NOT* respond well to aggressive questioning, and tends to counter it by blaming everything on communists or the French.

5 p.m.

Things Granny Jones remembers from December 1995

1. That American Airlines Flight 965 crashed in Colombia and only four people and a *DOG* survived.
2. That the *BLOODY* French were on strike again.
3. That Grandpa Jones beat AJ Schooler to become Captain of the Golf Club and Sylvia Schooler has never forgiven her.
4. That Major (Granny's dog before Geraldo, still allergy-causing, and with added drool issues) had to have emergency surgery after a fight with Mrs Ollerton-Grimshaw's cat Lincoln (Lincoln only lost some tail fur, but got off worse in the end, because Granny forced Mrs Ollerton-Grimshaw to have him put down on the grounds he was a threat to small children).
5. That Michael Jackson was Christmas number 1 only *GOD* knows why because *WHAT* did he think he was doing to his face? (Yet apparently Botox and an

unconfirmed, yet widely suspected, nose job is *FINE*.)

6. That Julia Hillsey-Knowles from number 47 put a light-up reindeer and sleigh in front of her gardenias (which lasted two days until Granny got a court injunction against it on grounds of it being a traffic impediment).

<u>Things Granny Jones does not remember</u>

1. Who Lola was going out with. Because according to Granny, Lola was living in a squat in Brixton by then, and only came home for New Year's Eve, and most of that she spent *OUT*, so feasibly it could be anyone in London and I would be better off asking Celia or Susie Fogarty who were squatting with her at the time.

Stan says he'll ask Celia tonight, only maybe it's best if I'm not there, in case the answers are too traumatic, plus I should probably stay indoors given my swollen eyes and red skin (Granny *ACTUALLY LET* Geraldo sit on her lap during the interview, because she said he was traumatized by Mr Cement giving him a menacing look this morning and might have a fatal heart attack if she left him alone for too long). He's going to come round in the morning to break it to me gently. Which is totally sweet.

Not that that means anything, Dr Sven. It is just the kind of thing a best friend would do. Not a *ONE TRUE LOVE*.

11 p.m.
I cannot sleep, Dr Sven. Because what if Celia can remember? What if she has told Stan already and it turns out that my father *IS* a drug overlord or something?

11.30 p.m.
I am still awake.

11.45 p.m.
Still awake.

12 midnight
OK, Dr Sven, I cannot wait any longer. I am going to Stan's. I *HAVE TO KNOW*.

12.05 a.m.
Stan was already on his way, in anticipation of me having a *MELTDOWN*. He said the only person Celia can remember Lola going out with is 'Julio', only according to Margot Hutt-Winner, who is now Mrs Julio, his sperm are immotile which is why they have adopted two Guatemalans and a Pole.

Which, on the bad side means I am still fatherless, but on the *GOOD* side means now I (and Stan) can get some sleep.

**Tuesday 26 October**

11.10 a.m.
OK. So I've just woken up, and clearly Imogen is now out of quarantine, because there is a note in her handwriting on the pillow telling me *a*) that I am due in PMS rehearsal in twenty minutes and *b*) that really I should not be sharing a bed with Stan until I have resolved my father issues. Which *a*) like *EWWWW* and *b*) is actually incorrect because Stan is not *IN* my bed, he is on the floor, only he *ISN'T* any more, because he has gone home, only *NOW* I am worried he has read *IMO*'s note and thinks I have unresolved issues with *HIM* which *I DO NOT*.

4 p.m.
Things Mr Burton learned in the PMS holiday workshop

1. That it is pointless organizing a holiday workshop because half the company will be in St Tropez, Barbados or Padstow and Mr Goldenblatt will be on a pilgrimage to Neverland.
2. That in fact PMS would be a lot more fun if half the company were permanently in St Tropez, Barbados or Padstow and Mr Goldenblatt lived in Neverland.

Seriously, it was the best rehearsal ever. No one tripped anyone up, no one got Slimfasted, or called a Fat-head Freak Show Baby (Fintan), or got a phone call from Fat Camp asking why she hadn't turned up for enrolment (Imo). We just sang 'It Must Be Love', and painted scenery, and tried to make alien contact by beaming Mr Burton's version of 'Space Oddity' into the stars on Len Cho's iPhone. In fact I kind of wish we were doing more rehearsals tomorrow instead of interviewing Denzil.

Oh, and Stan totally did *NOT* mention the note, or the bed, or unresolved issues. Which is totally *GOOD*, though doesn't necessarily mean he doesn't know about them. Not that there are any.

**Wednesday 27 October**

5 p.m.
That was a *COMPLETE* waste of a day. Because Denzil wasn't even there when we arrived at the barge, he was at Fiona Moon Twitchett's (who lives in a tepee in Bathhampton woods, except in extreme weather when she goes back to her Georgian mansion in Box), so we had to sit round Fish Knowsley's barge for *THREE HOURS*, which, believe me, is *NOT IN ANY SENSE* good because *a*) he likes to play the harmonica only he *CANNOT* play the harmonica and *b*) he *SMELLS OF FISH*. And then, when Denzil did get back, he said he was roadieing on a tour of West Cornwall with the Wurzels in 1995 and can't remember anything except the words to 'I've Got a Brand New Combine Harvester'.

Plus Ruby, who had been at Fiona's with Denzil, sharing a love of interpretive arts and crafts, i.e. making fertility brooches out of bits of old felt, is still sulking at my new look, even though I was not wearing over-the-knee socks and wedge heels, I was wearing wellies, due to canal hazards. She says I look like a *CAPITALIST TORY PIG* and *NO* my hair is *NOT* Debbie Harry/suffragette hair, it is *CAPITALIST TORY PIG* hair and that until I dye it back, or better, dreadlock it or shave it off, I am not welcome at her protests, or on the barge, or in vicinity of the Art College, the skate park, or the Mung Bean vegan café.

Imogen says she is just jealous in case my father turns out *NOT* to be a dreadlocked barge-dweller who eats beans out of the can for breakfast, but is Stringer Bell, i.e. rich *AND* controversial.

I am almost glad Imogen is going to her cousins in Pontypridd tomorrow. Although I am keeping my fingers crossed Dafydd is not there. I mean, I know it's legal, but seriously, fancying your *COUSIN*?

**Thursday 28 October**

10 a.m.
OK. So the list of interviewees has kind of petered out. Unless somehow we can unearth the mysterious Susie Fogarty who was in the squat with Lola. Though if she's anything like Che or any of the other weirdos they lived with, she's probably called Sunbeam and lives in Chichicastenango by now. Which, like, there's no way. Even with Imogen claiming she is totally that guy off *Without a Trace*.

So, I'm going to do something positive, i.e. I'm

going to go round Stan's to rehearse, which Mr Burton reminded me I am supposed to be doing every day, but *UNSURPRISINGLY* I'd kind of forgotten about.

11 a.m.
So that's weird, Stan says he can't rehearse because he's 'busy'. Only he won't say where or who with.

Harry says he will rehearse with me but frankly singing about being in love with your own brother is a little too Imogen for my liking. Plus Harry won £10 from Granny Jones in a game of Canasta so we're going into town for milkshake.

5 p.m.
OK. So totally *WEIRD* thing number *TWO* just happened, i.e. me and Harry were in Shaker Makers having Kinder Bueno and Banoffee Muffin milkshakes (which sound gross, but actually turn out to be amazing, which Ruby says is down to the level of transfats and third-world desecrating refined sugar in them and really I should go to Mung Bean for Fairtrade soya lattes only she has banned me from there so it's her fault if you think about it) and Blake came in, *WITHOUT* Sunday (Padstow) and asked if he could sit with us while he waited for his After Eight Mint milkshake, which meant I got to mention Imogen *TWICE* (that Imogen always has Reese's Peanut Butter Cup flavour, and that once she drank so many she was sick in someone else's handbag and they totally didn't notice) and it

would totally have been more only I had to spend at least four minutes explaining that Harry was *NOT* my illegitimate cross-race love child, he was my *BROTHER*.

And the thing is, he seemed kind of OK. I mean, he didn't call me Nemo, or After Eight milkshake me. He just said how he can't rehearse at home because the last time his dad caught him singing a Cher song he crashed the Range Rover, and that Coach Parry is not *IN ANY WAY* happy about the PMS thing either, because he caught him doing a grapevine on the touchline. Only Sunday won't let him leave, so he is stuck between a rock and the deep blue sea (which I know is totally mixing metaphors, but at least he tried *USING* one, I mean normally he just grunts). So I asked him what did *HE* want to do, and he said he'd like to be in a musical about England's famous victory at the Five Nations, with him as Jonny Wilkinson. And I said I meant more like now, at school, and he said he just wanted to do both. And then I thought that maybe Imogen is right after all and maybe he *DOES* have hidden depths. And I was totally about to ask if he wanted to rehearse at mine, only at that exact moment the Cooper-Willises came in and asked him what he was doing talking to me and Clint pea-shot Bounty-flavour transfat foam at me through his straw.

Which is probably a good thing. I mean, what was I thinking inviting a Mudhoney to the house from hell?

Plus then totally *WEIRD* thing number *THREE* happened which is that on the way home, I definitely saw Lily Rubenstein coming out of Stan's house. Which, like *WHY*?

I mean, they only have one scene together for PMS, for like two minutes, so why would they need to rehearse that?

7 p.m.
Not that I care. Just curious, you know?

**Friday 29 October**

10 a.m.
OK. So Stan is here. Because *a*) he has totally found Susie Fogarty (Celia called Harry's dad at MI5 and got the address in Cheltenham and a phone number. Which, like, why didn't I think of that? So I have called and left a message asking her to call me back immediately.) And *b*) he wants to rehearse. Now that he and Lily have finished doing whatever they were doing. Which he did not mention, and nor did I. But I totally wanted to. I mean WHY was she there, Dr Sven? WHY?

Anyway, we are going to do some kind of Cure/Kylie mash-up, which, if you ask me, Dr Sven, sounds WRONG on so many levels. But Stan says I just need to have some faith.

1 p.m.
I take it all back. The mash-up thing worked. I have NO idea how. But I guess it's like Kinder Bueno milkshakes, i.e. you think it cannot possibly taste as good as either the candy or the milk, but SOMEHOW it just does. Even better, in fact. Maybe Stan is right. Maybe I just need to have more faith in stuff.

1.15 p.m.
Though just because it turns out that The Cure and Kylie go together does *NOT* mean I think Imo's love mash-up analogy thing is any way correct. Believe me, Dr Sven, Buttercup Jones and anyone else would just be mash. Even Stan.

1.30 p.m.
OK. So Susie still hasn't called back. Stan says maybe she's on half term too, but if she is anything like Lola, which she is *BOUND* to be, she has no concept of *HOLI*days versus *WORK* days and so is probably more likely hungover or still out. So, if she hasn't called by two, which is late even by Lola's standards, then I'm going to try again. In a subtle, non-stalkerish kind of way.

2 p.m.
There is *STILL* no sign of Susie, so I rang, and *SOMEONE* picked up, but when I said hello, they hung up *IMMEDIATELY*. Which is not completely weird, because Lola has a tendency to do that, when she thinks it sounds like Mr Peason, our landlord, or the council, or Granny Jones, i.e. someone in a position of power, but the thing is, I don't sound like anyone in a position of power. At least I'm pretty sure I don't, because it has been pointed out that I say 'er' and 'um' at least ten times a sentence, which according to Imogen is a sign of low self-esteem, which for once, is almost definitely true.

4 p.m.

OK. So the Kylie/Cure thing is wearing thin now. I mean, there is only so much 'Spinning Around' I can do without barfing. Plus this is getting TOTALLY suspicious, Dr Sven. I have rung AGAIN, and a woman answered, and I said really quickly 'Hello, this is Buttercup Jones, you went to college with my mum Lola and I need to ask you some important and pertinent questions regarding December 1995,' but then I heard a noise like a chicken when you accidentally tread on one of its feet, and then she, whoever she is, HUNG UP AGAIN.

Stan says she DEFINITELY knows something, and it is probably causing disturbing flashbacks, and that the only answer is to turn up on her doorstep and DEMAND some answers. We are getting the train tomorrow. Stan said he will pay, and I said no, because he is ALWAYS paying for me, but Stan said I can write an IOU and he'll call it in when I'm a famous West End star. I said *a*) some chance and *b*) aren't all West End stars attention-seeking overly self-esteemed habitual joiners? But Stan just said I could break the mould. Sometimes I think he's the CRAZY one.

7 p.m.

Oh, and I texted Imo to tell her about *a*) the Blake milkshake saga and *b*) Susie, and she said I am totally forgiven but that she is at the Loaves and Fishes Christian convention in Lampeter, which she is NEVER going to forgive

Mr and Mrs Pritchard for, and that she is being forced to conceal *Heat* magazine inside her Gideon Bible which is really hard given the size differential, but that she will be round tomorrow night for *FULL DETAILS* and that this is *DEFINITELY MY TIME*, and that I should prepare to *MEET MY MAKER*.

I think this Christian thing may have got to her after all. She'll come back in a pinafore singing 'Kumbaya'.

9 p.m.
Or maybe not. Imogen has just texted to say she is adding Scott Pilgrim to her Top Five ideal men list, replacing Jesus. Which I'm kind of relieved about.

**Saturday 30 October**

8 a.m.
On scale of one to norovirus, I feel *TOTALLY TEN BUCKETS* of ill. Seriously, PMS is *NOTHING*. I would rather do a Lionel Richie/Green Day mash-up, *NAKED*, in front of the entire school, than this.

I mean, what if this *IS* it, Dr Sven? What if I'm about to find out *WHO* my dad is? *WHO* I have inherited my gingerness, height, and possibly liking for picking the top off an Oreo then licking the cream out of the inside from? (Because Lola has this weird aversion to the inside of Oreos; they totally freak her out for some reason.)

Stan says I can back out if I want, and he won't think any less of me, but that maybe it's one of those things in life that you just have to face up to, like tetanus jabs, or tax, or third albums being notoriously difficult.

I said I wasn't backing out. Imo has texted to wish me luck as well. Actually it was mostly to tell me that she is converting to Buddhism because Mr Megson, who is chief Covenanter, made everyone get up at 6 a.m. to wonder at God's work creating the sunrise, and Imo was having a dream about Scott Pilgrim which she would have preferred to wonder at for at least another two hours. But the thought was definitely there.

So, I guess this is *IT*, Dr Sven. Like Imogen says, I am going to *MEET MY MAKER*. Or one of them. Because the other I am totally aware of, which is *NOT* necessarily a good thing, especially as right now she is asleep on the sofa, with a chicken pecking peanut pieces out of her hair.

But what if he *DOES* turn out to be Steve Tyler?

Or actually *EVIL*? Stan says this is impossible or I wouldn't have turned out *NON EVIL*. But what about Luke Skywalker, Dr Sven? His dad was Darth Vader. You see my point?

4 p.m.
(3.30 First Great Western Cheltenham to Bristol Temple Meads)

Things I have learnt from my find my father fact mission to Cheltenham

1. That Susie Fogarty is now called Susan Hughes, and lives in a mock Georgian mansion with a dentist called Jeremy.
2. That she looks like someone from the Boden catalogue (which is this mail order clothes catalogue of mentally healthy-looking people doing mentally healthy things on beaches in Cornwall).
3. That she had a job designing Hallmark cards but is now too busy to work because she has twin girls called Ophelia and Amelia (who are also out of the Boden catalogue, and I mean *ACTUALLY*, they are child models).
4. That she has no idea who my father is, and really would prefer to have *NO* further contact with either me, *OR* Lola, on the advice of her psychiatrist.
5. That Cheltenham is just like here. Only flatter.

Which is so *NOT* what I expected (the Susie thing, not the flatness of Cheltenham, because, really, I am *NOT* someone who has the time to worry about geographical issues. Seriously. There is not enough room with Lola occupying most of my brain cells at any given minute). I mean, at first she slammed the door the minute she saw me, then after Stan kept his finger on the doorbell and she was forced to answer, because there is only so long you can listen to 'Au Clair de la Lune' for (I mean *WHO* chooses *THAT* as their

doorbell chime. Seriously, WHO? Imo had 'Onward Christian Soldiers' for a bit, but she 'accidentally' broke the connection and now they have a knocker in the shape of a crucifix), and then she totally denied she was even called Susie or had studied art, she said she did economics at Hull, but luckily Stan tricked her with a question about active government intervention in the marketplace and then she totally had to fess up.

So now I still have NO idea who my dad is, and we have exhausted ALL possible lines of enquiry.

Stan said something might crop up unexpectedly. I said, 'Like what, like Prince Charles is going to rock up and suddenly claim me as his own and anyway, like you care, because you're probably itching to hang out with Lily Rubenstein anyway.' (Which was kind of a shock, even to me, because WHY did Lily pop into my head at that precise moment, Dr Sven? WHY, I ask you?) Stan said, 'I know you're upset, Buttercup, but don't do an Imo, and don't take it out on me.' So I had to say sorry, which he claims he forgave me for, only now he is listening to sub-punk on his iPod and I still have no idea WHAT Lily was doing at his.

Not that that's important, I guess. Not in the scheme of things. I mean, I've just lost all hope of finding my father, why should I worry about a kooky cyber-hacker with a tendency to gossip and an ANNOYINGLY cute bob (I mean, it is the kind of hair I dream about, you know, it always looks neat and glossy, and the fringe is totally only about a centimetre long, which

me and Imo tried to copy once, using Lola's nail scissors, only I ended up more Frankenstein's monster than flapper girl. Seriously, Dr Sven, I looked like I had escaped from Arkham).

8 p.m.

Unsurprisingly, Imogen has a PLAN. It is: 'seize the day'.

I said I thought that the whole point was that I couldn't seize anything, i.e. forge any meaningful relationships with anyone, including myself, until I had resolved my genetic inheritance etc. But she says, according to *Cosmopolitan* (which she read at camp, because the travel size one is totally concealable inside *Praise Be*), it is all about *a*) having the serenity to accept the things I cannot change, the courage to change the things I can, and the wisdom to know the difference (which I TOTALLY recognize and I am pretty sure it is NOT from *Cosmopolitan*), *b*) bed hair (which is DEFINITELY from *Cosmopolitan*) and *c*) the HERE AND NOW (which could feasibly be from anywhere, including *Praise Be*).

She says instead of worrying about who Lola was snogging in December 1995, we should be concentrating on who she is snogging right now (well, not RIGHT now, as she is trying to deflea the chickens, but you get the picture) and making sure they are suitable father figure material and to that end she has drawn up a list:

Potential suitors for Lola Jones by Imogen Pritchard

1. Mr Megson (because his godliness would totally cancel out Lola's tendency to sin, plus, even though

he wears nylon trousers, he looks a bit like Dr Who from the side);

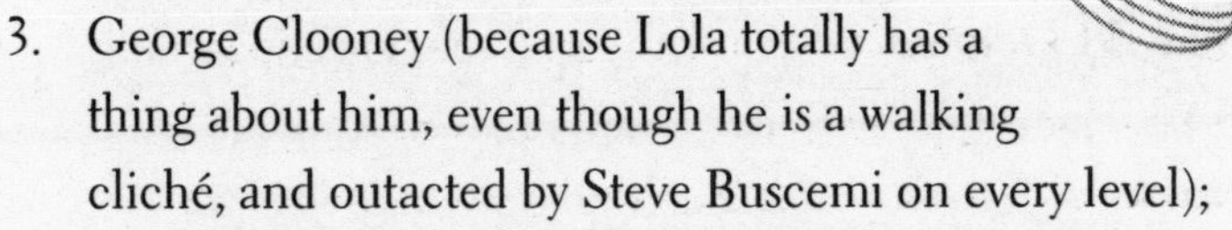

2. Fergal O'Shaughnessy (because then we could rescue them both from their messed up lives and someone would make a movie about it. With possibly Steve Buscemi as Fergal);
3. George Clooney (because Lola totally has a thing about him, even though he is a walking cliché, and outacted by Steve Buscemi on every level);
4. Mr Goldenblatt (because then both me AND Stan would have gay dads);
5. Mr Burton (because then we could be like Billy Ray Cyrus and Miley Cyrus and have our own father-daughter singing TV series).

And the thing is I think Imogen might actually be RIGHT. Not about the bed hair, because, as I have already explained, I do NOT do any hair very well, or about Steve Buscemi playing Fergal, or about a boyfriend for Lola at all (especially not Mr Burton. I mean, SO WRONG). But about the here and now, and concentrating on changing the things I can.

Because maybe who I am doesn't depend on who made me, but who I make of myself.

10 p.m.

I just read that last bit back and I TOTALLY sound like *High School Musical*. Imogen is infecting me with her absurd film dialogue/Christian camp speak. That or PMS is now somehow in my blood.

Clearly I am traumatized and need some sleep.

Tomorrow will be better. It will be a fresh start. A new dawn. A new day.

Oh my God. It's like it keeps spurting out of me in an unstoppable fountain of Zac Efronisms. Am stopping immediately before I make myself, or you, actually throw up.

**Sunday 31 October**

1 p.m.
OK. So I'm totally seizing the day. Or afternoon. i.e. I'm going to man up, or non gender specific up or something, and get ready for tomorrow's first ever solo rehearsal by channelling Judy, instead of lying in my bed feeling sorry for myself / IMing Stan about *The X Men*.

Prepare to be amazed, Dr Sven, I am totally making something, or someone, of myself.

5 p.m.
*OMG*, Dr Sven. I did it. I made someone of myself. Only not Judy, because 'Over the Rainbow' isn't in the show, despite lobbying from Imogen, and Mr Goldenblatt, but *MADONNA*. I swear I am totally channelling Madge. I even have the accent. Mr Burton is going to have a cow.

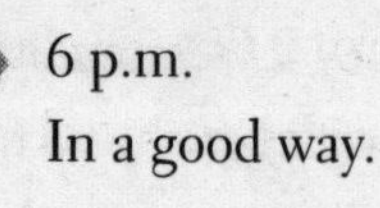

6 p.m.
In a good way.

# NOVEMBER

## Monday 1 November

Today's Top Three Mentally Compromising Occurrences

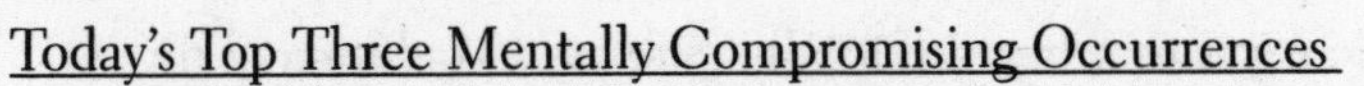

1. I got sent to Mr Kwame-Jones for uniform breaches AGAIN. This time it was for 'over-elaborate hair accessories', i.e. that my peacock feather hairclip (which was TOTALLY Imogen's idea) was obscuring Fintan Riley's view of the whiteboard, which, like, is a bit pot calling the kettle black, which is totally what I told Mr Kwame-Jones, only he said it was out of his hands, literally, i.e. Miss Hutchinson had already confiscated it, which Imogen said was a breach of my human rights, but which Miss Hutchinson said was 'tough luck, young lady'.
2. Blake Carrington asked if I could meet him at lunch tomorrow to 'go over lines'. WHAT DOES THIS MEAN, Dr Sven? Does it actually mean 'go over lines' or is it secret code for something I am not aware of, like doing jelly shots, or tipping cows? What IS tipping cows anyway? Is it ACTUALLY tipping cows? It is all totally confusing.
3. I am wearing Lola's pants. Which are NOT AT ALL regulation, i.e. they are not substantial waist-high heavy duty navy cotton, they are insubstantial, barely-covering anything black lace hipsters. This is because the washing machine is now COMPLETELY out of

bounds due to severe flood risk. And it was these or Harry's Incredibles Y-fronts.

*BUT* something good happened. Like, *REALLY* good. At least, I think it was.

So I was in rehearsal, totally making a Madonna of myself. Only the thing was, it felt all weird. The accent suddenly sounded kind of lame. And the Fuzzy-Felt brown dot on my cheek suddenly seemed more Hugh Cooper-Willis mole than beauty spot. And my voice kind of disappeared and I said I was sorry and that I was trying really hard to be Madonna and totally taking it seriously and seizing the day and everything. Only Mr Burton told me music wasn't about imitating someone else, it was about being yourself, and finding your own voice, which, like, is *SO NOT* what I want to do normally, which I told him. So then he made me close my eyes, and listen to the music, like *REALLY* listen, and think about what it meant for the Girl Next Door (which I had to get him to remind me, because the plot is *TOTALLY* convoluted, and slightly implausible).

Anyway, the point is, I did close my eyes, and tried to imagine how she felt about being ditched for the Bad Best Friend (only as I have never been ditched for anyone, let alone Sunday Henderson-Hicks, I had to imagine how I would feel if Stan decided he wanted to be best friends with, say Lily Rubenstein, which again I ask you, Dr Sven, *WHY*?) and *THAT*'s when the thing happened. Only it wasn't the thing Mr Burton wanted, because I didn't feel like me, because feeling like me involves feeling sick, paranoid, and mentally unstable. Instead I felt kind of good. The kind of good I feel when I'm singing with Stan. Like lost in the music, which I *KNOW* sounds like another Zac Efronism, but it is *TRUE*. I mean, for three minutes and nineteen seconds, I actually felt *HAPPY*, even while I was pretending to be sad. I mean, it was only Mr Burton, and I still have to do it in front of about five hundred strangers or, worse, people I actually know. But still, pretty cool, huh?

**Tuesday 2 November**

OK. So it turns out that Blake *ACTUALLY* wanted to go over lines. Which I guess I shouldn't be surprised at because he is *NOT* smart enough to do the code thing anyway. And it was fine, even given the fact that Imogen 'accidentally' popped in *SEVEN* times to ask me and Blake *URGENT* questions:

1. What time is rehearsal tomorrow? (Answer: at 3.15, like it always is.)
2. Do you think I should come in costume so I can get into the role, method-style. (Answer: Yes, as long as you don't also do that weird Dustin Hoffman impression thing.)
3. Do you think your fictional mother would wear a Kate Moss from TopShop leather vest. (Answer: No. That is the sort of thing Lola would wear, as well you know.)

4. Is that bag from Armani, Blake, because it is *JUST* like the one Chace Crawford has. (Answer: Oh, yeah, do you like it? I saw it on *Gossip Girl* last week.)
5. Oh my God, Blake, do you watch *Gossip Girl*? (Answer: Er . . . no. I accidentally turned it on when I was looking for *Top Gear*.)
6. Are you going to actually eat that peanut butter and Nutella sandwich, Buttercup, because if not, I will totally dispose of it for you in a suitable receptacle. (Answer: Here, have it.)
7. Are peanuts protein? (Answer: Just *EAT* it, Imo and go *AWAY*. We are *TRYING* to rehearse.)

And the thing is, Dr Sven, Blake did not seem *IN ANY WAY*, let alone a stalker way, interested in Imo. Which, like, *NOW* what do I do?

**Wednesday 3 November**

*OH MY GOD*. It is like Poppy Pringle is my fairy godmother. Which, like, is so *NOT* feasible, given her record on Slimfasting me. Only somehow, I have totally been granted admission to the Sidehicks in the form of a gold-embossed vellum invitation to Sunday Henderson-Hicks's birthday party on Saturday. Poppy gave it to me in rehearsal. (Sunday doesn't hand out her own invitations. Seriously, she doesn't even write them, in case she gets RSI from repetitive signature, so Poppy has learned to forge her signature for her. And her

mother's. And Mr Kwame-Jones's.
Seriously, she got sent to
Mr Kwame-Jones for faking a
note from Mrs Henderson-Hicks
so Sunday could get out of gym last year to go to H&M for the Kylie collection, only she just faked Mr Kwame-Jones's signature and told him he had already let her off and showed him the evidence to prove it.)

Anyway, the point is, I have finally been declared *NORMAL*. (Or at least not a total Mindy Matheson, who is in Year Eleven and has dry skin, which is totally not contagious, which I told the Cooper-Willises, but they still tried to make her carry a bell like the lepers in the Bible.) Either that or it is a totally elaborate plan to make me feel like I am *IN*, only it turns out that there isn't a party after all, and I am totally humiliated and videoed for YouTube in the process. Which is entirely possible, but also potentially paranoid, according to Stan. He is invited too, and so is Lily Rubenstein, which if you ask me is a *HUGE* mistake because any illegal snogging activity will be round the whole of Pennington by first period Monday. Although Imogen says that is probably the plan. She is just annoyed though because she *DID NOT* get invited, especially as she says she was the one who told Lily who told Alicia Beaufort who told Sunday that my mum once snogged a Rolling Stone, which is *TOTALLY* not true. It was Celia.

Anyway, the point is, Imogen has made me swear that I will spend the entire party hanging out with the Sidehicks to get the full story on Blake and Sunday and sow the seeds of doubt

in their minds that Blake is the right man for her. Which I have agreed to. Although, seriously, Dr Sven, I don't know how much more of the Sidehicks I can take. I mean, today, Finty Goggins-Smith actually asked me if they speak Latin in Brazil. I am NOT EVEN JOKING. It's like she has NO filter to tell her mouth when to open and when to SHUT THE HELL UP.

<u>Dumb-ass questions Finty Goggins-Smith has asked</u>

1. Do you think cats can read?
2. Is Liza Minnelli real?
3. What are breasts actually for?
4. How is Jerry still alive after Tom drops an anvil on him?
5. Does Diet Coke suck the calories out of chocolate?
6. Why do blind people even wear clothes?

Maybe SHE is the right one for Blake. They are totally matched IQ-wise. I mean, Sunday may be a complete bitch from hell, but at least she knows that Liza Minnelli isn't just made up.

Only Imogen says she is NOT a complete bitch, she is just misguided, which is why Stan totally needs to get off with her on Saturday too. Only Stan is not in any way keen on this. He says it will compromise him, as he has other 'irons in the fire', plus it would be purely prostitution, which he is not in favour of at all. (Although Ruby says all relationships are a form of prostitution. She is still not talking to me. Seriously, she came over before school this morning to have a shower, because Spike's bathroom is

being redone in Italianate marble, and Denzil only has a washing-up bowl and a squeegee, and she called me a scab when I was trying to eat my Fruit Loops (which, by the way, *GROSS*), which I pointed out was totally inappropriate, because I had not broken any picket lines, I was merely wearing lip gloss, but she started singing 'The Union Maid').

9 p.m.
Oh God. I have had a thought, which I should have had earlier, only I got sidetracked by the prostitution/ Ruby thing: you know when Stan said he had 'other irons in the fire'? Do you think he meant Lily Rubenstein? Maybe he doesn't just want her to be a best friend. Maybe he wants her to be a *GIRL*friend. I mean, she has that whole hairdo thing going on. And she plays the guitar. And last year on non-uniform day she came as Princess Amidala. In fact, she is kind of his dream girl, if you think about it.

Which I *TOTALLY* am. Thinking about it, I mean.

10 p.m.
Only, the thing is, *WHY* am I thinking about it? It's not like I have dibs on Stan as a friend. I mean, say he *DID* go out with Lily, it wouldn't mean the end of us, would it? I mean we could still hang out, and watch anime, and sing 'Fairytale of New York' and stuff. Plenty of people still have best friends

who are *GIRLS*, as well as having a *GIRL*friend. Like . . .

10.30 p.m.
Actually, they don't, do they. I mean, I cannot think of a single example.

Now what?

**Thursday 4 November**

1 p.m. (Geography)
Imogen's secret admirer is back. This time he has left her a single white rose and the lyrics to 'Every Breath You Take', which if you ask me, is *TOTALLY* worrying. Not that Imogen cares. She is so happy to be under the watchful gaze of a potentially murderous pervert that she doesn't even mind about missing the party on Saturday (plus she is going round to her new Gay Best Friend Titus Pelling's house to rehearse and, according to Imogen, probably watch Eurovision repeats and decide who is the hottest one in JLS). The question is, *WHICH* murderous pervert? *UNBELIEVABLY*, Lily Rubenstein, who is sitting behind me right now, has no idea. So I told her she is losing her grip on Pennington private lives, but she says she can't be expected to be in two places at once, and she was busy at Stan's first thing this morning so she missed the usual locker run. At which point I shut up. Partly because I was so *STUNNED* that she had been to Stan's without me knowing and partly because Mr Perkins told me to turn round

and concentrate on whether or not Belgium is a principality. Which it turns out it isn't. Only *a*) does this *REALLY* matter in the scheme of things and *b*) more importantly, *WHAT* was Lily Rubenstein doing, Dr Sven? That is what I want to know. And I would ask Stan, only he is sitting *NEXT* to Lily. Which is *COMPLETELY* weird. Because he always sits next to Fintan Riley at the back, because Mr Perkins says Fintan's head is an impediment to learning otherwise, only Madeleine Price-Waterhouse, who is normally next to Lily, is next to Fintan today, even though she normally says she can't be near him because he reminds her of Shrek.

Seriously, Dr Sven. Something is *UP*. And I don't like it being up. In fact I want it to be *DOWN*.

**Friday 5 November**

OK. So today in PMS, Stan hardly spoke to Lily at all. Which I know was partly because she was arguing with Mr Goldenblatt over her set design, i.e. hers involves painted chipboard and his involves suspended scaffolding walkways, a flight scene, and a glitter bomb. And partly because Stan and Mr Burton ended up doing this version of 'Smells Like Teen Spirit'. Which, like, rocked. Which, like, *I KNOW*.

But also because he spent a lot of it hanging out with me. Not doing anything. Just sitting around and messing about on his Cat Physics iPhone app.

Which I know is not exactly exciting news or anything. But it is kind of good. Only obviously a whole bunch of other *NOT* good stuff is going on, i.e.:

1. Imogen thinks she has Asperger's. She says she saw it on *Private Practice* last night and she definitely has issues with social situations. I said she doesn't have issues with social situations, the Sidehicks just hate her, and if anyone had Asperger's it was probably me, given my fragile mental health and the list thing, only then she got totally out of control and said it was *UNFAIR* because I have a broken home, a half-brown brother, *AND* an autistic spectrum disorder, which is just greedy.
2. It is Sunday's party tomorrow. And I have *NO* idea what to wear. And *NO* idea what to do or say in this kind of soirée situation either. I mean, I bet they don't sit around playing Who'd You Rather. Oh God. Maybe being *NORMAL* isn't all it's cracked up to be. I mean, I'd rather just stay in and laugh at the no-hopers on *Britain's Got Talent*. Or go round Titus's and rate JLS. Imogen says I am being pathetic and that she will come over in the morning to take control. But seriously, Dr Sven, I'm not sure I can go through with it. I mean, I feel like hurling already, and there are twenty-four hours to go. Plus she is still annoyed with me over the Asperger's thing and what if she tries to sabotage me?

**Saturday 6 November**

7 p.m.
OK, so on the positive side of things, Imogen has totally forgiven me for potentially being autistic, on the grounds that I am *NOT* in fact autistic, as proved conclusively by the Are You Autistic? quiz on Facebook, which claims I am just minorly obsessive, rather than fully statementable. Although Harry also took the quiz and apparently he should 'contact a medical professional immediately', except he didn't, he went to alphabetize his Horrid Henry books.

On the negative side, I now look like an extra from *Gossip Girl*. I am *NOT EVEN JOKING*. Seriously, Dr Sven, I have a tartan miniskirt, knee-length socks (not *EVEN* over-the-knee, which is, like, totally taking it up a notch), and a cloche hat. Imogen says next time she is going to get Titus to come too, as his gayness means he will totally be born with an innate ability to accessorize. This is *NOT GOING TO HAPPEN*. If I am any more accessorized I will look like a TopShop concession. I begged Imo to let me go with her to Titus's instead. She is taking round *Mean Girls*, *Funny Girl*, and *Top Gun*, which I said was completely *CLICHÉD* and what if Titus is actually into, say Steven Segal, or something, but Imogen said it was a genetic impossibility, as I would know, if I had any gaydar whatsoever. So instead I am about to enter enemy territory, with only a snakeskin clutch to defend me.

And Stan.

Stan will defend me.

Won't he?

12 midnight

OK. I think I may be having some sort of *CRISIS*, Dr Sven. Like a panic attack, or a nervous breakdown or something. Seriously, I have checked my symptoms (racing heart, inability to eat anything, shaking hands) on Google and it's either that or I am about to die from heart failure.

It all started out kind of fine. Except for Mrs Henderson-Hicks making me take off my Westwood heels (seriously, the woman has issues. I mean her house is *TOTALLY* white. And I mean *EVERYTHING*. It is like being inside a snowglobe, which, like, *WHY*? Because she is obviously totally dirt paranoid, because no one was allowed to wear shoes, or drink anything coloured, or apply lipstick anywhere other than the bathroom, which is fully wipe-clean) which totally ruined the knee-length sock look so that I just looked like a kind of insane slutty toddler. But despite this setback I was totally managing *NOT* to look like a giant *MISFIT*, and Alicia Beaufort offered to make me her special punch recipe (which totally *WAS* special, I mean have you ever tasted coconut juice and cranberry?) only about ten minutes after that it all kind of went horribly wrong:

The Bad Stuff

1. Lily Rubenstein showed up, looking even

more retro kooky than ever, and started doing ironic dancing to Motown hits with Stan, which is totally out of order because that is what *ME* and Stan usually do, which I totally pointed out to him, only he said I looked pretty tied up with Finty Goggins-Smith, which I wasn't, I was just explaining to her that she cannot catch 'helmet head' from snogging Fintan Riley.

2. I got stuck in the toilet queue with Lily Rubenstein (I am *NOT EVEN JOKING*), who said 'Isn't Stan *AMAZING*' (actual words), which made me even crosser than the ironic dancing, so, for some *INEXPLICABLE* reason, I reeled off a list of all the reasons Stan totally isn't amazing. And then Lily suddenly didn't need the toilet any more and when I came back out Finty said she had gone home with that 'boy from the show who isn't Blake', i.e. Stan, which meant I had to get a lift home with Alicia Beaufort, only I was sick out of the window of her dad's Maserati (I am obviously hyper sensitive to motion sickness), which apparently will strip the paint, and if it isn't covered by insurance (which, like, I am pretty sure it is *NOT*. I mean, since when do they put an 'abrasive vomit' clause into policies? Although, maybe they should. I should totally suggest this!) he is going to send a bill for the respray to Lola, and it is likely to be in the tens of thousands of pounds. Which, like, *HOW*?

So now *a*) I am even more potentially broke than ever, *b*) I *TOTALLY* forgot to do any of the Imogen 'Get Blake plan' stuff, plus *c*) what if Lily tells Stan what I said about him? i.e.:

1. That he makes this weird huffling sound when he eats.
2. That his left ear is half a centimetre higher up than the right ear.
3. That his feet are like freakishly big so that he can tip forward like one of those clowns without falling over.

Because it's not true. Well, it is true. Only not that I think they're gross. I mean, they kind of make Stan Stan.

And what about the stuff I didn't say. Like that he always comes with me to find Lola when she has forgotten to come home, or got lost, or got stuck in a public toilet in the library. (Seriously. That actually happened.) And that when I got tonsillitis he made sure he got it too (which I will *NOT* go into details of, but it involved spit) so I wouldn't be bored at home for a week. And that he's the only person I know who will cycle up a four-in-one gradient hill back from the giant supermarket just to get me Sour Skittles.

I mean, why didn't I say that to her? *WHY*?

4 a.m.

Oh my God. I know why. And I know why I feel like this. I'm not about to die of heart failure. And I'm not having a nervous breakdown. Although I may well do now that I have realized this:

I completely and totally *HEART* Stan Romer.

It's true, isn't it, Dr Sven? Imogen was right after all. Stan is my *ONE TRUE LOVE*. Oh God, I think I'm going to be sick again.

**Sunday 7 November**

Reasons why I SHOULDN'T go out with Stan Romer

1. He is my unofficial best friend. Or at least he was until I told Lily Rubenstein all that stuff about the huffling and the giant feet.
2. He has seen me wee in a paddling pool. Admittedly we were three. But, still. *EWWW*.
3. I do not look like Princess Amidala, who is his ideal woman, and Lily Rubenstein kind of does.

Reasons why I SHOULD go out with Stan Romer

1. He is my unofficial best friend. Or at least he was until I told Lily Rubenstein all that stuff.
2. He has seen me wee in a paddling pool, and is still my unofficial best friend. Or at least he was etc.
3. I don't care about Princess Amidala or Lily Rubenstein. Because *I LOVE HIM*.

What am I going to do, Dr Sven? I can't even tell Imo. I mean, she would *TOTALLY* tell Stan, which would be *HUMILIATING* beyond all previous known humiliations. Even:

1. The time I had to do the fifty metres breaststroke against St Hubert's in a gold bikini because Lola had used my

navy one piece to make a shark costume for Harry.

2. The time Lola came to my birthday party *DRESSED* in the same gold bikini because she 'felt a bit Princess Leia'.
3. The time Granny Jones asked a waiter to fetch her a gin in the Indian Eye, only it wasn't a waiter, it was Mr Kwame-Jones.
4. The time Imogen made me enter the school charity slave auction (*I KNOW*. Like *TOTALLY* non-PC, but this *IS* Pennington) and Stan ended up buying me for 10p, which would not have been so bad had Sunday Henderson-Hicks not just gone for £56 to Ms Nugent. Although not as bad as Blake Carrington going for £122 to Mr Goldenblatt.

2 p.m.
Oh God. Imogen has just texted to say she is coming over. What am I going to say, Dr Sven. Seriously, *WHAT*?

3 p.m.
OK, so actually I didn't have to say anything to Imogen, because she was way too busy telling me how totally gaytastic her night with Titus was and how he is already officially her new best friend (gay):

<u>Reasons why Titus Pelling is Totally Gaytabulous by Imogen Pritchard</u>

1. He has read *Pride and Prejudice*.
2. *Con Air* (starring Steve Buscemi) is in his

TOP TEN all time favourite films.

3. He is totally understanding of her protein-based dietary requirements, even though he says she has the figure of a goddess, which is, like, beyond gay.

I pointed out that *a*) everyone had read *Pride and Prejudice* because we are doing it for GCSE and *b*) *Con Air* is not very gay. But she said *a*) he read it last year, i.e. BEFORE we were doing it for GCSE, and AFTER she had come to non-uniform day as Elizabeth Bennet, which proves she is in tune with his gayness, and *b*) *Con Air* has Nicolas Cage sweating in a vest in it, and what is NOT gay about that?

Then I asked her about the bee thing but she says it was obviously self-harm because he was inwardly tortured by confusion over his sexuality.

THEN, and I don't know why, it just came out in an unstoppable garble, I asked her if she had seen Stan on her way down, so she said 'NO, why?' and I said, 'No reason', and she said, 'Oh my God you are totally hiding something from me did he get off with someone last night was it Lily Rubenstein because Titus says he saw them at Shaker Makers last week sharing a Farley's Rusks supersize, which is, like, gross, I mean why would you have that when you can have Wham® raspberry, or chocolate Pop Tart, or caramel Snack-A-Jacks flavour?' So I said, 'No, I just needed to ask him about Lat homework.' And then I totally deflected any further questioning by asking her about Titus's other Top Ten films, which totally worked, because she then spent half an hour explaining why *Lock, Stock and Two Smoking Barrels* is actually gay.

But the thing is, Dr Sven:

1. Maybe I'm wrong and he DID get off with Lily? I mean, what if she's there RIGHT NOW in his bedroom. Listening to Led Zeppelin. Or, worse, singing 'Fairytale of New York', WITH the accents.
2. Or worse, maybe they're in Shaker Makers sharing another Farleys Rusks supersize. Because, seriously, Dr Sven, they are totally an acquired taste, only I have NEVER acquired it.

So on top of having GOOD hair, Lily also shares his taste for exotic milkshakes. It is obvious, Dr Sven. SHE is his ONE TRUE LOVE.

Oh God, now I think I really AM having a nervous breakdown. And the only person who knows what to do when I feel like this is Stan. Only I can't tell him, CAN I?

In fact I don't think I can tell him anything EVER again.

**Monday 8 November**

OK, so it wasn't a nervous breakdown. But, on a scale of one to ten my life is still SUPER-SUCKY.

Seriously, Dr Sven, I don't know who I am any more. I mean, to be fair, I wasn't sure before, but now I am REALLY confused. Because every time I see Stan I turn into this gabbling FREAK, like he's a complete stranger, or George Clooney or someone. Like, he came up to me before first

period (when I was totally hiding out in the library, only clearly it's not such a great hiding place because Stan found me, and so did Imo, and so did Mrs Pimm the librarian who reminded me I have had *Silas Marner* out for two years and could she please have it back by Friday) and asked why I hadn't waited for him before school, which was true because I left at half seven, which is like a record, I mean usually I am still eating cereal in my pyjamas at quarter past eight. So I said I had to come in early to stack shelves, which is a total lie because Mrs Pimm does not let anyone do that after Finty Goggins-Smith ordered them by colour instead of the Dewey-Decimal system. But Stan totally bought it. He just shrugged and said 'OK', so then I felt bad about lying so I said I'd see him at lunch, only it turned out he was meeting LILY so I had to spend lunch listening to Imo and Titus discussing the number of calories versus fruit content in eight Jaffa Cakes while trying to watch Stan and Lily for evidence of snogging activity over the rim of my sandwich.

See. SUPER-SUCKY. Suckier even than Finty Goggins-Smith who got off with Hugh Cooper-Willis at Sunday's party, only it turned out to be Clint Cooper-Willis, and Alicia caught them in the downstairs wet room and hit Finty with a ceramic soap dispenser (white, obviously) and she had to have emergency nose surgery and now thinks her ears are psychic as well as her belly button because they hurt every time Katy Perry comes on her iPod.

Which Mr Goldenblatt is in no way happy about. Not the psychic belly button. I don't think he cares about that. I mean the Sidehick fallout, which caused total fallout at PMS after school because the Pipettes were supposed to be doing their synchronized swaying / 'Tide is High' harmony thing only Alicia won't stand next to Finty. Which means Poppy has to be in the middle, only she is the shortest, and Mr Goldenblatt said it was ruining the line and if they didn't sort it out then he may well have to step in himself, because he is exactly the right height in heels. Only they didn't sort it out they just started calling each other beeyatches, e.g.:

Alicia: It was your fault, beeyatch. You should have seen the mole.

Finty: I thought it was chocolate Magnum, beeyatch.

Luckily Mr Burton stepped in and said in fact no one was a beeyatch, not even Mr Goldenblatt, and that PMS is all about tolerance, and respect. Only Sunday said no it wasn't it was about show songs, and then another row started entirely involving Len Cho, Titus Pelling, and Norah Forbes about why under no circumstances could Marilyn Manson songs count as show tunes.

But anyway, my point is, love, and snogging, are dangerous things, Dr Sven. I mean, I do not want to end up with belly button delusion, or in a beeyatch off. My life is complicated enough already.

**Tuesday 9 November**

How do people do it, Dr Sven? Be in love, I mean, and continue to function normally, i.e. say, eat, or sleep, or study the Gross National Product of Belgium without *CONSTANTLY* drifting off into some kind of rapture about the back of his neck and getting sent to Mr Kwame-Jones for drooling on a textbook.

Seriously, Dr Sven, *I CANNOT* stop thinking about him. Even in Biology, when Mr Sylvester was making us slice open a rat's stomach, I was actually imagining what Stan looked like inside. I mean, is this *NORMAL*? Is this what love is like? Or is this a kind of mentally unstable extreme Buttercup Jones kind of love?

I would ask Imo, only, well, I can't, can I. Not that I'd get the chance. Seriously, it's like she and Titus are conjoined twins or something. He actually went into the girls' toilets with her at first break, and Finty threatened to set off the fire alarm, only Imo told her he was an honorary girl (which has totally confused Finty). And Len Cho is totally hacked off because now he has no one to play magnetic travel chess with at lunch, and has threatened to sack Titus from mathletes and Asian Entrepreneurs, because Imogen is compromising him academically, but Titus says it is a sacrifice worth making because *a*) he felt like a fraud because his dad only went to Hong Kong once on a stopover to Sydney, and *b*) he has met his soul mate. Which is *RUBBISH* because Imogen hates

maths, so *HOW* can they be soul mates. Plus, he is *GAY*. Which, when I actually managed to get Imogen on her own (in PE, because despite all Imo's pleas to Ms Nugent, Titus is not allowed to join the netball team) I pointed out, as well as that this whole thing was doing nothing for her standing with the Sidehicks, given Titus's reputation as a bee-eating freakshow, but she says once they realize his sexual status, even Sunday Henderson-Hicks will be begging her for access rights.

**Wednesday 10 November**

There is nothing else for it, Dr Sven, I am going to *HAVE* to tell Ruby, even though she is still not speaking to me over the whole makeover thing. I am just going to have to beg her forgiveness, because I cannot carry on like this. Seriously, in French today, Monsieur Leclerc asked me '*Qui est le President de France?*' and I sighed and said 'Stan'. I am *NOT EVEN JOKING*.

And PMS rehearsal was *TORTURE*, because I kept forgetting my lines, and when I sang it sounded like Lola singing along to the *Dora the Explorer* theme. Seriously, Mr Burton said I had gone two steps forward and about a hundred and ten steps back since my one-to-one rehearsal with him and had I forgotten everything about finding my own voice? And I said no, but I had temporarily lost it due to stressful personal circumstances, only then Stan asked what they were so I had to lie and say that Granny Jones had had a bad reaction to some lip filler and couldn't speak, which is totally plausible, but would possibly be a good thing.

And the REALLY stupid thing is, I'm not even stressed about doing the singing any more. I kind of like it, that losing myself thing. Although maybe I won't now that Mr Goldenblatt has announced that he has invited Cosmo Letterman from the National Musical Society Association to opening night, who it turns out is like the Simon Cowell of the amateur musical theatre circuit, and is talent scouting for national finals next term, which obviously Sunday Henderson-Hicks practically peed herself about. Only Mr Burton is totally not happy because he says PMS is about taking part, not being a star. But Mr Goldenblatt says that shows why he is totally unqualified to be director.

I seem to have gone off the point again. Which is totally another hideous side effect, because I thought I had got that kind of under control, only LOVE has set me back months in therapy. Anyway, the thing is I have texted Ruby and she has agreed to meet me at the barge tomorrow night.

Oh God, I hope she has some answers, because seriously, Dr Sven, if I carry on like this, I am going to end up in a bed next to Camilla St John Brice at the Manna From Heaven Christian Residential Unit for the Undernourished being intravenously fed peanut butter.

**Thursday 11 November**

Imogen is off the scale over the whole Cosmo Letterman thing. She is completely convinced that he is going to pluck her from obscurity, i.e. being my mother, and demand that the show is recast with her in the lead role, before he takes her to Hollywood to meet Kenny Ortega.

I am so not off the scale. Because *a*) weirdly, it kind of doesn't make a difference. Singing to anyone but Stan, or Mr Burton (which, I know, weird huh?) is pretty much vomit-inducing, so not even the Simon Cowell of amateur school choirs can make me feel more barftastic. And *b*) I am already way too barftastic over the whole Stan thing. Ruby thinks I am completely pathetic, i.e.:

<u>Ruby Tuesday Jones's Opinions on Love</u>

1. Love is mostly a construct invented by Hallmark/ Disney to sell cheap cards and cartoons.
2. That her and Spike have a deeper bond based on mutual respect, vegetarianism, and a hatred of *Hannah Montana*.
3. That Spike does not know this, because he was brainwashed at the age of seven by repeated exposure to *Sleeping Beauty* and *The Lady and the Tramp*.
4. That really I would be better off devoting my life to minke whales.
5. But if I am insistent on mooning around

like a loser, then the best I can hope for is that whoever it is will either *a*) go out with someone else so that I can see that he is a capitalist fascist pig or *b*) go out with me and utterly disappoint me so that I can see that he is a capitalist fascist pig.

Which, Dr Sven, is USELESS advice. Mainly because if I did devote my life to minke whales then she would only accuse me of copying her. And Stan ISN'T a capitalist fascist pig. He's Stan. Only I can't tell her that. PLUS I totally had to pay for it, i.e. I have had to agree to attend her anti-private school protest, in full battle wear, to enlist as many Pennington students as possible, and to dye my hair back to borderline ginger at the earliest opportunity. At least if I had asked Imo she would be totally on my side, and possibly had some answers that don't involve NOT being in love. Although they WOULD probably involve a balcony scene, me being ostracized from my family and a suicide pact.

**Friday 12 November**

Mr Burton is totally NOT OK with the Cosmo Letterman thing which he says is having a worse effect on rehearsals than Finty snogging the wrong Cooper-Willis, i.e. now everyone is singing over each other, overacting, and putting on massive jazz smiles, which he says do NOT look Broadway, they look insane. And which is not being aided by the fact that Sunday Henderson-Hicks got her dad, aka Mr Britesmile, to offer cut price tooth whitening for anyone in PMS, only Lucinda Ledbetter-Morpeth's smile is now so freakishly white she looks like she has used Tippex. Although this is not as bad as Norah Forbes who actually *DID* use Tippex. I am *NOT EVEN JOKING*.

On the positive side, I used the lull in onstage insanity to promote Ruby's protest thing.

Anti-private school protest sign-ups

1. Imogen, on the grounds that she might get arrested and tortured by fascistic police, which would make an excellent scene in the movie of her life.
2. Titus Pelling, on the grounds that Imogen is going.
3. Len Cho, on the grounds that the Asian Entrepreneurs are being denied new members due to them *a*) failing the English entrance and *b*) not being in the golf club.

Even Mr Burton said he was all in favour because the system places money and academic talent over artistic talent which is denying PMS new members (he has totally *NOT* seen the Potts brothers pretending to be Eminem). Only he is still on probation and does not want to get on the wrong side of the governors who already don't like him because he is still refusing to wear a tie.

In fact pretty much the only person who hasn't signed up is Stan. But that is not because he is boycotting the boycott. It is because *I HAVE NOT ASKED HIM*.

Seriously, Dr Sven, I am scared that if I actually speak in his vicinity, vomit, rather than words, will come out, which is so *NOT* an attractive look. Like, in maths today, he asked if he could borrow my solar calculator, and I had to run to the toilet, without even asking for a pass, so I ended up getting sent to Mr Kwame-Jones, just for *BEING IN LOVE*, which I totally told him, and also that is it *NOT* my fault because I do not *WANT* to be in love, I just want to be normal, and he said, 'Ah, the irrepressible animal urges of the lower classes', and just gave me a humbug, which I could totally tell Miss Hutchinson was *NOT* happy about because she started writing notes. It is probably because she invented the toilet pass system after the whole of 3B claimed they needed to pee during a film about glacier formation.

Plus now Stan is freaked out by the whole thing, which is unsurprising given that I have brought the *CRAZY* big time.

Oh God, Dr Sven. What if this drives him even further into the arms of Lily Rubenstein? Because her hair may be kooky, but the rest of her is definitely *NORMAL*. I mean, she is five foot five, she gets Bs in everything, she has a cat called Spot (he is stripy, it is ironic, but not embarrassing) and her dad is a civil servant. See, *NORMAL*. Whereas I am approaching six foot, with three unnamed chickens, and a dad who may or may not be Ron Weasley.

What chance do I have? Seriously, Dr Sven, *WHAT*?

**Saturday 13 November**

Not only is love making me ill, it is making me completely evil. *SERIOUSLY*:

<u>IM Conversation with Stan Romer aka YOUNGANGUSYOUNG</u> (who is this guitarist who dresses like a schoolboy, which if you ask me is just plain weird, only Stan says you have to see past the shorts and cap because he is the *GREATEST EVER* living guitarist except for Johnny Marr, only his name doesn't work so well in an IM name).

YOUNGANGUSYOUNG: Earth to Buttercup. Come in Buttercup.

YOUNGANGUSYOUNG: Seriously. Are you there?

B*CUP: Yes. I mean no. Kind of.

YOUNGANGUSYOUNG: What's going on? Are you bulimic? Or pregnant. Because Lily said you totally vommed this morning when you bunked French.

B*CUP: How does she know?

YOUNGANGUSYOUNG: She got it off Carey Cardew who got it off Alicia Beaufort who was two cubicles down relieving herself of breakfast.

B*CUP: Oh right, that figures. And *NO* I am *NOT* bulimic *OR* pregnant. Like, *EWWWW*.

YOUNGANGUSYOUNG: Thank God.

YOUNGANGUSYOUNG: Although I would totally support you if you were. Pregnant, I mean. Not bulimic. What is *THAT* about?

B*CUP: I know.
B*CUP: Hang on. Why would you support me? It's not like it's yours. Not that there is an *IT* to be anyone's. I'm *FOURTEEN* for God's sake. And men totally *SUCK*, as I have told you a million times.
YOUNGANGUSYOUNG: Oh yeah. So you did.
YOUNGANGUSYOUNG: So was it food poisoning or something?
B*CUP: I guess so.
YOUNGANGUSYOUNG: So listen, I could come over and we could watch a *DVD* or something?
B*CUP: Yeah. I mean *NO*. I might be contagious.
YOUNGANGUSYOUNG: From food poisoning? What about tomorrow?
B*CUP: Can't. I'm busy.
YOUNGANGUSYOUNG: Doing what?
B*CUP: Jesus, what's with the Spanish Inquisition Stan? I have to go to Granny Jones's, OK?
YOUNGANGUSYOUNG: Fine. I would say I'd come with you, only obviously you don't want me about.

And I so wanted to IM back and say no he should totally come with me, only I couldn't because *a*) I had just made it up, and *b*) know he's only doing it to make up for hanging out with Lily all the time because there is no way he actually wants to spend time with Granny Jones, I mean *NO ONE* does. Not even Geraldo.

So instead I said:
B*CUP: Don't you have to be at Lily's or something?

YOUNGANGUSYOUNG: Yeah. I do actually. See you around.
B*CUP: Not if I see you first.

Which was supposed to be funny. And it kind of was when we were twelve. But now I'm worried he'll think I mean it.

And I'm worried I do mean it.

See. EVIL.

**Sunday 14 November**

Clearly Stan hasn't passed on the message to Lily yet that I am NOT pregnant, because Imo has just called to ask:

*a*) When is it due?
*b*) Do I need to borrow a bigger bra?
*c*) Can she be the godmother? Or, better still, can we get it adopted by Jennifer Garner or Angelina Jolie and then the child can come and find me in sixteen years, which would be totally brilliant.
*d*) Is it true that the father is the man at Abrakebabra because Dorcas Wrigley who has a Saturday job at the bicycle shop next door told Len Cho who told Titus that I am always in there and it CAN'T be for the food because everyone knows it is made with dogs.

I said:

*a*) Never.
*b*) NO. Sadly.

c) OMG, are you serious? It's bad enough that I don't have a CLUE who my father is, without my non-existent baby suffering the same fate.

d) It was undercover work for Ruby trying to spot them importing Labradors, which they were NOT doing, because they DON'T use dogs, it is just normally horrible food.

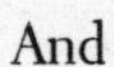

And

e) STOP CATASTROPHIZING (which I totally learned off GoShrinkYourself).

And then she asked if I wanted to go round to hers to make pink velvet cupcakes with Titus Pelling and I really wanted to say yes, only I remembered that I am *a*) babysitting Harry and *b*) supposed to be going round Granny Jones's, so I had to say no, because otherwise Stan might have found out. So now, thanks to all my lies, I have to spend the afternoon in the company of a Botox-addicted paranoid, a dog called Geraldo who makes me look like a Moomin, and a five year old who is currently obsessed with death.

Seriously, Dr Sven, I think, on top of being in love and all my other mental complications, I might be an actual compulsive liar. I mean, the evidence is all there:

<u>Big Fat Lies I have told in my life</u>

1. That I can play the kazoo.
2. That a chicken ate Harry's Woodcraft Folk

prizewinning raffia owl.
3. That my dad was Daniel Craig.
4. That I am completely and utterly *FINE* and am not in any way in *LOVE* with *STAN*.

OK, so the owl was totally plausible because we had actually just seen a chicken eat a paperclip. And the Daniel Craig thing was aged eleven to Sunday Henderson-Hicks, and it was Imogen's idea, and she totally deserved it because Sunday had told me her dad was the President, and it turned out he was President of Britesmile.

But, even so, this cannot be good for my state of mind. I mean, isn't telling the truth supposed to be therapeutic?

Only if I had told the truth to Stan, I would end up humiliated, or possibly dead from heart failure. And that's not too therapeutic. So, I guess it's kind of swings and roundabouts, huh?

5 p.m.
Seriously, Dr Sven, I can't stop. It's like I have lie diarrhoea.

<u>More Big Fat Lies I have told this afternoon</u>

1. That Granny totally does look 45 and not 50, which is what Dr Jolly said (and which is at least ten years under her real age anyway).

But what else was I supposed to say, Dr Sven? I mean, she is totally deluded beauty-wise. Not that she isn't beautiful, because she is, in an expressionless, odd-eyebrowed kind of way. And when she was young, she really *WAS* like a supermodel or something. I mean, she showed me an old photo album and she is a complete Greta Garbo. Only then I had a total Imogen moment, because behind the cover flap I found a picture of Lola and a boy with enormous red hair, who I thought might be an illegitimate brother who Lola had forgotten about, which would *TOTALLY* explain my gingerness, but it turns out it was 'Nervous Nigel' from next door at his eighth birthday party and Granny had refused to put the picture on display because Lola was doing a V-sign and Mrs Nigel had hydrangeas, which are common.

Anyway, my point is, I am going to try to be more truthful.

Plus I figure things can't possibly get any worse than the pregnancy scare thing. Can they?

Can they?

**Monday 15 November**

No. Still just generally awful. I still have no clue *WHAT* Belgium is *FOR*. And Mr Burton took me out of rehearsal to ask if I had anything to tell him. I said if he meant that I was pregnant and thus potentially compromising his show with morning sickness or a big fat baby belly then *NO I DID NOT*. He said, 'Er . . . no, I just thought, you, you know, seemed kind of, like distracted.' So I had to say sorry, and that I am definitely

*NOT* pregnant. But that I *AM* distracted. But he doesn't need to worry about it because I will be over him by the end of the week. And he said 'Him?' And I said, 'Er . . . actually, you know, I meant *IT*, not him.' And then luckily Finty Goggins-Smith fell over her own legs so then *HE* was distracted. And then Mr Goldenblatt moonwalked, so everyone was distracted. Seriously, Dr Sven, that man has more issues than me. If I didn't think he'd use it as a way of getting me expelled, I'd give him your website address.

**Tuesday 16 November**

And again. Still basically bad.

Because now Mr Goldenblatt has decided there will be a moonwalking dream sequence in the show. Only I have enough trouble walking forwards normally, let alone defying gravity at the same time. Seriously, I tried it down the language lab corridor and I actually reversed into a wall.

**Wednesday 17 November**

I *KNEW* it. I *KNEW* the basic low level nausea and mild panic was only a temporary blip until I developed full blown breakdown.

Because, somehow, I had totally forgotten I have to *KISS STAN*.

OK, so it is not a *REAL* kiss, it is a *STAGE* kiss, i.e. because of him being the Boy Next Door etc. etc., only I am not sure my brain can cope with the distinction and that my vomit reflex will kick into action anyway.

And I only have two days to do something about it because Mr Burton wants to rehearse all the duets on Friday while Mr Goldenblatt choreographs a Michael Jackson/Michael Bublé mash-up, which will totally take him all afternoon because he has to contend with *a*) the Cooper-Willis fallout, *b*) Fintan Riley's head, and *c*) Finty Goggins-Smith.

Two days, Dr Sven. Forty-eight hours. 1,440 minutes. 86,400 seconds (I googled it) before I am potentially sick into the boy I love's mouth (which Finty Goggins-Smith actually did at the May Ball. Only it turned out he wasn't the only victim because half of Year Nine went down with a vomiting bug by Monday and she got sent to Mr Kwame-Jones when she came back for indiscriminate snogging, which she pointed out wasn't ACTUALLY against the rules, only Miss Hutchinson proved it WAS, it is Clause 26 or something).

**Thursday 18 November**

8 a.m.
OK, so I've had an idea. I am going to appeal to Mr Burton's artistic nature and point out that maybe the Girl Next Door wouldn't kiss the Boy Next Door at all because she is pregnant and therefore totally hormonal and/or plagued by morning

sickness and thus afraid of vomming in his mouth. Brilliant, huh?

Oh, and if he says no I am either going to *BEG* for mercy, or claim I have cooties. Which I am not even sure what they are, or even if they are real, but Imogen says thirty-five per cent of American teen films feature their absence at some point as a valid reason for kissing to ensue.

2 p.m. (Citizenship)
So *THAT* didn't work.

I mean, I went to Mr Burton's office at lunch, which is actually part of the stationery cupboard because Mr Goldenblatt had dibs on Ms Millington's old office because he has claustrophobia and an allergy to erasers, according to Lily Rubenstein, and anyway, he was in there playing this song on the guitar (and I am *NOT EVEN JOKING* he is better than Stan. Better even than Johnny Marr on 'Last Night I Dreamt' maybe, not that I would *EVER* tell Stan that, although that's kind of not a problem now anyway) and I told him the stuff about hormones and/or morning sickness but he said this wasn't a Ken Loach film, it was a high school musical and I needed to just go with the flow. Only I said I wasn't really that good at going with the flow, and besides, the whole plot was kind of implausible if you think about it, and maybe she wouldn't go out with anyone at all and would just run off to London to find fame and fortune or found a co-operative, which is what Ruby said should happen (and I totally had to plead with her not to stage a boycott on these grounds). Only then Mr Burton got really weird and said actually it *IS* totally plausible because it actually happened and I said 'To who exactly?' and he said, 'Er . . . to me. Yeah.' At which point I should have totally said something like 'Oh, I'm so sorry,' or, even better, '*SHUT UP*', but no, instead I burble, 'Oh my God you are totally the Boy Next Door. This is like the movie of your life. Only on stage. And without any celebrities. Although that's probably a good thing, because what if you ended up with say Ashton Kutcher playing you? I mean, *HOW* humiliating. Not that I'm saying he is anything like you. And I think I'll shut up now.' And he said 'OK. Um. Great.' And I said, 'Except, did you marry her?' And he said 'Like, who?' and I said 'Like, duh, the girl next door.' Which I totally regretted immediately because saying 'Duh' to a teacher is totally banned by Miss Hutchinson under Clause 35, only Mr Burton *DIDN'T* say I had to go and see Mr Kwame-Jones, he said, 'No, it . . . er . . . totally turns out I wasn't her type after all.' So I said, 'Oh I'm so sorry. Did she go back to Blake, I mean Too Cool Boy?' And he said *NO*, actually she ran off to London to find fame and fortune and he has never heard from her since (only with some 'ers' and 'likes' and 'ums' in there). And then his eyes went all Stan cow-like, so I said I had Latin, but that that song he was playing before was really good and he should put it in the show, and then I went before he cried, because if he cried, I would cry, and in my fragile emotional state I am

. sure I could stop right now.

So now not *ONLY* do I have to kiss Stan tomorrow, but I have the weight of Mr Burton's entire life story riding on it. I mean this isn't any old kiss, it's the first kiss *AND* the last kiss.

It's a *MOVIE* kiss.

Oh my God. Imogen is going to *FREAK*.

**Friday 19 November**

The good thing

I did not kiss Stan today. This is because Mr Goldenblatt accidentally got exposed to a rogue cola-flavoured eraser in the staff room, according to Lily Rubenstein, so his jazz hands were too shaky to do any choreography, which meant we all had group rehearsal of 'ABC'. And it turns out that Alicia and Finty have totally made up, because Alicia has dumped Clint. Or is it Hugh? I forget. Anyway, she's going out with whichever one she didn't dump, and Finty has decided she fancies Norah Forbes so for once the Pipettes did not end rehearsal threatening legal action against each other for misuse of jewellery, shoes, or Hubba Bubba.

The bad thing

I now have to kiss Stan on Monday. Which I know I should be happy about because I have three days' reprieve. Only, in reality, that means three more days of feeling like I have eaten bad Nandos.

Oh, and Imogen *FREAKED*. Only not until this morning

because she wasn't in last night to do any freaking because she was round at Titus's AGAIN (I reminded her about the official best friend contract thing, and that any changes would require a signature, but she says Titus is not a best friend he is a GAY best friend which is a different thing entirely and TOTALLY allowed, if not encouraged). Anyway, Imo said:

*a*) 'OMG, are you SERIOUS? This is, like, OMG.'

*b*) 'I TOTALLY bet it is Lauren Laverne. She is like girl candy to overgrown emo types.'

*c*) 'But kissing Stan is NOT like kissing say, Heathcliff, or Robert Pattinson. Because Stan, as you have pointed out like a MILLION times, is like a brother, or something. So it will be more like kissing Titus, because there is no tension because of the gayness.'

And then she totally snogged Titus in front of me (and half of the Year Sevens who were waiting to go into History, only obviously Mr Goldenblatt was busy stabbing himself with an EpiPen), to demonstrate this point. Which I told her was COMPLETELY risky because what if Blake finds out? But Imogen says she hopes Blake DOES find out, because according to Lily he has not snogged Sunday on Pennington grounds for two weeks, which is like a record because normally you cannot walk through the quad without coming within a metre of them exchanging spit, and Sunday is completely paranoid he is going off her, which totally explains the illegal Wonderbra that

she got sent to Mr Kwame-Jones for.

The thing is, Dr Sven, if kissing Stan *IS* like kissing Titus, then what does that say about me and Stan? Plus then I totally have to *FAKE* it being a movie kiss. Which is bad, right?

But if it *ISN'T* like kissing Titus, i.e. if it's like kissing Heathcliff, if he weren't a glowering bully, and totally made up, i.e. the earth totally moves and violins or something start playing in the background, then *WHAT AM I GOING TO DO*? Seriously, *WHAT*? Because I know that in *NORMAL* circumstances, this should be a *GOOD* thing.

Only I'm pretty sure that, given all the millions of reasons I have previously cited, i.e. that there is nothing *NORMAL* about the circumstances whatsoever, this is *BAD*.

*VERY BAD*.

**Saturday 20 November**

Sometimes I think Harry is the only sane person around here, and he is the one who is on the autistic spectrum (allegedly, according to Facebook, so probably *NOT AT ALL*). Seriously, Dr Sven, because he is in total agreement that the kissing thing is implausible, and possibly the entire plot. On genetic grounds, which I am not sure I understand, and so cannot repeat here. But I can repeat the facts about kissing he then reeled off, which have pretty much put me off the whole idea full stop.

Harry Jones's Facts About Kissing

1. You exchange between ten million and one BILLION bacteria in a kiss. Which, like, EWWWW.
2. Several diseases can be passed on during kissing, e.g. glandular fever and herpes.
3. A woman in China had her eardrum ruptured during a kiss. (Seriously. Her boyfriend actually sort of sucked it out.)
4. Bonobo monkeys do French kissing. (Which is just plain weird.)

I mean, why is this kind of information NOT on the school curriculum? WHY? (Except the Bonobo monkey thing, because I'm not sure that's educational, just disturbing.) And, for that matter, why is kissing even ALLOWED on school premises? I mean, just because it's a stage kiss doesn't mean I won't catch some vile disease or get my eardrum sucked out, does it? At this rate I will go off the whole concept of kissing anyone EVER.

**Sunday 21 November**

11 a.m.

Except that I haven't.

Seriously, Dr Sven, I can't stop thinking about kissing Stan. And the thing is, I keep trying to fill my head with Imogen telling me it will be exactly like kissing Titus, and Harry telling me if my eardrum doesn't get sucked out I will probably catch herpes or glandular fever, but my head keeps telling them to shut up because it is far too busy imagining how nice it might be.

Oh God. There *IS* something wrong with me, isn't there? I mean, it *CANNOT* be normal to obsess about kissing your second best friend to the extent that it has been impossible to eat anything for twenty-four hours. I am *NOT EVEN JOKING*.

And on top of this worry, I am supposed to be rehearsing lines, only I can't ask Stan for *OBVIOUS* reasons, and Imogen, who is normally totally keen on coming over here in case it involves infidels, has decided that Titus's gayness trumps this and has gone round to his to watch *Lark Rise to Candleford*. And Harry is at Granny Jones's watching Made for TV movies.

Which leaves the chickens, or Lola. And I'm not sure who would be less helpful.

5 p.m.
I think I might be having some sort of complete meltdown. Seriously. I have been lying on my bed staring at the ceiling for an hour. I cannot speak. I can barely hold the pen to write this.

I should have asked the chickens.

Oh God. Why, *WHY* did I ask Lola?

Transcript of conversation with Lola Jones. (Some words may have been changed due to current brain meltdown.)

| | |
|---|---|
| Lola (aka BND): | Because it's you, it's always been you, Lulu. |

Buttercup (aka GND): How could I not have seen it. You're my Romeo. My Morrissey. My Boy Next Door.

Lola: Are you sure I haven't seen this before? Isn't it the one with that woman from *Titanic*, what's her name? Kate Beckinsale.

Buttercup: (sighs) Winslet. No. As I said ONLY five minutes ago, it is totally original material written by Mr Burton.

Lola: Right. Wait, not *Titanic*?

Buttercup: God, Lola, for the millionth time, NO!

Lola: Right, sorry. What happens next?

Buttercup: And then you kiss me. And I try not to throw up.

Lola: Why, are you ill, baby?

Buttercup: Give me strength. NO, I am NOT ill.

Lola: Oh, right. You're pregnant. Brilliant. I forgot.

Buttercup: No. Well, yes. But that's not why I feel like throwing up. The throwing up is real. The pregnancy is fake.

Lola: Does he know?

Buttercup: What? Oh for God's sake. I feel sick,

| | |
|---|---|
| | in *REAL LIFE*, because I have to kiss *STAN*, OK? You know, the Boy Next Door? |
| Lola: | Right. God, how tedious. |
| Buttercup: | What? |
| Lola: | Well, it's so uninspired. There's a whole world of men out there to explore. |
| Buttercup: | Gross. |
| Lola: | I mean, why settle for what's on your doorstep. |
| Buttercup: | But that's ridiculous. What if your boy next door is, say, Robert Pattinson. Or George Clooney? I mean even George must be someone's boy next door. |
| Lola: | Ooh. Whose is he? |
| Buttercup: | Maybe you should have stuck with your boy next door. Then I wouldn't be so *MESSED* up. |
| Lola: | What? Nervous Nige? No. Or did I . . .? |
| Buttercup: | *OMG*. |
| Lola: | No, definitely not. Because he was like, a brother or something. Like Stan. |
| Buttercup: | Stan isn't my brother. |
| Lola: | No? Riiiiight. Cousin, I meant. |
| Buttercup: | Pardon? |
| Lola: | Oh yeah, because of your dad being Fidel. Possibly. |

Buttercup: *WHO* is Fidel?

Lola: Che's brother. Only I think he's really called Miles. Or is it Giles? Anyway, yeah. I'm sure I told you.

Buttercup: *NO YOU DIDN'T!*

And I swear, Dr Sven, I totally wanted to do the fingers in my ears lalala thing, only this time, I really needed to hear every word.

Only now I kind of wish I hadn't. Because it turns out that Lola had some kind of epiphany when she was watching *Lunar Jim*, and remembered that when she was living in the squat with Celia, Fidel (aka Miles or possibly Giles) came to stay and they totally ended up snogging *ETC*. Which means that not only is my dad *NOT* the calm-inducing, law-abiding, house-fixing genetically superior father figure I had hoped for but instead *EXACTLY* the kind of flaky, establishment-defying, stupid-name-bearing loser that I had feared, but:

Stan is my *COUSIN*. I am not even *JOKING*.

It totally makes sense I guess: why we like all the same stuff (except Princess Amidala, because *WHY* would *ANYONE* like a woman with hair that crazy?) and why I like him so much.

Not because he's my *ONE TRUE LOVE*. But because he's like related to me.

I mean I guess it could be worse, it could be Che, which I wouldn't have put past Lola. Seriously, once her and Celia both went out with this man called Guy for a month until he decided he couldn't keep up.

OMG. I've gone off the point. Which is, basically, OMG. I mean, I am a good person. I don't drink. Or take drugs. Not even aspirin, because I read they can thin your blood, and I get dizzy enough as it is up here.

So why is this happening to me?

Why Dr Sven? WHY?

**Monday 22 November**

11 a.m.

(D-Day (aka Kiss Rehearsal Day), French)

<u>Two people I would rather be right now</u>

1. Marie-Antoinette on the guillotine.
2. Sophie. You know, the one who had to make the choice between which of her children she was going to let die.

Lola says I am totally overreacting, that it doesn't change anything, and that now I can kiss Stan knowing there is nothing to worry about because he is my cousin. But I am NOT overreacting, it changes EVERYTHING and I can never look at Stan normally again let alone KISS HIM. Legal or not, it's just too WEIRD.

And now Imogen wants to know what I am so totally freaked out about. But I CANNOT tell her, Dr Sven. Not just because of the totally off the scale 'I am undone' potential, but because she is BOUND to tell Stan, in some misplaced 'this is the kind of thing that happens in *EastEnders*' fit, and I don't

want Stan to find out.

Oh God. Stan just looked at me. Maybe he *KNOWS*. Maybe because we are related we have some kind of telepathic thing going on.

I have to stop thinking about him. I am going to immerse myself in conjugating *'manger'*.

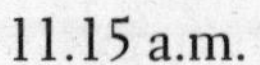

11.15 a.m.
OK. I think I may have put him off the truth. But only because I was reciting '*Je mange, tu manges* etc.' so loudly that Monsieur Leclerc had to ask if I had a hearing impairment. So now Stan just thinks I am deaf, or stupid, which is totally preferable to the truth. But I'm not sure how long I can keep this up. Because it's only 240 minutes to the kiss.

11.16 a.m.
239 minutes.

11.17 a.m.
238 minutes.

11.18 a.m.
OK. I will stop now. Because this is just making it worse. Which, believe me, I *DID NOT* think was possible.

5 p.m.
OK. So the good bit is, I did *NOT* kiss Stan.

The bad bit is that now he thinks it is because I find him so utterly physically repellent that I would rather kiss a dead orang-utan, which I can't even be bothered to explain, but believe me, it's not as bad as it sounds. AND which is so NOT true, Dr Sven. But I CANNOT tell him that, oh, actually, it's because it turns out I love you only you're my COUSIN, which is legal and all, but still Channel 5 shocktastic *Mermaid Boy* documentary material.

Mr Burton says we will have to work on the kiss at home when we don't have an audience, if THAT is what is worrying me. Which I said it was, which was only half a lie, because believe me, you really DO NOT need Lily Rubenstein giving you the evils because you are getting to snog her ONE TRUE LOVE, because you think he is your ONE TRUE LOVE, only it turns out you are both extras from some *Chat* magazine article about inbreeding. Mr Goldenblatt offered to demonstrate, but I said that I would rather not have to kiss him, given that he is a TEACHER. Only he said he had meant he would take my part, which Stan totally objected to.

And the thing is, none of this would have happened if it weren't for PMS. Seriously, PMS is the root of ALL EVIL. It is like Pandora's box or something. I mean, if you think about it, if we hadn't joined, Stan would never have met Lily, which would mean I would never have got jealous, and fallen in love with him, and told Lola, and found out he was my COUSIN. Do you believe in miracles, Dr Sven? Because I'm thinking that my only hope of sanity

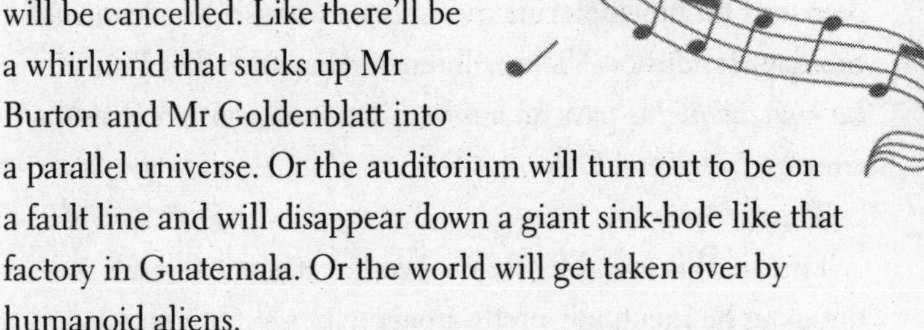

is that, maybe, just maybe, PMS will be cancelled. Like there'll be a whirlwind that sucks up Mr Burton and Mr Goldenblatt into a parallel universe. Or the auditorium will turn out to be on a fault line and will disappear down a giant sink-hole like that factory in Guatemala. Or the world will get taken over by humanoid aliens.

Then all this can stop. And everything can go back to normal.

Can't it?

**Tuesday 23 November**

OK. So it's not a whirlwind, or a sinkhole, or aliens. But something *MIRACULOUS* has definitely happened.

Thanks to Blake's try-scoring skills (or whatever they are called) on Saturday, Pennington First XV are now playing in the finals of the West of England Schools Rugby Tournament on the *SAME DAY* that the musical opens, and Coach Parry says there is no way the school minibus can get back in time from Tiverton because it is already on go-slow after the Pony Club took it to the Horse of the Year Show and brought back a Shetland, which means that Blake Carrington, i.e. Too Cool Boy, i.e. second male lead, is *OUT OF THE SHOW*.

He has begged Mr Kwame-Jones to consider couriering him back on a motorbike, but Mr Kwame-Jones said school funds are in deficit due to the new hand-dryers and he cannot afford to be paying for motorbikes, or Ms Nugent will start making demands for helicoptering the lacrosse team to Roedean, and Sunday Henderson-Hicks will reissue demands that *Penny for Your Thoughts* pays for a monthly skincare giveaway and a column by Cheryl Cole.

Thank God.

I mean, this is bad for Blake, because against all odds it turns out he is actually pretty amazing in a slightly spooky Zac Efrony kind of way. But it is BRILLIANT for me because now the show might NOT go on. Which is karma, or Yin and Yang, or something philosophical and tattooable anyway.

Not that anyone else seems to share my joy. I mean, Sunday Henderson-Hicks actually passed out in shock, although Poppy Pringle says it could also be that she has been existing on Special K and Diet Coke since she found out that Cosmo Letterman was coming to the show. She is now being force-fed Nutriment in Miss Hutchinson's office before anyone calls the Manna From Heaven Christian Residential Unit for the Undernourished.

And Imo is totally hacked off, because with Blake out of PMS she has NO chance of luring him into her weird gaytastic web of love at the after-show party, which apparently she and Titus have been plotting for the last week, involving an 'Under the Sea' theme, a jazz quartet, and compulsory corsages. (Seriously, don't ask.) And Stan is annoyed because he has just paid £30 to restring his guitar just for the show. Which I did say was totally gutting. But then he said maybe me and him could rehearse anyway, because he's thinking of doing something with a Led Zep/Judy Garland mash-up, which totally freaked me out and I had to run to the toilets before I barfed all over him.

See. It's not just my mental health at stake. It's the sanitation of the entire school.

**Wednesday 24 November**

Yet *NO ONE* seems to care about this. Because *UNBELIEVABLY* the show *WILL GO ON* after all.

Mr Burton has done an emergency recasting so that now Len Cho will be playing Too Cool Boy which is *a*) implausible because Len Cho is not in *ANY WAY* cool. I mean, he actually wears days of the week underpants. Plus *b*) his breath is worse than Geraldo's. Imo says I am overreacting (seriously, where does she get this from? *SHE* is the one who is perpetually overreacting) and that I just need to impose a moratorium on crisp consumption the night before the show, and anyway, it could have been worse because, according to Titus, who got it off Lily Rubenstein, Mr Goldenblatt offered to take over the role *AGAIN*, but luckily it turns out it is actually against The National Schools Musical Society rules and Mr Goldenblatt does not want to compromise his chances with Cosmo ever so slightly more than he wants to sing 'Man In The Mirror' in a pair of skinny jeans.

I said this was cold comfort, which Sunday Henderson-Hicks

actually agreed with (although Finty Goggins-Smith got completely confused. Lemsip was involved. I don't need to elaborate). She is threatening to sue Mr Burton for ruining her stage career by casting her opposite an amateur with a pitchy C. *AND*, amazingly, she has *DUMPED* Blake. She says it is the final straw in their coffin (which I know is mixing metaphors, but you *DON'T* argue with Sunday when she is in the middle of a dramatic monologue) and that she is sick of him putting rugby before her career, and her oral health (because she was planning on using tongues for realism, only not so much with Len Cho).

The only person who *IS* happy is Imogen. I swear she actually thanked God, and crossed herself, even though she is not a Catholic, she just thinks it looks stricken and ingénue-ish. Because not only is Blake now actually single, but it's his birthday on Saturday night and she is going as Titus's plus one, even though he will be minus one within five minutes of arrival, but Imo says that is the whole point of gay best friends. Imo says I *HAVE* to go as well, and I can be Len Cho's plus one. But I said I had my own invite, and frankly, if I do go, which is unlikely, it will be *ALONE*.

Only I should have probably checked who was in earshot, because Stan (who is, like, *ALWAYS* my plus one, even to Lettice Henry's party when we were seven, and neither of us even liked Lettice, we only went for the party bags, which had Limited Edition Lego in them) said 'Charming' and stormed off with Lily Rubenstein towards the music rooms.

Though why does *HE* care? I mean he can be Lily's plus one, anyway. Which is at least *HONEST*. I mean, seriously, I cannot plus one my own cousin to a party. Not unless I move to Alabama or Norfolk or something.

**Thursday 25 November**

1 p.m. (Latin)
How do you write a sigh, Dr Sven? Because believe me, that is what I have been mostly doing all morning. Because Imogen is excelling even her own previous boy obsession behaviour over Blake. Seriously, she spent the whole of maths writing down the exact script for their kiss on Saturday night, including extended dialogue, a balcony, and a suicide pact. I am *NOT EVEN JOKING*. I mean, OK, he's single, but there is *NO WAY* Blake Carrington is going to say he is going to kill himself if Mrs Pritchard 'cruelly contends to cut short our true love'. Plus, as I pointed out, the whole stalker letter thing has stopped, so even if it was Blake, it's obvious he has moved his affections elsewhere. But Imogen said *a*) it is only because he knows he has her love now, which will be consummated snog-wise on Saturday night at midnight, on a raised patio area, if a balcony proves unavailable, *b*) stop trying to ruin everyone else's love lives just because I am a sad singleton, and *c*) thank God Titus understands her.

It's Titus I feel sorry for. Although Imogen says gay men live for overwritten dialogue and suicide pacts. Which I am not sure is true, except that he did write Blake's part. Plus he seems happy enough. I mean, the bee-eating has stopped.

And I guess I should be grateful. At least Imogen is too wrapped up in her own *90210*-style fantasy to even notice that I am in UTTER TURMOIL.

Not that it wouldn't be nice to be able to tell someone. Someone real I mean. Because, no offence, Dr Sven, you are totally BRILLIANT, it's just that you don't have a box of tissues or a packet of Jaffa Cakes, which are ESSENTIAL crisis food. And you don't say stuff like 'OMG it is totally like the time etc. etc.'

In fact you don't say anything at all. Or at least you won't until I find £500. Which, by my calculations, could be at least two years, seven months, and three days away.

5 p.m.
OK. See, this is what happens when you have no one to fess up to and your online shrink is not doing any shrinking. Because I ended up telling Mr Burton. I am NOT EVEN JOKING.

I mean, even I can't believe it. I was in rehearsal. And I was singing 'Endless Love' with Too Cool Boy, i.e. Len Cho, i.e. COMPLETE UNCOOL MATHLETE GEEK. When out of nowhere I just burst into tears. So Mr Burton told Len to have a crisp break, which he was totally willing to do, and then said it was obvious my . . . er . . . like, distraction, was, like, still totally distracting me. Which, like, duh. Only I did not say that. I said, 'Oh my God. I'm in love with this boy. Only he doesn't know. And

I can't tell him. Because it is totally, like, FORBIDDEN.' So then he asked if he was Muslim, or Jewish, and said that he could talk to the boy's parents if that was the issue. Which I said it wasn't. And that please please could he not tell anyone especially not Imogen. Or Sunday. Or Mr Goldenblatt. So then he said he was good at like . . . er . . . keeping secrets. But that . . . er . . . coming clean, is, like, the best policy. Only I pointed out that coming clean totally did not work for him and Girl Next Door i.e. she went off to London anyway. And he said, 'Yeah. You're right. But, like, you're not me, Buttercup.' Which, like, duh. And then he said maybe now would be a good time to try singing 'Jolene'. Which it turns out, it totally was, because I was all upset, and vulnerable. And so Mr Burton says well that is how I can put my feelings to good use, i.e. I can channel them for my character. Which he is right about. And I guess I feel a little bit better. But only a LITTLE bit. And that's not enough, Dr Sven. Not nearly.

**Friday 26 November**

It never ends, Dr Sven. Seriously. I mean, I managed to get through the morning without having to listen to *a*) Imo and Titus's endless pre-nup rehearsals, *b*) Lily Rubenstein going on about how AMAZING Stan's chord changes were last night when they were ALONE in her BEDROOM, or *c*) Finty

Goggins-Smith wondering whether rabbits will ever grow wings, (thank God for the language lab headphones, which, even though they are greasy, and totally unflattering, block out any noise other than Monsieur Leclerc asking you to *écouter et repétér*) when I get cornered at my locker by Blake Carrington who practically BEGS me to come to his party tomorrow.

I KNOW! So I said, 'Yeah, right, because, what? Some friend of yours fancies me, only when I show up they call me a freak and lock me in a room with a Weimaraner, FOR FUN, like last year?' Only he said no, and sorry about that. And also for the time they poured treacle in my trainers. And the time they shut Alfie Watson-Jackson, who has a growth disorder, in my locker (which I didn't even know about, so he must have totally worked a way to get out, which means maybe he has a career as a midget escapologist). So I said 'Why then?' And he said it's because he organized the party months ago, only now the Cooper-Willises spend most of their time giving him grief over being in PMS, and Sunday hates him, which means so do the Sidehicks, only they're all still coming because there's a swimming pool and they got St Tropezed specially, so Saturday night is going to be hell if there isn't at least one friendly face in the room. Which is, like, me. Which is, like, oh my God!

And then I thought, maybe it's just because he wants me to bring Imogen as my plus one, which I totally asked him, only he said, 'Aren't you bringing Stan?' So I said, 'I doubt it. And anyway Lily Rubenstein is bringing him.' And he said, 'Oh. I thought you two were like an item or something.' And I said, 'You thought wrong.' (Which is totally borrowed off Imo and she is going to kill me if she finds out I used it before her, especially with Blake.) And he said, 'Oh well, cool. See you there?' And then my mouth just went ahead and said 'yes' without consulting my brain, because if it had, it would have reminded it that I am supposed to be going to the theatre with Granny Jones (which, like, I KNOW. But she has to have someone with her to explain what is happening because she refuses to wear her glasses on vanity grounds and contacts make her eyes itch). So NOW not only do I have to endure the full horror of Blake's party and the Imogen balcony suicide scene, plus very likely watch Stan snog someone who has better hair than me and ISN'T his cousin, I have to get shouted at by my own grandmother.

5 p.m.

In a case of unprecedented serendipity (I so like that word, don't you? Although I did go off it for a bit when Imogen started overusing it and claiming everything was serendipitous, which it wasn't, it was coincidental, which is an entirely different thing) Granny has had a bad reaction to a face peel and is refusing to leave the building.

So, problem solved. Or at least, A problem solved. Which is not that bad. Because I'm pretty sure I have no chance of sorting out world peace, or the chicken and egg conundrum, or the WHY I'M IN LOVE WITH MY COUSIN thing any time soon.

**Saturday 27 November**

7 p.m.

Hey, Dr Sven. So, I am all dressed up (in a black lace faux-fifties thing, in case you were wondering, which you're probably not, but maybe it will reveal some important detail about my current mental state. Or the state of my wardrobe at least) with somewhere to go (i.e. home of Blake Carrington, i.e. previous enemy territory until tonight on grounds of being *a*) mock Tudor, *b*) gated, and *c*) too far to go to play knock-down ginger). Only the thing is, I don't *WANT* to go. I mean, I know I kind of said that it would be nice to get through the rest of Pennington classified by the Mudhoneys as *NOT WORTH BOTHERING ABOUT* rather than *COMPLETE FREAK*, but I'm pretty sure I didn't ask to be spending my Saturdays at one of their infamous house parties, at which I guarantee that at least three of the following things will happen:

Pick and Mix events at Pennington Parties

1. That one of the Cooper-Willises will shout 'scrum' and then about fifteen fat-necked, polo shirted red-faced rugger bores will all jump in a pile in the middle of the room breaking several glasses and someone's nose.
2. That one of the Sidehicks will spend two hours locked in a bathroom snogging one of the Cooper-Willises.
3. That another of the Sidehicks will spend two hours

locked in a bathroom sobbing because other Sidehick is snogging said Cooper-Willis in the other bathroom.

4. That several people will have to wee into Red Bull cans due to bathroom occupation.
5. That Finty Goggins-Smith will drink out of one of these cans.

See. Why would I want to go to one of these things? *WHY, I ASK YOU*!

7.15 p.m.

Oh God, sorry for shouting. I know it's not *YOUR* fault, obviously.

It is *IMOGEN'S* fault because she is the one who is so desperate to snog Blake, and to do it in front of a receptive audience, potentially on mobile phone camera so she can upload it to YouTube later.

And possibly Blake's. Because he is so desperate for me to come although why I am not completely sure. Unless maybe he *DOES* fancy Imo after all and he wants me to bring her as my plus one.

But then why didn't he just invite her in the first place?

7.20 p.m.

Oh God, Dr Sven. I have just had a *HIDEOUS* thought.

What if Blake is so desperate for me to come because he

fancies **ME** not Imo? I mean, he did say I am a friendly face. And what if he wants to **SNOG** that friendly face? Oh God. My life is more implausible than an *EastEnders* plot and just as **DEPRESSING**. **SERIOUSLY**, Dr Sven, **NOW** what am I going to do?

7.30 p.m.
Kiss Blake?

Or is that **TOTALLY** off the scale? I mean, I **KNOW** Imo fancies him and everything. Plus he is a total rah who thinks Jack Wills and Jack Johnson are at the cutting edge of fashion and music respectively (only without knowing what respectively means).

But at least he's not my cousin. And maybe if the kiss was like, totally movie kiss, i.e. with earth moving and violins, then I would forget Stan, and Imo would forgive me because it is my mental health at stake, plus I could tell her about Stan and she would be so consumed with 'I am undone'ing she would forget that I have completely stabbed her in the back.

I mean, it's possible, at least in the scheme of my ridiculous life.

Don't you think?

1 a.m.

OK. So, the good thing is that Blake does **NOT** fancy me.

The bad thing is that I kissed him **ANYWAY**.

You are not going to believe why. Even **I'M** not sure I believe why. And I'm in love with my own cousin.

Events unfolded as follows (more or less, although

my brain may be clouded by the *HORROR* of what actually did unfold) which also reminds me: note to self: *CHANGE NAMES*. Seriously.
Because this is bigger than Imogen's breasts. Metaphorically speaking:

Timetable at Blake Carrington's Birthday Party (theme: *Twilight*, not that anyone told me, though as I was wearing black lace I did not stand out too much, unlike Len Cho who wore a werewolf costume)

8 p.m. Arrive at Carrington House (I am not even joking), whence am immediately assaulted by a Labradoodle called Monty.

8.15 Join queue for downstairs toilet.

8.45 Finty Goggins-Smith emerges from downstairs toilet.

8.46 Clint Cooper-Willis emerges from downstairs toilet.

8.47 Alicia Beaufort and Poppy Pringle emerge from downstairs toilet (clearly they are either *a*) experimenting with open love square or *b*) very ill).

8.59 Finally gain access to downstairs toilet. Note that face is definitely dog-allergy affected so that I now look like Snorkmaiden.

| | |
|---|---|
| 9.15 | Rory Cardew (brother of Carey, also Mudhoney, also stupid) attempts to fly like a vampire from the pool-house roof. Does not succeed but death averted due to soft (though wet) landing in pool. |
| 9.16 | Finty Goggins-Smith and Imogen join in one colossal display of idiocy/failure to delineate myth and real life, and have panic that water will melt vampire. |
| 9.17 | Rory emerges from pool unmelted *UNSURPRISINGLY*. |
| 9.30 | Imogen and Titus gain control of iPod dock and put on playlist including ironic Eurovision entries. |
| 9.35 | Sunday Henderson-Hicks decrees Eurovision not ironic, just pants, and ousts Imo's iPod for own iPod and playlist heavy with Pussycat Dolls, i.e. opportunities for synchronized dance routines in very small outfits. |
| 9.36 | Blake Carrington says was actually enjoying Eurovision and reousts Sunday's iPod. Frantic iPod battle ensues with much ousting. Sunday wins battle, but not war, according to Imo, who takes Blake's defence of Eurovision as confirmation that he is her *ONE* and will be snogging her drunkenly in the |

downstairs toilet by midnight.

9.37 Buttercup points out that is not exactly *Romeo and Juliet* balcony scene as rehearsed.

9.38 Imogen tells Buttercup *a*) scene is not reliant on balcony as she is expert at romantic dialogue, having watched *The Notebook* seven times in last three days, *b*) in any case she is planning on manouevring him to the raised pool area once he has his tongue in her mouth and he is utterly at her mercy, and *c*) butt out and mind my own business.

10 p.m. Clint Cooper-Willis shouts 'scrum'. Several fat-necked red-faced rahs jump into pile on the oak flooring and writhe sweatily.

10.01 Imogen points out homoerotic nature of scrum and suggests Titus joins in.

10.02 Titus declines on grounds that he has weak femurs.

10.05 Scrum disbanded to reveal four broken glasses, one spilt bottle of Fanta and

| | |
|---|---|
| | Finty Goggins-Smith who got caught in crossfire and appears to now be dead. |
| 10.06 | Finty declared not dead, just stunned, and is revived by squirting Chanel in her eyes. |
| 10.15 | Sunday Henderson-Hicks, Poppy Pringle, Alicia Beaufort, and Finty Goggins-Smith (partially blinded) perform routine to 'I Kissed a Girl'. |
| 10.20 | Imo and Titus perform routine to 'Bad Boys'. |
| 10.25 | Sunday challenges Imo to dance-off. Imogen accepts. Titus, Finty, and Blake declared judges. |
| 10.30 | Judges argue over who gets to be Simon Cowell. |
| 10.35 | Finty Goggins-Smith is Simon Cowell. Blake is Piers Morgan. Titus is Amanda Holden due to ability to cry at will. Dance-off begins. |
| 10.40 | Buttercup Jones feels tap on shoulder. Has momentary panic is grim reaper. |
| 10.41 | Is not grim reaper, is Blake Carrington who says he has no interest in dance-off and does Buttercup want to go up to his room. Buttercup confirms that Imogen completely engrossed in hip thrusting and agrees. |

| | |
|---|---|
| 10.42 | Buttercup and Blake arrive in room. Buttercup notes plethora of Jonny Wilkinson posters (makes mental note to tell Lily Rubenstein she is utterly *WRONG* about Zac Efron thing). |
| 10.43 | Conversation takes place as follows (and this is where you will utterly need to sit down, Dr Sven, if you aren't already. Although really you should be, because working whilst standing up is bad for your back and your concentration): |
| Blake: | This party sucks, huh? |
| Buttercup: | (worried is trick question) Oh, I don't know. |
| Blake: | It's not a trick question. |
| Buttercup: | Oh. OK. Then yeah, it totally sucks. But they always do. |
| Blake: | That's why I invited you. |
| Buttercup: | Because I suck? |
| Blake: | Er . . . no. Because you totally don't. |
| Buttercup: | Oh. |
| Blake: | So where's Stan? |
| Buttercup: | I don't know. I'm not his keeper. |
| Blake: | No. Right. Look, I need to tell you something, Buttercup. |

| | |
|---|---|
| Buttercup: | (Puts finger on Blake's lip in fashion completely borrowed from Imo, and previously seen in various key cinematic moments.) Don't. We don't need words. We just need this (kisses Blake on lips). |
| Blake: | (Pulling away frantically as if being kissed by Gorgon of hell, or Miss Hutchinson.) God, no, Buttercup. That's not what I meant. |
| Buttercup: | (Having checked breath discreetly for traces of garlic.) I'm sorry. I . . . I thought— Oh God, it's the hives, isn't it? |
| Blake: | Are there bees? |
| Buttercup: | What? No. Monty. The dog. I'm allergic. |
| Blake: | And I'm gay. |
| Buttercup: | (In head.) And I am undone. |
| Blake: | What's undone? |
| Buttercup: | Sorry, I could have sworn that was in my head. |
| Blake: | So, the gay thing. |
| Buttercup: | Are you serious? But, I mean, you're kind of so totally NOT gay. I mean, you wear bad-fitting jeans. And what was Sunday all about? |
| Blake: | I know. But you don't understand the |

pressure I'm under.

Buttercup: Pressure YOU'RE under. OH MY GOD. Try being me. THAT'S PRESSURE. Which, like WHY are you telling me anyway?

Blake: Because you're different too.

Buttercup: Yeah, well I wish I wasn't.

Blake: You're not going to tell anyone, are you?

Buttercup: No. So you didn't send Imogen a poem telling her she was Rubenesque.

Blake: What's Rubenesque? Is it like Rubik's Cube?

Buttercup: As I thought. And you're sure you're gay? I mean like, TOTALLY?

Blake: Totally. I mean. One time I was watching wrestling and Blake junior—

Buttercup: OK, TOO MUCH INFORMATION.

Blake: But—

Buttercup: No, I will put my fingers in my ears and sing lalala if you say another word. My head is already WAY too full of out of bounds things.

Blake: Really? Like what?

But at that EXACT moment . . .

10.57 p.m. Door bursts open to reveal sweating

Imogen Pritchard and Sunday Henderson-Hicks demanding to know why Piers Morgan is not judging but is in bedroom with person who is not *EVEN* contestant. (I am *NOT EVEN JOKING*, is like film, isn't it, except is *HORRIFYINGLY REAL*.)

11.00 Buttercup explains Blake was just telling her something. Blake, in visible potential outing panic, says, 'Yes. She was telling me that she *WILL* totally go out with me,' and kisses Buttercup on lips in full view of Imogen and Sunday.

11.05 Blake removes tongue from mouth of Buttercup but Buttercup still completely unable to speak due to shock.

11.06 Alicia declares it is new Pennington French kissing record, as previous Sunday/Blake record proved void due to loss of contact for more than one second.

11.07 Sunday and Imogen unimpressed with record, and with entire snogging episode and storm off together followed by Simon Cowell and Amanda Holden.

11.08 Buttercup regains use of brain, and tongue, and potentially stomach, and declares she has to leave before she

vomits on
Jonas Brothers
bedspread.

Which brings us pretty much up to date, Dr Sven. So, in case you have missed anything (though *HOW* this would be possible as I have pretty much told you every single event, down to what I eat for breakfast) and also in order to ascertain just what level of pantsness my life has spiralled into, I have made a detailed assessment of my situation, as follows:

<u>Buttercup Jones's Pants-O-Meter of Life</u>

1. My mother is still a failed conceptual artist called Lola.
2. My dad is a fake revolutionary called Fidel. Who also happens to be the uncle of my official best friend, i.e. Stan, i.e. my cousin who I am totally in love with.
3. Imogen is not speaking to me because I have snogged Blake Carrington whom she hearts more than Heathcliff.
4. Titus is not speaking to me because Imogen is not speaking to me.
5. Sunday Henderson-Hicks is totally going to Slimfast me on Monday for snogging Blake before she has snogged someone else (although I totally bet she immediately went and snogged one of the Cooper-Willises in order to claim victory).
6. Blake is gay and I am the *ONLY* person in the entire

world to know this, and it is like a hideous red button with a 'do not push button' sign on it, which, like, is *TOTALLY* impossible not to push.

7. I have a face like boiled hippo.

Oh God, it is *TOO* depressing for words. In fact I am adding that to my list of potential mental health issues and going to bed, which is a definite sign of depression according to Imogen.

1.35 a.m.

Or is that not getting out of bed?

1.40 a.m

It *IS* not getting out of bed, but *WHATEVER*, I am still totally hacked off, not least because Imo will probably *NEVER* tell me stuff like this again so in fact I probably *WON'T* get out of bed tomorrow anyway.

**Sunday 28 November**

1 p.m.

OK, so I got up. But only because I am too long for the bed and my legs start to get pins and needles, and then I start worrying I am getting some kind of terminal disease. Anyway, the point is, I have rung Imogen and it is clear she is definitely *NOT* speaking to me because Mrs Pritchard said she has possible consumption, and I know for a fact that the last time she claimed that was when we had our vaccinations and Sunday told her it was in

the buttocks, and she had totally failed on the cabbage soup diet. Plus consumption is *TOTALLY* made up.

2 p.m.
Harry has googled consumption and says it *ISN'T* made up, it is TB, which is undergoing a resurgence due to malnourishment, crowded living conditions, and a culture in some areas of spitting in the streets. But as Imogen is an only child, eats for two, and has not been anywhere near the Twerton estate since she got over her crush on Dane Perry, child motocross legend, then she *DOES NOT HAVE IT*.

3 p.m.
Ooh, the phone is ringing. Which is a miracle given Harry has been using the handset as a space transmitter. And I really must stop writing and answer it immediately in case it is Imo!

3.10 p.m.
It was *NOT* Imogen. It was, unbelievably, Mr Burton checking up on me. He said he was . . . er . . . worried that I was going to pull out of PMS with the whole, like, distraction thing. I said *a*) no, because, *AMAZINGLY*, singing is about the only time I do not feel like barfing right now and *b*) he is so not my father or anything so he does not need to check up on me. Although it is very kind, thank you. Which it is. But also kind of weird, don't you think?

4 p.m.
Now it is the door. And there is no way this can be Mr Burton because he does not know where I live because Miss Hutchinson has firewalled the school address log ever since Lily Rubenstein hacked in and started sending random objects to several Year Twelves. Oh, God, please let it be Imo.

5 p.m.
Either God is not listening. Or does not like me. Or has some kind of weird plan for me that I am totally *NOT* getting right now. Because that was *NOT* Imo. It was Stan. And just in case you cannot imagine how *OFF THE SCALE* our conversation was, which I find hard to believe as it is clear that things are so *NOT* normal between us at the moment, then I am reproducing it here in its entirety (except the bit at the front door because that just involved him asking to come in etc. which is neither interesting nor relevant):

Stan: So, what happened last night?

Me: Nothing . . . Why? What have you heard?

Stan: That you and Blake Carrington exchanged saliva in front of most of Pennington.

Me: Oh. That.

Stan: So it's true?

Me: Kind of. I guess. How do you even know though?

Stan: Carey videoed it on her mobile and

texted it to Lily.

Me: Oh God. I think I'm going to hurl.

Stan: Do you need a bucket?

Me: No. I think I have swallowed it. So, you've seen it?

Stan: Two seconds of it. Because Fintan's head got in the way. Why did you do it, B? I mean I thought you thought he was a fat-necked rugby rah.

Me: I do. I mean I did. He's not though. But it's not what you think.

Stan: So what is it then?

Me: I can't tell you.

Stan: I don't know what's up with you. You used to tell me everything.

Me: I know.

Stan: So you and him. You're . . . together?

Me: No. Yes. I don't know. I think so.

Stan: OK. Right, well, I guess that's it then.

Me: What's what?

Stan: Just that, I always thought that me and you . . . You know.

Me: No I don't know. *WHAT?*

Stan: God, don't make me say it, Buttercup.

Me: Say it.

Stan: That we'd be together. One day. God. Sorry. I shouldn't have said anything.

Me: . . . (Stunned into silence, which, I *KNOW*, right?)

Stan: Say something.

Me: (Through hand clamped on mouth.) Can't.

Stan: I should go.

Me: (Nods head frantically.)

Stan: Forget it. What I said. I just hope the old Buttercup is in there somewhere (pushes skanky blonde dyed hair behind my ears). I miss her. I want us to be like we used to.

Me: (Still nodding.)

Stan: See you. Good luck at school. You're going to need it.

(Followed by *TOTALLY* awkward goodbye where we both got stuck in my doorway, so in the end I just went back and retched in toilet and then lay down on bed, and he let himself out. And *BELIEVE ME* I totally needed to lie down. Because, if I am reading this right, which has been known to not be the case, but this time I am pretty sure I have it down, then *STAN LIKES ME*. And not just in a *FRIEND* kind of way but in a *GIRLFRIEND* kind of way. Which, like, *WHAT ABOUT LILY*? Unless she is totally not his *ONE TRUE LOVE* but is someone who he is just

snogging in a Sidehick kind of way. Which is so not Stan-like. But anyway.

And, the thing is, I would give anything for things to go back to how they were before. Only now it's not just about the hair, there's like about a million other lies that I have somehow wrapped myself up in. And underneath it all, the 'real Buttercup' is his *COUSIN*.

10 p.m.
But oh my God he *LIKES* me.

10.05 p.m.
Could we?

10.10 p.m.
No. Because we are *COUSINS*.

10.15 p.m.
Only it's not *ACTUALLY* illegal. I checked on Wiki.

10.20 p.m.
But it is icky. Like, *EWWW*.

10.25 p.m.
Still. He likes me.

**Monday 29 November**

8 a.m.

I do *NOT* feel good, Dr Sven. Because

*a*) I have to go to *SCHOOL* where I will get completely lynched by Imogen and Sunday Henderson-Hicks and possibly half the upper school.

*b*) I am snogging Blake Carrington, despite the fact that he is *GAY*, a fact that only I know about, which is annoying, because

*c*) I want to snog Stan, who it turns out *LIKES* me, because he doesn't yet know that I am his *COUSIN*.

Seriously, Dr Sven, this is the *WORST DAY EVER*. And I would stay at home only the more days I stay away the more 'inversely proportionate this is to transgressions being forgiven/forgotten', according to the mathletes who have a formula for this. And for everything. i.e. The 'worse it will be' (in non-geek language). Plus by the time I did go back the rumours would have escalated to me having snogged Blake *AND* several Cooper-Willises and being pregnant with twins but no one knows who the fathers are.

4 p.m.

I was right. It *WAS* the worst day ever:

1. The mobile phone fake gay kiss snoggathon video has been uploaded to YouTube and has had 12,789 hits so far, including Mr Kwame-Jones, according to Lily

Rubenstein, who obviously I am not talking to, but she told Carey Cardew who told Norah Forbes who told me, because only two people speak to her anyway.

2. Blake begged me to do a repeat live version of the snogathon in the canteen at lunchtime because Coach Parry caught him with a suspect magazine in his bag at practice this morning (*Grazia*, which he claimed he was going to put in Titus's locker, which Coach Parry said was OK, but even so he needs back up).
3. Imogen happened to be walking past at the time on her way to the salad bar (which she totally negates by drowning the lettuce in squeezy bottle mayonnaise) and said, 'I'm embarrassed to be white', (which is not *EVEN* relevant, and I know for a fact that it comes from *Hairspray*, but still is *NOT* nice) and Blake defended me (which on reflection he should *NOT* have) by saying she made him embarrassed to be a boy, which again, makes no sense, but also did not make Imogen in any way happy, because then she totally *MAYONNAISED* me. So I ketchupped her back and then we both got sent to Mr Kwame-Jones (who wasn't there, he was at a governors' lunch getting shouted at by Mr Ledbetter-Morpeth) so Miss Hutchinson asked me for detailed reasons behind the fight, only I told her to ask Imo, and then she told her to ask me, and then it got out of hand so we both told her, only I corrected the bit

where Imogen said I had flung myself at Blake against his wishes, and she said she did *NOT* have unrealistic expectations of love, while Miss Hutchinson took notes (which, like, *WHAT*?). And then she said we are on a warning, and any more shenanigans (she actually used that word) from either of us and she will suspend us, and that we should think ourselves lucky that the governors rejected her request to reinstate caning. So I pointed out that only Mr Kwame-Jones can actually suspend anyone, which he has never done, because as scholarship students we are all victims of social injustice. (He thinks anyone who didn't go to Eton is a victim of social injustice, which, like, has he *SEEN* the size of the Henderson-Hicks swimming pool?) Only she pointed out that under clause something or other, if Mr Kwame-Jones is off the premises for longer than two hours, all his powers pass to her, and she is not afraid to use them. Which I totally believe.

4. In PMS I got tripped up during 'Man in the Mirror' twenty-two times and it is *NOT* because I have baby giraffe legs, which is what Sunday Henderson-Hicks claims. And then I was so freaked out I ended up telling Mr Burton that it is *ALL* his fault that my life is so *COMPLETELY* awful and that he should never have cast me in the first place. Only instead of sending me to Mr Kwame-Jones *AGAIN*, he took me into the stationery cupboard/office and said that he totally . . . um . . . understood, that

it . . . er . . . like, sucks being a teenager (he totally used that word, which, like, respect), especially one who, like, doesn't look like a . . . er . . . walking Abercrombie and Fitch advert, and that some day I will, like, realize that not being 'normal' is actually pretty . . . um . . . damn cool. Which he is wrong about, but it's the thought that counts, and I totally didn't deserve the thought.

5. Stan is just giving me totally 'I am *SO* disappointed in you' kind of expressions. Which, like I *KNOW*. Because even I am disappointed in me.

5 p.m.

Great. Now Blake has texted to say he needs to see me and is coming over. So by this time tomorrow the fact that I live in some kind of hippy hell with three chickens and a stuffed mongoose will be common knowledge in the Penn locker rooms. Plus *WHAT* does he need to see me about? It cannot be snogging because what is the advantage in doing that round here where no one can see?

5.05 p.m.

Unless he has decided he is not gay after all, or is bisexual (which Lola totally claims she is, but is a lie, she is just trying to be clever *AGAIN*) and actually wants to snog me for real. Seriously, this *CANNOT* happen. Not even *EASTENDERS* could come up with that.

7 p.m.

Blake wanted to say sorry. For the fight, and for the Miss Hutchinson thing, and for totally using me as a decoy, which he said he only did because *a*) his life on the rugby team will be over if they find out, because Coach Parry sacked Charley Bott-Johnson just for using moisturizer to stop his thighs chafing and *b*) he *DOES* really like me (which I did panic about, but he said *NOT* in a saliva-exchanging kind of way, which, like, thank God) and that he wants us to be friends, because I am '*DIFFERENT*', i.e. *LIKE HIM*. I said being different *SUCKS* big time, and that I am definitely *NOT* like him, i.e. I am *NOT* gay, as evidenced by fact that I am in love with my own cousin, i.e. Stan, who is definitely *NOT* a girl, because I have seen it (paddling pool incident). And I *ACTUALLY* told him this (which goes to show that Imogen is totally right about the Gay Best Friend thing and that somehow they telepathically get you to confess everything).

But then I remembered that being gay does not disqualify him from being a total Mudhoney jerk, so I *BEGGED* him not to say anything on pain of death, and I did actually threaten him with a pair of pinking shears (from the time Lola thought she would make a fortune from recycled plastic bag bunting) at this point. Only he said he is an expert in keeping secrets (which if you think about it, is totally true. I mean not even Sunday guessed and she has had her tongue in his mouth for seventeen minutes forty-one seconds, according to Lily Rubenstein). Then he said that the Stan thing must be AWFUL and asked me for every detail, which I totally gave him (see?) even though I did not expect him to understand half of it because it is way complicated and involves too many dates and men with various pseudonyms.

But it turns out that maybe I was wrong about him in more ways than just the being straight thing, because then he just said, 'Are you sure.' And I said, 'Which bit? The Hare Krishna restaurant?' And he said, 'No, that's he's 110 per cent your cousin,' which is, like, a lame sport cliché, only I didn't point this out, because he was TOTALLY right. Because I am NOT 110 per cent sure. I am not even 100 per cent sure. I mean, I only have Lola's word for it. Not that I think she was lying about Fidel, because what would be the advantage in that? Plus he is totally her type, i.e. he is deluded, jobless, and a minor aristocrat.

But the thing is, Dr Sven, what if there was someone else? What if she has still not remembered another freakishly tall, borderline ginger, big-lipped man that she once snogged? I mean, it's TOTALLY possible.

8 p.m.
Isn't it?

8.05 p.m.
Oh my God. It IS totally possible. Which would mean I totally CAN snog Stan in a non-hicksville kind of way. Only it would

be in a him-cheating-on-Lily kind of way, which is *NOT* good, but at least is not *Take a Break* magazine material.

I am going to write a plan, Dr Sven. The list kind that comes with several satisfying points. And possibly two different kinds of pen. And then I am going to find out the *TRUTH*.

**Tuesday 30 November**

Buttercup Jones's Plan to *a*) Identify Her Father, *b*) Potentially Kiss Stan Romer (if he is not in fact her cousin), *c*) Restore Status as Official Best-Friend with Imogen Pritchard, and *d*) Tackle Rampant Homophobia in Private School System

1. Find out where Fidel lives.
2. Go to Fidel's house and ascertain if he looks in *ANY* way like a potential father.
3. If the answer is *YES*, then phone Ricki Lake immediately for space on programme (as cannot afford DNA test otherwise).
4. Once I have the answer, confess all to Imogen, in spite of 'I am undone' potential.
5. Get Ruby to organize a protest about anti-gay nature of rugby and sport in general.
6. So that Blake can come out and still be Mudhoney *AND* complete Gleek, because Pennington is now embracing of difference in every way.

Isn't it great? I wrote it in Chem, when we were supposed to be doing something with lithium, only my partner is Imogen and she refused to let me touch the Bunsen burners or the tweezers because my 'treacherous hands' might contaminate the results. Which, like, HOW? Only clearly Mr Sylvester has seen the video on YouTube and agreed with her because he made me sit at the back with Fintan. Anyway I have shown it to Blake and he says he will totally help me, except for the coming out bit because he does not want to be mayonnaised every day until he goes to college (I did not point out the likelihood of this is, like, zero), which is sweet. Although I am not banking on his help actually being totally helpful. I mean, I know I said he was not the single-celled amoeba that I had thought, but he still plays contact sport and wears CKOne.

Anyway, the point is, I have a plan. Now all I have to do is find Fidel. And how I'm going to do that without Stan is anybody's guess.

Oh, and get through PMS rehearsal tomorrow without getting my legs broken.

# DECEMBER

**Wednesday 1 December**

OK. So PMS was really really so *NOT* good. Seriously. I have a bruise on my thigh that is actually purple and the shape of Brazil. And Mr Burton says he cannot move me away from Sunday in 'ABC' because the only other place is in between Finty Goggins-Smith and Alicia and they will just Hubba Bubba me.

But you know what, I don't care.

Because Blake found Fidel.

I am *NOT EVEN JOKING*.

To be fair, he looked him up in the phone book under Harrington-Bovey, which is not totally CSI, but still, I didn't think of it. And anyway, it turns out there are only two, and one is called Margaret, who is definitely not my father, unless he has also had a sex change, which I guess given Lola's track record is possible, except that the other one is called Miles (not Giles). Which *HAS* to be him.

So, I am going to go up to London on Saturday. Blake can't come because he has rugby practice and he says he is going to keep up the pretence until the world, or at least Pennington, is a more accepting place. I said it would be *VERY* soon, once my plan is complete. And Ruby, who suddenly appeared from the kitchen like some kind of dreadlocked genie, says it will be by tomorrow because it is her anti-private school protest, which I am totally under duress to come to as part of our agreement.

So then I had to apologize because I am pretty sure that Imogen and Stan and the rest of Penn will *NOT* be coming any more. So then Blake said he would come to make up for it. Only Ruby said he looked like a spy, i.e. his collar was turned up, which is a giveaway for someone with land and a Range Rover in Ruby's book. Which he is. Except that he is also secretly gay. Which I did *NOT* say (because Blake kicked me with one of his Timberlands, which, like, *OW*. He could seriously do with gayer footwear), I just said he was different. Ruby looked dubious, but said OK because even she admits beggars totally can't be choosers.

So on the downside I have to embarrass myself *AGAIN* in front of the entire staff and student body tomorrow. But, you know what, Dr Sven? I don't care. Because my plan is *WORKING*!

**Thursday 2 December**

8.45 a.m.

OK. Now maybe I do care. Because it is quarter to nine in the morning and instead of *a*) being at school in *b*) regulation Pennington uniform, i.e. a navy blazer with a crest of triumphant elephants (though *WHAT* are they triumphant about, Dr Sven? That is what I would like to know), pleated skirt rolled up to reveal at least a ruler's worth of thigh, and over-the-knee socks, I am *a*) in the kitchen wearing *b*) combat trousers, wellies, and camouflage make-up. I pointed out to Ruby that, given her anti-war stance, the military wear is hardly appropriate, but she said it is metaphorical military wear which is entirely justifiable, plus she is worried the police might try to kettle us so we need to be fully equipped. Hence also our weapons, i.e. washing up bottles filled with dirty water from the chicken coop.

I am not at all sure about Denzil coming, given the smell. Or Harry, given that *a*) he does not even *GO* to school, private or not, and *b*) he is dressed as some sort of reptile, but Ruby says it will make a good picture in the *Chronicle*, it is just a shame we cannot reveal who his father is, as the celebrity endorsement could do wonders for our cause.

So now we are just waiting for *a*) Spike to arrive with a tent and emergency rations in case we have to form some kind of Greenham Common camp on the perimeter fence and *b*) Ruby to finish her list of demands.

8.55 a.m.

Spike is now here with fourteen loaves of bread, nine tins of chick peas, and a bag of something that looks like dried hops, but which I suspect is not. He said it is enough to feed the five thousand that they are fully expecting to join the picket line. It isn't, and they won't. Plus the tent is only a two-man one because the tepee still smells of sewage from Glastonbury. Seriously,

Dr Sven, I *REALLY* hope we do *NOT* have to build a perimeter camp. Although if we actually even get to school it will be a miracle because Ruby is *STILL* writing her list of demands.

9 a.m.
Ruby has *FINALLY* finished her list of demands, which I have reproduced below, only with no spelling mistakes, or peace signs, or flower doodles:

<u>Required Outcomes of Pennington Protest</u>

1. All entrance exams to be abolished.
2. All fees to be abolished.
3. Uniform to be abolished.
4. Pennington to admit at least ninety per cent of pupils who have never shopped in Jack Wills or Joules, or been to Padstow on holiday.
5. The canteen to ban all meat products, and adopt Freeganism and food foraging.
6. Rugby and lacrosse to be replaced with creative dance for boys and self-defence for girls.

I think she may be being a little ambitious on, well, pretty much all of them. But Ruby says they are immovable, like ourselves, i.e. we will not be leaving until every single one has been met.

11 a.m.
*UNSURPRISINGLY* the protest is over. With the following outcomes:

Actual Outcomes of Pennington Protest

1. I have been suspended. I am *NOT EVEN JOKING*. It is because Mr Kwame-Jones was at the dentist, and he ended up having a bad reaction to either the gas and air or Mr Llewellyn, so he was off the premises for two hours and eighteen minutes, which meant Miss Hutchinson was in charge, and she pointed out she had already given me a warning, and had the taped evidence to prove this.
2. Ruby now has a restraining order on her and is not allowed within five miles of Pennington, which Miss Hutchinson said she should have done when Ruby was actually *AT* the school, because then they might still have working showers in the swimming pool, and which means she is pretty much not allowed to leave the vicinity of the barge. *EVER*.
3. Blake has been given a merit award for trying to *STOP* the protest, which he totally *WASN'T*, he was trying to pull me off the crease before the photographer could see me, only Miss Hutchinson clearly refuses to believe that that could be humanly possible.
4. There is going to be a photograph of me in next week's *Chronicle* and believe me I *DO NOT* look in any way revolutionary. I look like a racist who has possibly wet their pants.
5. The school is *STILL* private, there is turkey on the menu

for lunch, and Miss Hutchinson said at no point will self-defence lessons be allowed because last time they tried it four Year Eights ended up in hospital with broken arms. Seriously, Dr Sven, it could *NOT* have gone worse, even by my standards, which, let's face it, are pretty disastrous. I mean, like, *a*) no one else showed up except Blake and he had a balaclava on, *b*) we didn't arrive until after everyone was *IN* school, meaning a picket line was *POINTLESS*, so Ruby said we had to go and stand outside Mr Kwame-Jones's office instead i.e. on the cricket crease. But *c*) Miss Hutchinson saw us and got Mr Heckles the groundsman to turn on the sprinklers, and Ruby started screaming that it was a chemical weapon, and then *d*) everyone just ran, leaving me in the middle of the crease, with a wet stain on the front of my combats, a black face, and a tin of chick peas in my hand. Which *e*) is *EXACTLY* when the photographer from the paper decided to show up.

Ruby said it is still a triumph. She is *WRONG*. I mean, seriously, what is triumphant about *ANY* of the above?

11.15 p.m.
Oh wait, I forgot. Something good *DID* happen. At least, I think it's good, i.e. I am *OUT OF PMS*.

Mr Burton was totally *NOT* pleased, and part of me felt bad as well because *a*) he is *SO* into this musical and *b*) singing is pretty much the only time that I feel good, you know, kind of *NOT* like a loser with growing out roots and a gay fake boyfriend.

But, like I said, it's probably for the best because at least this way all the Hubba Bubbaing will stop. Plus I was totally supposed to be concentrating on being ordinary this term, and PMS is like the opposite of that. Only Mr Burton said, 'But you're not . . . er . . . ordinary. You're, like, extraordinary.' Which is nice and all, but kind of the problem. Which I told him. Only he said, 'You just, kind of, have to believe in yourself, Buttercup.' Which I said was a bit rich because he didn't even have the guts to use his own song in the musical. Then he said he had his . . . er . . . reasons. Then I was about to say something else only Imogen showed up and demanded my part, as she is official understudy, which she had got in writing, so Mr Burton totally had to concede. So now she is totally off the scale of Imogen-ness.

Unlike Titus who now has to be married to Fintan Riley.

Or Mr Goldenblatt who says it is like casting Kathy Bates as Juliet.

Anyway, it's good, isn't it? I mean, I don't have to be in PMS any more. And I've made Imo happy again. By accident. But it's a start.

3 p.m.
Oh. And I've thought of another good thing (see, positive thinking): I can go to London *TOMORROW*, instead of learning about Belgium's punitive tax system.

I have bought a train ticket with Granny's credit card. Which is totally the only advantage of being freakishly tall, and of knowing that the pin number is the same as Geraldo's birthday.

And I KNOW it is supposed to be for 'life or death' emergencies only, and I KNOW Granny kind of meant stuff like the water being cut off, or having to shop in Lidl. But this is WAY more important than that. This is about whether you can snog someone without either *a*) vomming or *b*) Lily Rubenstein selling the story to *Heat* for £10,000. Which IS pretty much life or death, if you think about it.

**Friday 3 December**

9 a.m.
OK, so the Universe is TOTALLY smiling on me today because ANOTHER good thing happened. Which is that Blake came round before school with a DIY DNA testing kit. I am NOT EVEN JOKING. He said it is left over from the time Sunday Henderson-Hicks thought her dad might actually NOT be her dad, due to him being unable to hit top C or appreciate a jazz canon. I said was he? Blake said yes, it just skipped a generation or something. Anyway I asked how come he still had one. And he said that they were on two for one at Specialdrug. (It is lucky that Imogen doesn't know about them. She would totally be trying to get DNA off Prince William. Seriously.)

Anyway, Blake says this way I won't even have to tell Fidel

about him possibly being my father. I can pretend I am doing a project on the Nineties for history at school and flatter him that he is a key figure in the underground movement. (I did not even know he knew words like underground!) Then I just need to get one of his hairs. I said yanking hairs out is *HARDLY* discreet. But he said I just need to find a hairbrush or something. So I said what if he's bald. And Blake said 'Bathroom floor?' Which, like, *EWWWWWWWW*, but also, totally CSI!

Now all I have to do is get the train, get to Fidel's flat, get a hair and get home again.

I mean, what could be easier?

10.25 a.m.

Oh my God, Dr Sven. Did you notice that? I am not having negative thoughts or doubts *AT ALL*.

Maybe after today I won't even *NEED* your help any more. Maybe all my questions will be answered and all my issues will evaporate like cheap nail varnish remover.

11 a.m.

This is good, right? I mean, I *TOTALLY* don't want him to be my dad, because, like, duh, the Stan thing. But if he is, well, then I will *FINALLY* know. Which can *ONLY* be positive.

Maybe I will have one of those moments, you know, when I see him and it will be like on *Surprise Surprise* (which is this *COMPLETELY* lame TV show that is rerun on satellite where some woman with enormous teeth reunites long lost people and everyone sobs and Imogen is *DESPERATE* to go on there and be reunited with anyone, preferably her real mother, if she turned out to be Cher or Michelle Obama rather than Mrs Pritchard) and I will *KNOW* we are related.

11.45 a.m.
Except I *REALLY REALLY REALLY* don't want him to be my dad.

12.15 p.m.
OK this is it. I am on the underground. And I am going to stop writing now because even though it is completely clear that there is *NO* barometer of *NORMAL* in London (seriously, the man next to me is wearing moon boots and a turban) I am starting to feel *SICK* and I think I might need my writing hand to cover my mouth when I start gagging.

Wish me luck, Dr Sven. I think I might totally need it after all.

7 p.m.
<u>Evidence that Fidel (aka Miles) Harrington-Bovey *IS* my father</u>

1. His hair is black. Which, like, I *KNOW* is not the same as mine, except that *OBVIOUSLY* if you were an aspiring revolutionary, you would totally *DYE* your hair.
2. He is not a midget.
3. He totally remembered Lola. In fact, his eyes *ACTUALLY* filled with tears at one point.

4. He flipped his mobile open and shut fifty-six times, i.e. he has potential OCD issues, i.e. *COMPROMISED MENTAL HEALTH*.

<u>Evidence that Fidel Harrington-Bovey is *NOT* my father</u>

1. His lips are normal sized.
2. He has a dog. It is a bull terrier called Dido. Which, like, I *KNOW*.
3. He does *NOT* heart Sour Skittles. Not *EVEN* the purple ones. And I offered at least three times.
4. There was no *Surprise, Surprise* moment at all. He thought I was from the council coming to check he is eligible for disability benefit. Which, he totally *ISN'T*. Except possibly on OCD grounds.

So, anyway, thank God Blake *DID* get the DNA test thing. And thank God he is going slightly bald and that his hair has moulted on the sofa. Seriously, it was covered in them.

I mean, *OBVIOUSLY* if he is my dad I will tell him then, but the whole teary-eyed thing was worrying me and I did not want to push him over the edge into full breakdown without a definite answer. Which I will have in *FIVE* working days, i.e. next Friday morning according to Mr Singh, who was the duty pharmacist at Specialdrug (currently being sued by Superdrug under the Trades Descriptions Act, and countersuing on the same grounds, according to Lily Rubenstein).

So now all I have to do is *WAIT*. Which will be fine. I mean a week's not that long. It will *FLY* by.

Won't it?

**Saturday 4 December**

11 a.m.

Oh God. I don't know how much longer I can take this. I mean, I didn't think it was possible but I am actually *BORED* and *TERRIFIED* at the same time.

Seriously, there is *NOTHING* to do except worry about the DNA thing.

Like what if he *IS* my dad? Will he want to come and live with us and potentially compromise my mental health even more with the mobile phone thing and evidential adoration of Lola? Plus, I *WONT* get to snog Stan, which is a *BAD THING*.

But what if he *ISN'T* my dad. Then the chances are it *WILL* turn out to be someone like Fergal O'Shaughnessy. Plus I *DO* get to snog Stan (Lily Rubenstein issues dependent), which is a *GOOD* thing, but equally nausea-inducing and mental-health compromising.

How did I *EVER* think this was a good idea?

Though on the plus side, I have got my appetite back. It is the sitting around. It just seems to make me hungry.

2 p.m.

I have actually eaten an entire packet of KitKats. I am *NOT*

EVEN JOKING. And the thing is, I didn't even know I was doing it. Seriously. I was watching the Cartoon Channel and the next thing I knew I had eaten five. No wonder there is an obesity problem. It is all the unemployed wondering about their genetic inheritance whilst watching daytime TV with nothing but junk food or urine samples in the house. I have total new-found sympathy for their plight.

And I KNOW I could go out or something. Only OUT involves the risk of bumping into *a*) Imogen, *b*) Sunday Henderson-Hicks, and *c*) Stan. And I am not on any of their Top Ten People to Bump Into lists. Plus there is no way Stan is going to fancy me at the moment. I am wearing slippers and have chocolate stains all over my T-shirt. It is so NOT a good look.

3 p.m.
Oh thank God. The door. I was totally in the process of opening the mini Twixes, which, like NOOOOOO.

5 p.m.
It was Blake. My new GBF. Which I am still totally trying to get used to. Especially as he was wearing an England rugby hat and an All-Blacks shirt. Which I said he kind of needed to change, especially when he comes out. Only he said he is definitely NOT coming out. Which I said was unfair as I had done my part of the deal, i.e. gone to London and got the

DNA etc. so now he had to do his, i.e. come out and rejoin PMS. Only he pointed out that we hadn't made a deal, which I totally checked fifteen pages ago, and annoyingly it turns out he is right. But *THAT* is not the point, which I told him, the point is that it is important to *BE HIMSELF*, and besides there are already loads of gay people at Pennington, e.g. Ms Nugent (who is the chair, and only member, of the Pennington Lesbian and Gay Society), Mr Goldenblatt (who is not out, but is not really trying very hard to be in either) and Titus Pelling. Only Blake said Titus is *NOT* gay. So I said Yes he is. And he said No he isn't. And that went on a few minutes until Blake said I had *NO* gaydar *WHATSOEVER*. So I said fine, then who *IS* gay, Mr 'in tune with everyone's sexuality'? And he said that is not the point. Which is true, even though the diversion would have totally cheered up my otherwise obesity-threatening afternoon. The point is that it is *NOT* good that Blake is not being true to himself. I mean, I know I am always moaning about not wanting to be myself. And I did dye my hair. And wear knee-length socks and stuff. But the thing is, if I *KNEW* who the real me was, maybe I could *TRY* to be true to it. Which I am totally trying to do with the Dad and Stan thing.

**Sunday 5 December**

So you'd think I'd be happy because today was like the first major PMS run-through and instead of waving my jazz hands around in a syncopated line-up of drama freaks and geeks, I am in the privacy (bar chickens) of my own bedroom, which two months ago I would have given Jimi Hendrix's actual plectrum for. Only the thing is, instead of silently contemplating this stroke of complete luck, I am singing Elton John ballads. I am NOT EVEN JOKING. It's like some weird compulsion. A new manifestation of CRAZY. And not under my breath, but full-on vibrato. I mean, WHAT IS THAT ABOUT? It totally confused Lola who said she thought I was out of PMS, which she said is a shame because she has tickets for everyone including Granny Jones. I said well they can all still go (except Ruby because of the restraining order) just that I won't be on stage. Which she seemed to think was fine, which, like WHERE is the parenting in that? Maybe they'll enjoy it more though. I mean, I'd be bound to trip over a Sidehick, or miss a top C. And Imo's not that bad really. At least she's enthusiastic. OK, to the point of looking like a demented hamster on a sugar rush at times, but that counts for something, doesn't it?

It does to me, anyway.

**Monday 6 December**

OK, so I totally offered to teach Harry for the day to alleviate my boredom/panic/weight-gain but it turns out that Granny Jones is taking him horse racing for a maths lesson. She says if he can master spread betting then he can conquer the world.

I did not even bother to point out the issues with this. Because at that point *Helicopter Rescue* came on and I was transfixed by a cow being winched off a cliff.

2 p.m.
If I watch any more TV I think I may develop Type 2 diabetes. I am trying to console myself with the thought that if I was at school right now I would be mindless with boredom at something to do with Belgium.

Oooh. Which is a point. I wonder what is happening at school right now. What if Imogen has seen the error of her ways and has started a mass sit-in in the canteen until I am unsuspended and Miss Hutchinson is replaced by someone with less attitude and more words per minute?

4 p.m.
Blake has just texted. He says the following things have happened:

1. The lacrosse B team lost 87–3 to St Hubert's and are being relegated to the comprehensive league. Except only one other comp plays lacrosse, because it is POINTLESS, and ARCHAIC, so they have to commute to Essex every other week or give up.
2. Finty Goggins-Smith passed out in Bio, because Mr Sylvester told her corneas were permeable and she tried to breathe through her eyes.
3. Imogen got sent to Mr Kwame-Jones for mayonnaising

Sunday Henderson-Hicks in Latin (which has taken over from Slimfasting due to fire power from squeezy bottle advantage).

Whereas here I have:

1. Watched TV.
2. Eaten processed food.

Three more days to go. This is TORTURE, Dr Sven. Seriously. I mean, not on the scale of Guantanamo, but still, NOT GOOD.

**Tuesday 7 December**

Food consumed
Four Pop Tarts
Two segments of orange (real, not Terry's chocolate)
Two chicken drumsticks
A box of Apricot Wheats. (Actually delicious. Like crisps. But apricotty.)
Two mint KitKats
Two normal KitKats
One KitKat Chunky
(and then I stopped due to definite onset of nausea)

TV watched
*Helicopter Rescue*

*Homes Under the Hammer*
*Loose Women*
*Murder She Wrote*
*To Buy or Not to Buy*
*Deal or No Deal*
(TV also stopped due to nausea levels)

Interesting events
A chicken laid an egg in the hen house (this is the first time it has not been in the microwave, washing machine, or under my bed, so in the Jones house scheme of things, is kind of groundbreaking, although in the REST OF THE WORLD scheme of things is PANTS).

**Wednesday 8 December**

Food consumed
Six toffee apples
Four Frubes
A packet of frozen peas
A box of Apricot Wheats

TV watched
*Helicopter Rescue*
*Homes Under the Hammer*
*Loose Women*
*Murder She Wrote*
*Quincy* (daring channel change from yesterday)

*Deal or No Deal*

Interesting events at home

None.

Seriously. Nothing happened. I am actually thinking of going round to Granny Jones's tomorrow. Even a bloaty faced rash and some barely disguised insults might be more fun than this.

Plus, I've kind of realized something. You know I said that PMS was the cause of everything *BAD* and that it was ruining my life blah blah blah. But, and it *SO* pains me to admit this, I actually *MISS* it. Can you believe it? And not just the singing feeling. But all the other small stuff. The dumb stuff. Like which Cooper-Willis Alicia is snogging now. And whether Finty thinks dwarves are bigger than elves and that *NO* Alfie Watson-Jackson is not an elf.

And it's dress rehearsal tomorrow, and, like I know Imogen is going to be off the scale with drama. And Stan is going to be having second thoughts and trying to find some crazy way to get himself off stage. And Mr Goldenblatt is going to be trying to find some crazy way to get himself on stage and spotted by Cosmo Letterman. And Mr Burton is going to be going plain crazy.

And the thing is, maybe Mr Burton was right. That I just need to believe in myself. What if it's OK not to be ordinary? What if it turns out I kind of like being *EXTRA*ordinary?

Oh God. I think I might have made a big mistake, Dr Sven. Huge.

**Thursday 9 December**

OK, ignore what I said last night. It must have been some new kind of crazy brought on by junk food and boredom. But I'm not bored any more. Not because anything actually *HAPPENED*. But because I am too busy being consumed by panic because tomorrow is DNA-*DAY*.

Oh God, Dr Sven. I know it is good to get it over with, and I know I have possibly said this before, in fact I have *DEFINITELY* said this before, only this time is it actually *TRUE*, because I *CANNOT* feel any worse than I do now.

And normally it would make me feel so much better to tell someone about it, i.e. Stan or Imo, only telling them now will kind of defeat *EVERYTHING*. And yes I *KNOW* I have you. But you are, with all due respect, kind of unresponsive at the moment. Which I *KNOW* is not your fault. But which still, basically, *SUCKS*.

9 p.m.

OK. I am totally sorry about the outburst earlier. But this is like *WAY TERRIFYING*. I mean have you any idea what it feels like to be about to find out if a man called Fidel is actually *NOT* your biological father, which means that your best friend is *NOT* your cousin after all, so you *CAN* snog them? *HAVE YOU*?

I thought not. Because *NO ONE* can come close to understanding just how *FREAK SHOW* my life is right now.

Except that the *Chronicle* didn't run the wet-pant black-face picture because some C-list actress was doing something in a crinoline. Which Ruby says is an outrageous media black-out conspiracy. But which I say is one less mentally-compromising thing to worry about.

**Friday 10 December**

8.30 a.m.
I cannot eat. Which, given my junk consumption levels in the past few days is probably a good thing. Except that I am pretty sure I need some calories to keep up the level of shaking that my hands are doing right now. Lola actually asked if I was going cold turkey.

8.45 a.m.
OK. I cannot wait any longer. I am going to Specialdrug to see Mr Singh. Wish me luck, Dr Sven. In quarter of an hour I will find out if I can kiss Stan without ending up as the subject of a Channel 5 documentary.

9 a.m.
The post is not in yet. And Mr Singh says I cannot wait inside because I am putting off other customers with my dark circles, poor skin, and tremors. He has told me to buy some Tropicana and come back in an hour.

10 a.m.
The post is still not in and I have drunk my bodyweight in orange juice (no bits). I am *SO* complaining to Royal Mail. Once my hands can hold a pen. And I have peed.

11 a.m.
OK. I thought the post had arrived. But it turned out to be Lily Rubinstein's little brother Noah in a Postman Pat outfit. How was I to know the Post Office doesn't have a dwarf on its staff? It totally should. Maybe I will complain about that too.

2 p.m.
The post has *FINALLY* arrived. Delivered by Fish Knowsley. Which, like, they won't employ a dwarf, but they let a man who smells of mackerel and thinks hurdy-gurdies are an instrument deliver the post? *WHATEVER*. I am going to open it now. Here goes. Oh, I am undone!

2.05 p.m.
I retract the ill-timed 'I am undone'. Because the test results are *INCONCLUSIVE*. Something to do with one of the hairs not actually being human, and the other showing only a ten per cent match. So one is, in all probability, Dido's, and one might be Fidel's, but equally might be some other random fake revolutionary.

I am not a *FREAK*. I am an *IDIOT*. *HOW* did I think this was ever going to work? And the worst thing is, I can't even go and live with my dad to get away from it because I still have *NO IDEA* who it is. There is nothing else for it. I am going to transfer to Broadmead. Getting beaten up and wearing polyester trousers has to be better than facing up to Stan at Pennington. Blake will have to find a new pretend girlfriend. And Imo can give Titus a contract making him best friend and not just GBF. Because I am never going through those gates again. *EVER. FOR ANYBODY*.

5 p.m.
Except that I have just got a text from Blake.

> GET TO SKL ASAP.

I have texted back:

> Y?
> BLAKE: NIKE
> ME: ?
> BLAKE: JUST DO IT
> ME: HAHA. AND AGAIN Y?
> BLAKE: TELL THE TRUTH.
> ME: WHATEVER. OK.

Which, like, what *IS* it about GBFs? They have some kind of spooky power to get you to do anything. Because I *AM* going. Because he asked me, and he is the only friend I have, even if he does wear golfing socks. And because he is right. Hiding at Broadmead is not the answer. Because the trousers aren't long enough and I would look like a failed Audrey Hepburn in her Capri pants era. And because I need to tell the truth, even without the DNA thing. Because I'm sick of it, Dr Sven. I can't go on feeling this bad. And maybe it will totally be like in the films and a weight will be lifted or something. That or I'll be mayonnaised within an inch of my life. But I guess there's only one way to find out . . .

'The Boy Next Door'. A play, with music (which you will totally have to imagine because I do not have a volume button on this diary), by Buttercup Jones

OPENING. HALLWAY OF A PRIVATE SCHOOL SOMEWHERE IN THE WEST OF ENGLAND. A FREAKISHLY TALL FOURTEEN YEAR OLD BURSTS IN FROM STAGE LEFT AND RUNS STRAIGHT INTO…

A 36-YR-OLD WOMAN WITH DAZED EXPRESSION (LOLA) AND A FIVE YEAR OLD IN A SHARK OUTFIT (HARRY).

LOLA: Buttercup baby. I thought you were in detention. Or something.

BUTTERCUP: *SUSPENSION*. But I have to tell someone something. Something important.

LOLA: Oh my God. I *KNEW* it. You *ARE* pregnant.

BUTTERCUP: For the *MILLIONTH* time. *NO*! I haven't even kissed anyone. Unless you count Blake. Which, oh God, I can't even go into.

ENTER ELDERLY LADY WITH ABNORMALLY SMOOTH SKIN ON FACE, SMALL DOG UNDER RIGHT ARM AND TWEEDY-MAN ON LEFT ARM.

GRANNY: Buttercup Jones, what on *EARTH* do you think you're doing?

BUTTERCUP: I know I'm suspended. It's just—

GRANNY: I mean the hair. Good Lord, Buttercup, those roots. I am booking you in with Renaldo next week.

MR CEMENT (for it is he): I thought that was the dog.

BUTTERCUP: Geraldo. There is a fine difference. But only a fine one.

ENTER THIRTY-SOMETHING MAN IN RAMONES T-SHIRT UNSUCCESSFULLY HIDDEN UNDER JACKET (MR BURTON).

BUTTERCUP: Mr Burton, I need to tell you something. I—

(Pause as little tinkling sound occurs as Mr Burton spots DAZED WOMAN)

MR BURTON (ashen-faced): Lola Jones.

LOLA: Wow. You're like psychic. Buttercup, he's psychic.

MR BURTON You . . . er . . . don't remember me?

LOLA: Don't take it personally. I don't remember quite a lot of things.

GRANNY: I do though. Nervous Nigel from next door. You used to follow Leona around like a dog [although not like Geraldo, who actively avoids Granny Jones], when you weren't

playing that appalling guitar.
MR BURTON: Until you, like, got environmental health to . . . er . . . enforce a noise curfew. Oh . . . *AAACCHOOOO*. God, sorry, it's the dog. Can you—*AAACHOOO*.
GRANNY (stepping back to avoid sneeze residue and thrusting dog into liver-spotted hands of tweedy man): Oh, so I did. (Pauses for reflection) I always thought you were mentally deficient. Yet here you are teaching. So the band never made it. What were they called. The Fruit Pastilles?
MR BURTON: The Fruit Bats. I . . . er . . . quit. I went to the . . . um . . . Royal College. And, like, qualified as a music teacher. But that's, like, not . . . (turns to Lola) You really don't . . . er . . . remember me?
LOLA: Sorry.
MR BURTON: New Year's Eve. We . . . um . . . you know . . .
LOLA: We what? (Pause for flash of light to indicate epiphany) *OH*. Did we? Wow.

ENTER OVER-MADE-UP BALDING MAN IN WHITE TUXEDO.
MR GOLDENBLATT: Nigel, you *HAVE* to come now because Cosmo Letterman is sitting behind Fintan Riley's father who is also cranially *AFFLICTED*.
MR BURTON: What?
MR GOLDENBLATT: FAT HEAD FAT HEAD!
MR BURTON: Right. Er . . . sorry. I have to go. Lola . . . it's . . . um . . . good to see you.
LOLA: Yeah, right. Sorry, what was your name?

EXIT MR BURTON STILL SNEEZING
STAGE RIGHT, AND FAMILY
STAGE LEFT.

SPOTLIGHT FALLS ON
BUTTERCUP.
BUTTERCUP: *OH. MY. GOD.* It's possible. It's
*TOTALLY* possible.

ENTER BLOND A&F MODEL TYPE MALE ON THE
BACK OF A MOPED, DRIVEN BY SECOND A&F
MODEL TYPE MALE.
BUTTERCUP: Where did you get that? And who is that?
BLAKE: I can't tell you. Well I can. But I don't have time right
now. What have I missed?
BUTTERCUP: Oh, nothing. Just that, I think . . . No,
I know . . . Mr Burton is my dad.
BLAKE: Like your dad dad?
BUTTERCUP: No my great-uncle dad. *YES* my dad dad. What
are you doing here anyway.
BLAKE: I had an epi—epi—
BUTTERCUP: Epiphany.
BLAKE: One of those. That's who this is. He's Cain. He's a
full back for St Olave's first XV. *AND* is playing Captain Von
Trapp in their production of *Sound of Music*.
BUTTERCUP: Seriously? That is like—

BUT THEY ARE INTERRUPTED BY A BLONDE

GIRL EATING MALTESERS, FOLLOWED BY A BOY CARRYING MALTESERS.
IMOGEN: *WHAT* are you doing here? You are totally expelled. Titus, get Mr Kwame-Jones. She has to be escorted off the premises at *ONCE*.
BUTTERCUP: Imo, I can explain. Everything.
BLAKE: No. Let me. Imogen, I'm gay.
IMOGEN: No you are not. I have totally gaydar.
BLAKE: Yes I am.
BUTTERCUP: He is, Imo.
IMOGEN: You treacherous witch.
BUTTERCUP: What?
IMO: This is totally *TYPICAL* of you. I get a gay best friend so you go and get one as well. You are stealing my thunder and I am . . . (pause while Imogen makes two and two add five) Ooooh. *OH MY GOD*. Blake, you can totally go out with Titus.
TITUS: But I'm not gay.
IMOGEN: Yes you are.
TITUS: No I'm really not. I'm in love with you, Imo. But . . .
IMO: With me?
TITUS: Yes. Didn't you get the letters?
IMO: Oh, I am undone!

ENTER FOUR DEVILS IN ANGELIC DISGUISE, LOWERED FROM HEAVENS ON SPARKLING UNICORN CHARIOT.
SUNDAY: Oh my God. I am totally going to catch gayness.
BLAKE: Sunday. I should have told you. I—

SUNDAY: Shut up. It's like transferring through the air at me.
BUTTERCUP: Oh grow up, Sunday. You sound like Finty.
FINTY: Are unicorns, like, real?
EVERYONE: Shut up, Finty.

EXEUNT ANGELS IN PUFF OF DRY ICE.

BUTTERCUP: There's something else, Imo.
IMOGEN: Oh my God. YOU'RE gay and in love with me too.
BUTTERCUP: No. I'm in love with Stan.
IMOGEN: Stan. What, Stan Stan?
BUTTERCUP: Yes.
IMOGEN: Stan who you said was like a cousin or something.
BUTTERCUP: YES. Only it turned out he actually possibly WAS my cousin, because Lola had slept with Che's brother Fidel. Only the DNA test came through and, oh it's a long story. But he's not my dad. 110 per cent.
IMOGEN: That is such a cliché.
BUTTERCUP: I know.
IMOGEN: OH MY GOD. I have got it. You have to go on stage. You have to kiss him. It is totally like in that episode of *The OC* when—
BUTTERCUP: No, Imogen. It isn't like anything. And, anyway, I'm banned, remember.

ENTER LUDICROUSLY UPPER-CLASS BLACK MAN IN BESPOKE SUIT, AND SMALL WOMAN WITH BAD PERM AND ILL-FITTING MAUVE JACKET, IN MORE DRY ICE.
MR KWAME-JONES: No, you are unbanned. It is not your fault you resorted to violent protest, you are a victim of social injustice.
MISS HUTCHINSON (taking notes): No she's not.
MR KWAME-JONES: I must insist. She is. Her poor breeding and wrecked home life are all that is to blame. She should be applauded for rising above her lowly upbringing to take a stand against the chains of the class system.
BUTTERCUP: Well, not really, but thank you anyway. *OK*, I have to ask. Miss Hutchinson, *WHY* are you always writing this down?
MISS HUTCHINSON: I'm . . . It's for PTA minutes.

ENTER KOOKY-HAIRED GIRL HAND IN HAND WITH ANGLO-CHINESE BOY WITH QUESTIONABLE BREATH.
LILY: No it isn't. She is writing a novel. Which she is hoping to sell for a quarter of a million so she can give up being a school secretary and join the Romance Novelists Association. Aren't you?
MISS HUTCHINSON: No comment.
BUTTERCUP: Um. Lily. Hi. How much did you hear?
LILY: Enough.
BUTTERCUP: Are you and Len, you know?

LILY: Yes. Not that it's anyone's business.
BUTTERCUP: That's kind of rich.
LILY: Whatever.
BUTTERCUP: So, what was with you and Stan?
LILY: I was helping him.
BUTTERCUP: With what?
LILY: Making you jealous. Which, like, totally worked. Oh, and writing you a song.
BUTTERCUP: Oh. Hang on. Really? What song?

VOICE OFF: This is your five minute call.

FOLLOWED BY MUCH EXEUNTING, LEAVING ONLY IMO AND BUTTERCUP IN THE SPOTLIGHT.
IMOGEN: One thing: if he isn't, who *IS* your dad.
BUTTERCUP: I . . . I can't . . . It's . . . complicated.

VOICE OFF: Beginners please.

SCENE CHANGES TO BACKSTAGE AREA. A BOY WITH A LOW SLUNG GUITAR IS WAITING IN THE WINGS. ENTER FREAKISHLY TALL GIRL.
BUTTERCUP: Stan?
STAN: Buttercup? But I thought . . .
BUTTERCUP: I know. There's kind of been a change.
STAN: Of plan?
BUTTERCUP: Of heart.

STAN: So you're the girl next door?
BUTTERCUP: And you're my boy next door.
STAN: Well, two doors up on . . . Wait. Really?
BUTTERCUP: Really.
STAN: So the kiss?

THEY ARE INTERRUPTED BY THE OPENING BARS OF 'ABC'.
BUTTERCUP: Wait. The song. Lily said you wrote me something.
STAN: You'll hear it.

SCENE CHANGE TO STAGE.

THE FINAL BARS OF 'A GIRL NEXT DOOR' (MUSIC AND LYRICS N. BURTON AND S. ROMER) FADE.

THE BOY NEXT DOOR LETS HIS GUITAR DROP AS HE STANDS. THE GIRL NEXT DOOR LOOKS UP (HE HAS STACK HEELS ON) EXPECTANTLY.

THE SPOTLIGHT TIGHTENS.

THEY KISS.

FINTY GOGGINS-SMITH FALLS OFF STAGE.
BUT NEITHER OF THEM NOTICES.

**Saturday 11 December**

So, Dr Sven, that's pretty much how it went. Only there were more bits with Sunday refusing to kiss Blake in case she started liking La Roux or something. And one very confusing bit where Len Cho forgot he wasn't playing Too Cool Boy any more and Sunday didn't know who to refuse to kiss.

But you get what I mean. Pretty amazing, huh?

And the kiss? It was everything and nothing like I imagined. The earth totally moved *AND* stood still at once. It was a first kiss. A *MOVIE* kiss. Just I hope not the last.

And I don't know what's going to happen next. I mean there's kind of a lot of stuff to tell him. Like about my dad.

I mean, *OH MY GOD*. I should have guessed it was Mr Burton. The shaved head to disguise the gingerness. The height. The dog allergy. And he totally *DOES* have mental issues. I mean, he loved Lola for a start.

Oh. And I have to tell Lola as well. Because despite the mash-up being the song that he totally used to play at her through the walls, she *STILL* hasn't got it yet. And, maybe they could get back together. I mean, it's kind of romantic, don't you think.

Or am I sounding like Imogen?

Oh. And Imogen totally doesn't know. Because of the 'I am undone' potential. And because she'll totally tell Titus (they actually kissed last night. And he even managed to keep up the movie dialogue. Although Imo says he is totally going to need lessons in the big dip moment, because she leant backwards and he totally didn't hold on and she knocked herself out on a stage weight) and he will tell Len, who will tell Lily, and I will still end up as Pennington's biggest ever freak show.

So much for being ordinary, huh?

Oh, and UNBELIEVABLY PMS got through to the finals of the National Musical Society Association Awards. Cosmo Letterman said I reminded him of a young Judy Garland. I am NOT EVEN JOKING.

And the thing is, Mr Burton was right after all. That being extraordinary suddenly felt OK, when I was up there on stage, in front of everyone. I felt at home. Better than at home, given what that's like. I guess what I'm saying is, I've found somewhere that it's OK being me.

But don't think you're off the hook yet, Dr Sven. Because I may feel all floaty and fantastic now. But come next term, I'm pretty sure you'll still have some therapeuting to do.

If that's a word. And if I can find £500. And a big enough envelope.

Because I'm still not sure if this is one amazing mash-up. Or the beginning of Buttercup Mash.

# Forget Dr. Sven, write to Joanna Nadin!

Jo is a self-confessed **Facebook** ADDICT, and you can get in touch with her on the **Buttercup Mash Facebook page**: the place to be for all **Buttercup Mash** lovers, and I am NOT EVEN JOKING!

talk to other **Buttercup Mash** fans

watch the hilarious **Buttercup Mash** trailer

download wallpapers

ask Jo your questions

To visit, search 'Buttercup Mash' on www.facebook.com *

* For fans aged 13 or over, in line with Facebook terms and conditions.

Hey there,

So maybe you've already read the book, in which case I hope you totally hearted it. Or maybe you're just sneaking a peak at the end first, in which case, I like your style.

Whichever, I just wanted to say that I hope Buttercup has made you laugh (a lot), cry (a little), and especially think (but not too hard, this isn't Dickens you know). Because while Buttercup is a lot about family, and friendship, and how to cope with them, it's also about being you, which can also take some coping with. And I hope it's made you realise that whoever you are, and whatever you look like, it's OK to be you, and it's OK to be different. Even if you do some pretty Buttercupish things. I mean, take some of mine:

1. When I was fifteen I looked like a man in a permed wig. I am NOT EVEN JOKING. Google Robert Plant and you can see for yourself.

2. The following year I tap danced on stage to 'New York, New York' in a peach lycra body con dress with 32DD breasts and a very unsupportive bra.

And I'm still doing them (although more in a kind of Lola way now):

3. The first time I was supposed to meet the Prime Minister, I got banned and had to hide in the toilets because I was wearing combat trousers, a see-through top and a silver puffa jacket (I know, time to call the fashion police, but it was 1998).

4. The first time I did meet the Prime Minister I curtsied. YES, actually factually curtsied. Although at least my top wasn't see-through.

5. Last week I did the shopping in a gold lamé ballgown under my parka, because I could not be bothered to get changed.

6. I am still so short that my daughter asked me if she 'will grow up to be an elf too?'

See? Buttercup.

But life's kind of more interesting that way. And I hope it stays like that.

Jo x

## WHICH BUTTERCUP MASH CHARACTER ARE YOU?

1. A FRIEND STANDS YOU UP AT THE CINEMA. DO YOU:

a) Go and watch the movie on your own. You've wanted to see it for ages.

b) Stamp your feet and leave endless messages on your friend's phone demanding to know where she is.

c) Call one of your other friends—if they have other plans cancel them to spend an evening with you.

d) Cinema? You don't have time for that—there are polar bears to be saved.

2. WHAT WORD WOULD YOU USE TO DESCRIBE YOURSELF?

a) Confused.

b) Romantic.

c) Fabulous.

d) Angry.

3. IT'S THE GLEE CLUB PRODUCTION! YOU'RE MOST LIKELY TO BE:

a) Backstage, where no one can actually see you.

b) The romantic heroine, of course!

c) The director—people always do as you say.

d) Outside the hall protesting about school funds being spent on something as trivial as glee club.

4. YOUR PERFECT EVENING IS:

a) Hanging out in the basement jamming with your best friends.

b) Being swept off your feet by a handsome prince or a gorgeous vampire!

c) Strutting down the red carpet to an exclusive VIP party.

d) Picketing the pizza parlour for using endangered tuna.

5. WHAT'S YOUR STYLE?

a) Kind of individual, though you hate to stand out too much.

b) You love to be noticed, so anything that helps that is great.

c) Anything with a label, darling.

d) Combat trousers, boots, flak jacket.

6. WHAT'S YOUR GREATEST FEAR?

a) Making a fool of yourself in front of lots of people.

b) That life won't be like it is in books.

c) Never being spotted by Andrew Lloyd Webber.

d) Climate change. And accidentally eating meat.

7. WHAT IS YOUR FAVOURITE WORD?

a) Totally.

b) Drama.

c) Gucci.

d) Propaganda.

8. WHO IS YOUR IDEAL BOYFRIEND?

a) The boy next door, who's also your best friend.

b) A romantic vampire.

c) The most popular guy in school.

d) A vegan tree dweller.

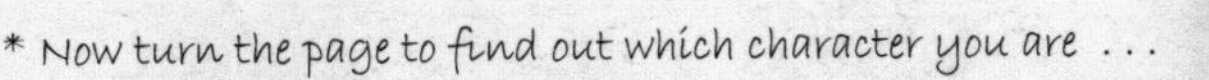

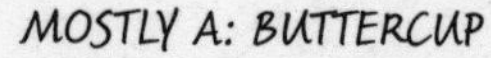

MOSTLY A: BUTTERCUP

You're a loyal and caring friend. You lack confidence in your talents and you need someone to bring you out of your shell at times. But once you're sure of what you're doing, you go for it 100%. Although you probably don't realize it, you're a popular person with a great individual style and people admire you for not following the crowd but just doing your own thing.

MOSTLY B: IMOGEN

You're a dazzling ray of light, which is fine by you as you need everyone to notice you. You love a bit of a drama and never like to be kept in the dark about anything. You're confident in your style and your abilities and although you sometimes appear a bit flaky, you'd do anything for your friends and they love you to bits. Life's never dull when you're around!

MOSTLY C: SUNDAY

You're the leader of the pack and all your friends look up to you. You're popular, cool and always look super-stylish. You love to party, you love to shop and you generally love a good time. You live for the moment and try not to think too much about the future, although you have a feeling you're destined for great things!

MOSTLY D: RUBY

You're a force to be reckoned with and you care deeply about things that are important to you. You'd do anything for your friends, in fact there's nothing you like more than a friend in need who you can defend and go into battle for! The frivolous side of life is not for you—there are far more important things to be doing.

## TWENTY QUICK-FIRE QUESTIONS FOR JOANNA:

| | | |
|---|---|---|
| 1. | BBQ or Sunday roast? | Sunday roast |
| 2. | Stilettoes or Sneakers? | Stilettoes |
| 3. | Ben and Jerry or Haagen Daz? | Ben and Jerry |
| 4. | Chocolate or Vanilla? | Chocolate |
| 5. | Pink & fluffy or Cool & creamy? | Pink & fluffy |
| 6. | Night in or Night out | Night out |
| 7. | Ketchup or Brown sauce | Brown sauce |
| 8. | Half full or Half empty | Half full |
| 9. | Star Wars or Star Trek | Star Wars |
| 10. | Skate or Surf | Skate |
| 11. | Mountain or Ocean | Ocean |
| 12. | Cats or Dogs | Cats |
| 13. | London or Paris | Paris |
| 14. | Acoustic or Electric | Acoustic |
| 15. | Chill out or Freak out | Chill out |
| 16. | Truth or Dare | Truth |
| 17. | Sunset or Sunrise | Sunrise |
| 18. | Listening to advice or Giving advice | Giving advice |
| 19. | X Factor or Strictly | Strictly |
| 20. | Vampires or Werewolves | Vampires |

Also by Joanna Nadin, for older readers,
the hilarious Rachel Riley series

Rachel Riley is on a mission to sort her life out . . . and it's not going to be easy! Follow her highs and lows, friendships and relationships, in this fabulous series.